MAYBE IT'S FATE

WESTON PARKER

D1516970

BRIXBAXTER PUBLISHING

Maybe it's Fate

Copyright © 2020 by Weston Parker

All rights reserved. This book or any portion thereof may not be reproduced or used in any manner whatsoever without the express written permission of the publisher except for the use of brief quotations in a book review.

The novel is a work of fiction. Names, characters, places and plot are all either products of the author's imagination or used fictitiously. Any resemblance to actual events, locales, or persons – living or dead – is purely coincidental.

First Edition.

Editor: Eric Martinez
Cover Designer: Ryn Katryn Digital Art

FIND WESTON PARKER

www.westonparkerbooks.com

DEDICATION

To all my amazing readers who love a good love story. This one is for you. Life just has so many misunderstandings, doesn't it? But I've found in my short time as a husband who loves the heck out of his wife that working through the miscommunications has been key. That's what this fun, fly by the seat of your pants romance is all about. I'm hoping you love it.

Weston

CHAPTER 1

LINDSAY

Every little girl grew up dreaming about her wedding day. We dressed up in poofy white dresses, strung decorations over everything, and said our "I dos" to our teddy bears, Barbies, or the poor neighbor kid who had gotten stuck playing with us that day.

Or at least, I'd heard that was what little girls were supposed to do. Several movies had sequences about it in them and countless books I'd read described exactly that.

Maybe I'd skipped that phase of my development because I'd never done any of that as a child. I'd spent my days pretending to be a big-shot executive. I dressed up in some of my grandmother's finest suit jackets and shoes and used my grandfather's post-it pad as a checkbook.

Our neighbors' kids didn't get stuck marrying me. They simply had to work for me.

My christening gown had been the last poofy white dress I'd owned before this one. Frankly, I'd rather have been christened in a well-fitted corporate outfit rather than the frilly monstrosity my mother picked out for me.

"Fifteen minutes, everyone!" The wedding coordinator clapped her hands from the doorway of the bridal suite. "Only fifteen more minutes to go."

Ember, my best friend, maid of honor, and walking beacon of skepticism about any man I'd ever dated, downed the last of her champagne. "Are you sure you're ready to become Lindsay Cummings?"

She snorted when she said Will's last name—again—and applied a layer of gloss to her lips. Her burgundy gown had so many layers of tulle that it covered her all the way up to her chest when she sat with her knees crossed like she was doing then.

I cast a critical eye at my own appearance in the mirror, trying to come to terms with the fact that I looked like a fairy-tale princess gone horribly, horribly wrong. "How many times are you going to ask me that?"

"As many times as it takes to make sure you really want to do this." Her hazel eyes found mine, and in the reflection of the full-length mirror, I could see the worry darkening them. "We're wearing the equivalent of an explosion in a princess-dress factory in some third-world country. Was that really what you wanted to wear on your wedding day?"

"I wouldn't know. I never thought about it." The dress was a disaster though. There was no way around it. "You know how much it means to Will that we're wearing his mother's designs."

She snorted and reached for another glass of champagne from the tray sitting on the coffee table in front of her. "I love you, but these aren't *designs*. They're her hobby and she's not very good at it."

The mis-stitched lace on my bodice agreed with her. As did the uneven hem and the fact that I had a ribbon tying the back of the dress together instead of the buttons we'd planned.

I hadn't even picked up any weight to have caused the change of plans. In fact, I'd lost a ton in the run up to this day. My fiancé's mom and wedding-dress maker had simply realized she didn't know how to neatly sew buttons onto a dress if they weren't the ordinary type of button.

I sighed, turned away from the mirror, and snagged a glass of champagne for myself.

"It was important to him. Despite what you might think about him, Will is a really nice guy. He deserves to have whatever he wants on his wedding day."

"And you don't?" She rolled her eyes at me. "All I'm asking is if you're sure this is really what you want. Will can be as nice a guy as he wants to be. It still doesn't mean you have to marry him."

"We've been together for a year. We're both thirty-one. It's time to get married." I took a swig of the sickly sweet sparkling wine masquerading as champagne in the glass. "I've spent my life getting to where I wanted to be in my career. Will was the right guy at the right time and you know it."

So what if I didn't feel butterflies when I looked into his pale green eyes? Butterflies weren't real anyway. No one really felt them. They were the figments of the imaginations of people who took creative license for a job. Period.

Ember shook her head. "He was *a* guy at *a* time. I don't know anything about the *right* part of either of those two statements."

I sank into the plush armchair opposite hers. At least the hotel we'd chosen for the wedding was nice. It was a perfectly respectable establishment close enough to Houston that our guests wouldn't have to spend the night.

The bridal suite Ember and I were getting ready in had a nice sitting area, a nice big bath, and a nice balcony. It was, well, nice.

My parents were downstairs, ready and waiting, which was nice too. We'd never had the greatest of relationships, but I was truly grateful that they'd made the trip from Dallas, where they'd retired.

"Let it go, Em. Will and I are compatible in every way. We enjoy each other's company. He doesn't drive me crazy, doesn't fool around on me, and we have a good time together."

She leaned forward, fought with the tulle to have somewhere to rest her elbows, and looked me right in the eyes. "If you're in love with someone, they're supposed to drive you crazy from time to time. You shouldn't just have a good time with them. You should be counting the hours until you get to see them again."

"That's just the way it is in stories. It's not real life. Real life is knowing there's dinner waiting for whoever gets home last. It's being able to live with a person's quirks and loving them anyway."

"That's just my point, though. You don't love him." Ember never pulled any punches. The girl was as straightforward as a mid-summer's day was long. "I mean, think about it. You guys schedule your private time and you never do anything outside of it."

Damn all those tequila shots at my bachelorette party. I never should've told her that. "There's nothing wrong with keeping to a healthy schedule that both parties have agreed to and can live up to."

She slammed her back into her chair and widened her heavily made-up eyes at me. "Fifteen minutes twice a week is not healthy for a newly engaged people, hon."

"Twenty-five minutes with time for foreplay included," I grumbled. "That's perfectly acceptable."

"That's what I'm saying. Perfectly acceptable doesn't cut it." She pointed a French-tipped nail at the window. "Do you really think there would still be civilization out there if people only had sex on the clock? Hell no."

"There are a *lot* of people out there who schedule it."

"Sure, but for a man with the last name Will has, you'd think he would at least make it enjoyable enough for you not to only want to schedule it."

I was never drinking tequila again. It was official. "So what if his prowess isn't overwhelming. It's not underwhelming either. It's just whelming enough. There's nothing wrong with scheduling."

"Scheduling it is fine for parents and whatnot, but you're a young couple who's supposed to be in love. Yet you're never just spontaneous."

"Spontaneity can't be planned," I replied dryly. "You, of all people, know how much I love my planner."

"Professionally? Sure. Your personal time doesn't always have to be planned though. What do you do if you find a really good show on TV on a Saturday night? You can't plan that kind of binge-watching."

"That's different." I scooted forward on my chair and took her hands in mine. "I appreciate that you're trying to watch out for me, but it's time to let it go. It might not seem like it, but in my own way, I do love Will."

"If you say so." The furrow between her brows told me she wasn't convinced. "It's not too late for us to sneak out the back."

I squeezed her hands. "I can't tell you how much I love you for knowing just how honestly you mean that, but I'm fine. I've spent too much time planning this to bail out now. This is the right thing for me to do."

Her eyes caught mine and she let out a heavy sigh, shrugging as she withdrew her hands to pick up her champagne again. "If you change your mind, let me know. I parked near the back entrance just in case."

"Thank you." I really meant it. "I'll keep that in mind, but I'm ready. We have our honeymoon in Fiji for a week, everything's already booked and paid for, and after that, I'm hoping to convince Will we need to find a new apartment. I'm ready for this next chapter in my life, Em. I promise."

"You still haven't decided whose place you're going to stay in from now on?" She sucked in a deep breath. "Come on, Linds. You're getting married *today*."

"I know. We just—"

A sharp knock at the door interrupted us.

I frowned at my friend before glancing down at the ornate watch on my arm. "It can't be my dad yet. He's nothing if not punctual and he still has a few minutes."

Ember pushed herself up with her palms on the armrests of her chair and glanced at me. "Stay put. It's bad luck for anyone to see the bride before the wedding, right?"

"Right." An uneasy knot formed in my stomach. I wasn't the most intuitive person, but something had seemed off to me all day.

It wasn't that I didn't want to marry Will or wasn't sure of my decision. It was something else. Something a lot more turbulent.

Shifting in my seat to face the door even though most of my body was still hidden behind the chair, I watched Ember swing it open to reveal our preacher. His cheeks were red and his gray hair messy, like he'd been tugging at it a lot.

His gaze rested on Ember, but I heard the anxiety in his voice. "Have you seen Mr. Cummings? He was due downstairs some time ago, but he's not there. He's not in his suite either. There's no answer there."

She shot me a look over her shoulder. "Maybe he beat us to the punch on the whole leaving out the back idea."

"I'm sure there's a reasonable explanation." My heart didn't pick up speed at all, but my hands started shaking. I buried them in the millions of layers of my skirt and, for the first time, was thankful for such a big dress. "I'll give him a call. We'll let you know where he is in a minute or two."

The preacher bowed his head and Ember closed the door, all traces of her joke gone from her expression. "You don't think he really left, do you?"

"I don't know." For all the jokes and teasing and reassurances that we were doing the right thing, even I wasn't convinced. I couldn't disregard the possibility that Will might not be, either.

Rummaging through my tiny purse, I found my phone and hit my last dialed number. A tiny sigh of relief flooded me when the call connected. "Will? Hi. Where are you? The preacher's looking for you. If you guys have gone out for cigars or something, it's time to come back inside."

Faint sounds of a moving car hit my ears before he said anything, and my heart sank. "I can't do it, Lindsay. I tried to, and God knows I wanted to be able to, but I just can't."

The phone trembled against my ear and my voice came out thick. "Why not?"

"We're just not right together. I love you, you know? I do, but you're like a roommate to me or a friend. I know you feel that way too. I've already spoken to my parents about it and they've agreed to paying for everything, okay? You don't have to worry about a thing. I've taken care of it."

My chest just about caved in on itself, but even in that moment, I knew it wasn't heartbreak causing it. It was just good old-fashioned humiliation. I had been stood up, left at the altar.

Most of the guests down there were his. Only a handful or so were mine, but even then, all of those people would now have a story to tell about a wedding where the groom didn't show up.

That wasn't what killed me, though. It was that I should've admitted it earlier too. "You're right. I love you too but not in that way. Be happy, Will. Keep in touch."

I disconnected the call and tossed the phone down in the layers on my lap. Ember planted her hands on her hips and took a deep breath. She might not have heard what he said, but she sure as heck had gotten the gist of it.

"Right. I'll go tell everyone the wedding is off. You stay right here and I'll sneak you out the back in a few minutes." She bent over to kiss my forehead. "Don't worry, babe. No one will even know you're still here."

CHAPTER 2

JAXON

Clear blue skies met us as we made our approach into Houston. The city spread out down below like it was one of those toy miniatures at the mall.

Joe, the co-pilot, grinned at me. "I don't know why it's always such a rush coming home, but it really is."

"Yeah, always." It used to be more of a rush back in the day when I was coming home after fighting and flying in a different country for months at a time, but he wasn't wrong. "Funny thing is, I only left two days ago."

"You do the run to the Pacific Islands often?" he asked while checking his dials.

I shook my head. "I've only been flying commercial for a few years. They started me out on shorter-haul flights. Once I started long haul, I was on the Europe track for a long time."

He laughed. "If they've got someone like you paying your dues first, it's no wonder it's taken me so long to get on the international track."

"You're here now." Joe and I had gotten to know each other a little earlier on in the flight, but then we'd switched out for naps, and this was my first real chance to speak to the kid properly without pleasantries and basics being in the way. "It's not all it's cracked up to be, flying international, but it pays the bills."

"I'd say." He smiled but returned his attention to the controls while we were landing. When we were safely on the ground, he stuck his hand out to me. "It was an honor flying with you, sir. I have to say, you're nowhere near as intimidating as I thought you were going to be."

"Why would you think I was going to be intimidating?" I unbuckled my seatbelt. "I have the next few days off and I'm planning on seeing my mother. What's intimidating about that?"

"I didn't know that." He undid the latch on his own belt and darted his gaze out the window. "Your reputation precedes you, Jaxon. I know there are a lot of you former Air Force guys flying for us now, but it never makes it any easier to actually meet any of you."

"You did a great job." I clapped him on the shoulder after I got up, grabbing my suitcase as I opened the door. "I'll see you around, Joe. Stop being so afraid of people just because of what they did in a previous life."

I tipped my hat, which I was contractually obliged to wear outside of the cockpit. Then I left the kid to his own devices and made my way into the terminal.

As soon as I stepped out, I was surprised to see a familiar face waving at me. "Jaxon! Oh, my baby boy. I've missed you."

My mother flung her arms around me like it'd been weeks since she'd last seen me, but I dropped my case and hugged her back. "What are you doing here, Mom? I thought we were having dinner at your place."

"We were, but this way, I didn't have to wait until then to see you." She let go of me and stepped back. "It feels like you're always away these days."

"We have our weekly dinner most weeks," I said, picking up my suitcase again before wrapping my arm around her shoulders. "We had our dinner last week. What gives?"

She shrugged, glancing up at me with laughter dancing in her eyes.

"Maybe I got tired of cooking and wanted my son to buy me dinner for a change."

I laughed and hugged her closer to my side. "I knew there had to be a reason you came to the airport when you knew I was going to come see you anyway."

Batting her eyelashes at me, she pointed at a steakhouse I knew she loved near the end of the terminal. "AJ's never hurt anybody and that place is as good of a reason to drive out here as anything."

"Really? As good of a reason to drive out here as your own son?" I gave her a little shake and she laughed again.

"With the amount of hours I've spent waiting for you to come home in this wretched place, those people have become my family just as much as you are."

"You'll have your steak medium-rare with a baked potato and veggies then, huh?" I couldn't even argue with her about the hours she'd spent waiting there for me. The staff there knew her order as well as I did by now.

Even though it'd been a few years since my last deployment, they'd never forgotten her. She smiled up at me and wedged herself out of my grip. "Actually, I'm on a diet now. I'll have the grilled chicken breast and a salad."

I eyed her scrawny figure. "No one even knows how you ever gave birth to someone the size of me. You don't need a diet. You need a steak or four."

"Mrs. Scott, it's so good to see you," the hostess said when we walked up to her stand, cutting off whatever retort Mom had been about to come up with. She turned her attention on me, and her cheeks grew red. "Hey, Jaxon. We haven't seen you for a while."

I shrugged. "I've been in and out. You got a table for us?"

"For you? Always." She took my mother's arm and led her to a table near the bar but kept sneaking glances at me over her shoulder.

I wasn't being immodest when I said Tiffany was always like that. Rumor had it that she and a few of her pals had a thing for ex-military guys.

Well, it wasn't really a rumor. I'd heard it from some guys I knew personally.

Mom loved AJ's, though, and she loved Tiffany right along with it. She even gave her a kiss on the cheek before she sat down. Tiffany smiled at her. "I'll be right back with your menus and Dustin will be your server tonight."

"Thank you," Mom said. "You don't need to bring us menus. Tell Dustin we'll have our usual."

She winked at my mother, then at me. "You got it."

As soon as we were alone, Mom turned her brown eyes to mine. "So, what enchanting tales do you bring me of the great big world this time?"

"I was gone for two days," I said.

She arched a brow at me. "That doesn't change the fact that I haven't seen you in a week. I don't even know where you've been, which is why I'm asking. Tell an old girl some stories about the world outside of Texas."

"I've told you a thousand times I could get you a seat on a plane anywhere you wanted to go."

She rolled her eyes. "Did I say I wanted to go anywhere? I just want to hear the stories about where you've been. Lord knows, you've traveled enough for the both of us."

"I went to Fiji on this last leg," I said. "Australia before that. Quit making it sound like I've seen the world. You know I mostly see the insides of airports and hotels."

"Only because you're not making the most of this opportunity." She made her eyes big as she stared at me. "You're thirty-eight, Jaxon. Live a little."

"I've lived plenty, thank you very much."

Sighing as she shook her head, she spread a cloth napkin over her lap, flattening it before bringing her eyes back to mine. "I've always tried to teach you to chase the moments, but you've forever been too busy trying to catch the next flight instead."

"If you knew about half the things I've done, you definitely wouldn't be saying that." I flashed her a teasing smile. "Have I told you about that bar in Singapore—"

She lifted her hands. "I never said I wanted to know about it. I just want you to have some fun while you still can. You're no spring chicken. One of these days, you're going to look like me."

Mom's face barely had any sign of wrinkles. Her eyes were bright, and even though she'd never dyed her hair, it was still a rich auburn color. "I don't see anything wrong with that."

"You will." She thanked Dustin when he brought our coffees. Then she turned serious again. "When are you going to start exploring these wonderful places you fly to?"

"Actually, I've been thinking of doing just that." It'd only been for the last fourteen hours that I'd been thinking about it, but it was true. "I got to talking with a man in the airport lounge before takeoff. He'd spent the last two months in Fiji. Seemed to think it was the best place on earth."

"Fiji, huh?" She dipped her head from one side to the other. "That could be nice."

"Yeah. The guy kept talking about how beautiful it is, and I think it'd be nice to see it. I've done the route now so I might stay for a little bit sometime."

"You should go," she said. "Didn't you say you have some days off?"

"Yeah, but to make it worth my while, I'd have to see about getting some extra days off." Not that I didn't have vacation days saved up. I had the damn things coming out my ass. "I'll check with the airline to see when I can take them."

"As long as you don't fall in love with somebody over there, I'm all for it. I need you here with me, and I'm not going to Fiji."

"Well, that escalated fast." I grinned at her. "I wouldn't be going to fall in love with a local girl and spend my life sipping out of coconuts while teaching at a flight school. It's called a vacation. You know how that works, right?"

"Right, but I also know how life works." She gestured to my phone, lying on the table. "Call the airline. Ask them about some time off. It'll be good for you to take a breather."

"I didn't actually mean I was going to call right this minute."

She frowned at me. "Why not? You've only got a few days off. Optimize them. Adding to them is better than wasting them."

"Jesus." I shoved my hand through my hair. "I haven't even showered since I got off my last flight and you're already pushing me onto the next one?"

"As if that's something new to you." Mom waved a hand at my phone again. "Go on. Even if they approve your leave, you don't have to get back on the plane while you're still in your uniform. I'm sure they'll have a flight once you've showered and changed. Just don't let life wait on you any longer, Jaxon."

Relenting with a sigh, I picked up my phone and looked up the number for our HR department. The receptionist was nice, but she couldn't help me. "I'm afraid the woman who runs that part of the department is out right now. I'll pass on the message to call you."

"Don't worry about it." I made eye contact with my mother. "I'll call her back again another time. It's nothing urgent."

Mom huffed out a short breath at me, but even she couldn't bring someone back into the office who was already out for the day.

I shrugged when I hung up. "She's out. I'll call her back. I'll see Fiji one of these days, Mom. It doesn't need to be today."

CHAPTER 3

LINDSAY

I sat on my couch with my feet tucked in underneath me, staring at two birds in a tree in my backyard. My long hair was tied in a messy bun on top of my head and my face was bare of any makeup. A cup of tea dangled between my fingers in my lap, but it was probably cold by now. I didn't really know how long I'd been sitting there since I made it, but I'd only had about half of it.

My thoughts were racing, but at the same time, my mind was at peace. It was difficult to explain how I felt. I guessed I didn't really know how to feel. Who would know how to feel less than a day after being left at the altar?

No one expected that kind of thing to happen to them. I was no exception.

A key turned in my lock at the front door, but I didn't get excited. It wasn't Will coming back to beg me to give him another chance—not that I wanted him to.

Ember was the only person with a key to my place and she used it liberally, never bothering to call ahead anymore.

"I've got breakfast," she said. "Tell me you haven't eaten yet."

"Not since yesterday," I replied, not moving from my position. The scent of freshly baked goods preceded my friend into the room, making my stomach grumble. "You're an angel. Please tell me those are from Newmarket Bakery."

She grinned, throwing herself down beside me before stretching her legs out in front of her and propping her feet on the coffee table. "You know it. Best sticky buns in town. I got us Super Fudge Brownies as well, since it's a special occasion."

"Why is it a special occasion?"

"It's not every day you get stood up on your own wedding day." She reached out to pat my leg. "How are you holding up?"

"I don't really know." I shook my head before leaning it back against the couch to look up at the beams in my ceiling. "I just didn't see it coming. I feel like there had to have been some kind of sign that I missed. I should have at least suspected something."

"Will isn't exactly very in touch with his emotions. He's on one solid level all the fucking time. How do you think you could have suspected it when the inflection of his voice never even changes?"

"He's not that bad." I rolled my eyes at her. "You can stop ragging on him now. He's out of the picture, remember?"

"How can you say he's not that bad when he ran out on you just yesterday? You should be ranting and raving about what a total and utter dick he is."

I lifted a shoulder and released a breath through my nose. "I honestly don't feel like ranting and raving about him. I understand why he did what he did. I might even be a little bit relieved. It just came as a surprise, is all. I thought I was the one settling, not the other way around."

"Trust me. You were the one settling." She flicked a hand at a photo of Will and me on the mantel. "You're eleven years younger than him, you're gorgeous, and you don't even have one bald spot. He is almost exclusively bald spots."

I smacked her in the arm. "He's very sensitive about his hair situation. Don't be mean. He really isn't a bad guy. He's going to make some woman very happy one day."

"As long as it isn't you." Opening the stamped brown paper bag in her lap, she dug into it and extracted a treat, handing it over to me.

"He might be a nice guy, but that doesn't mean he's the right guy for you."

"Pray tell then, who would the right guy for me be?" I tore a bite off the mouthwatering pastry and waited patiently while she moved her lips from side to side in thought.

"Someone fun. Possibly a little spontaneous. Hot obviously. He'd have to be smart, too, and funny." She snapped her fingers and smirked. "I'd also vote for a guy who doesn't only do missionary."

"Why are you so obsessed with my sex life?" I laughed. "I swear you're more invested than I am."

"That's only because you don't know what you're missing." Her smirk melted away. "You deserve the best of everything, my friend. You just don't seem to realize it. That's all I want for you. The best."

"Well, that seems like a bit of a tall order at the moment." She didn't miss the edge of emotion in my voice.

Reaching out to pull me into a hug, she held me tight before releasing me just as abruptly. Her hands landed on my shoulders and she looked into my eyes, her hazel ones fierce with determination.

"Oh no, you don't. I get that this came as a massive shock to you, but it doesn't mean that you don't deserve to be happy or that you won't be. It's not a tall order. It's a completely realistic order. You just need to find the right guy. It'll happen."

"Says the woman who believes humanity is broken and that everyone she meets has an ulterior motive?" I gave her a sad smile. "Maybe you're right. Maybe people are just shitty."

"Obviously, they are." She winked. "But there are good people out there. Like you. You're good. If anyone can find another good person out there, it's you."

"I did find a good person. He just didn't want me." I stated it as fact because that was what it was.

Ember pursed her lips before letting out an exasperated huff. "You didn't want him either. Not really anyway. It was a convenient relationship for both of you. That's it. It should never have gone as far as it did."

I didn't immediately protest against her assessment. I couldn't

16

because I was pretty sure she was right. The day after being left at the altar, I should've been heartbroken but I wasn't. I was more concerned about what this meant for my plans for the future than the actual breakup.

"It went as far as it did because both of us felt like the time was right. It was the next logical step to take. As it happens, I am now completely out of logical next steps."

"That's the best news I've heard all week." She flashed me a slow grin when I frowned at her, clearly seeing my confusion. With a roll of her eyes, she sat back on the couch and gave me a pointed look. "It's good news because it's going to force you to stop trying to force your life into a daily planner. Or any kind of planner, for that matter."

"How is that good news?" My heartbeat faltered at the mere thought of having to shoot from the hip or make decisions on the fly. I had to-do lists to make my to-do lists. It allowed me some measure of control in life—not much, but it was better than nothing.

My best friend knew me more than well enough to know where my thoughts had gone. She was much gentler when she looked at me again.

"It's good news because sometimes we just need to let things happen. You and Will both tried to force this, and obviously, neither of you were completely ecstatic about the prospect of your impending nuptials. You approached the whole thing like a business deal and left all the details, like your fucking dress, to his mother." She rolled her eyes. "I mean, it was your wedding dress for God's sake. Surely, you couldn't have felt like it was an extra little thing that didn't fit in any other category."

"Will said it meant a lot to his mom to take care of it," I said meekly. I had no other excuse. "At least I've learned from this experience what I don't want in a dress."

"There we go." She smiled. "You found a silver lining."

I let out a very unladylike snort and reached for a brownie. "It's not much of a consolation. I still don't know what I'm supposed to do from here. Knowing what I don't want in a wedding dress when I don't even know if I'll ever get married isn't exactly useful."

17

"Do you still want to get married?" she asked. There was no judgment in her tone, only curiosity.

Ember never understood why I wanted to get married in the first place. As much as she talked about finding the right guy, it was only because she thought that was what I wanted.

I shrugged. "We'll see. Trying to plan it that way didn't work and I'm not sure if I can live with the alternative of just waiting and seeing if it ever does."

"I'm not sure there's any other way to do it," she said sympathetically. "On the bright side, you've got a couple of weeks off work now, don't you? You have plenty of time to wrap your head around all this."

"That's part of my problem." I blew out a breath. "I already took time off for the wedding and the honeymoon and I'm just going to be sitting around the house. I don't need time to wrap my head around stuff. I need to get on with my life. You know how much I hate empty days in my planner, and I'm staring at almost two weeks of empty days now."

Her teeth sank into her lip before she perked up. "So go on your honeymoon."

"What?" I scoffed and held up my hands. "No, that's a terrible idea. It would be the most depressing thing in the world to go to a romantic resort booked for my honeymoon alone."

"Why? It's a vacation that's already been paid for. Someone has to go on it. It'd be even more depressing if all that money went to waste."

"It'd be infinitely more depressing to sit on the beach in fucking Fiji drinking cocktails by myself while watching couples do activities and stroll around hand in hand."

"The only parts of the sentence I heard were 'fucking Fiji' and 'drinking cocktails on the beach.' There's no way that could be depressing, and if it is, you just order more cocktails."

"You're insane." I folded my arms, but my gaze flicked to the clock on the wall. "There's no way I'd make the flight anyway. It takes off in four hours."

"It takes less than forty minutes to get to the airport from here. You're already packed, aren't you? Being who you are, I doubt you were leaving it until this morning before having your suitcase ready to go."

"Of course, I'm packed but I haven't even showered." Nibbling on the inside of my cheek, I realized that—logistically, at least—she was right.

There was no reason why I couldn't go. I had time to get cleaned up, grab my things, and make it to the airport with time to spare.

My passport was ready. My airplane ticket and accommodation at the resort was booked and paid for, and I already had the time off work.

If I didn't go, I was staring down the barrel of doing nothing for much longer than I'd ever done nothing for before. I could go back to work early, but I didn't really feel ready to face the pity and the "are you okays?" from everyone there.

Staying here would mean having to face that from family and friends who came around to check on me. I'd been getting messages about it all morning already.

"You're really thinking about it, aren't you?" she asked, excitement sparking in her eyes as she bounced on the cushion.

I nodded. "Any way you could come with me?"

She sighed and shook her head. "Unlike you, I don't have all my ducks in a row to take off in such a short amount of time. There's also the tiny issue of not having a paid-for plane ticket."

"Good points." I stared at her for another beat before slowly getting up. "I'm going to do it. I'm going to go on my fucking honeymoon. Alone. Screw it. I'm not sitting around here being felt sorry for and wondering how to get on with my life. I'm just going to get on with it."

She clapped her hands and followed after me when I took off to my bedroom. "I'll help get your things together and go drop you off at the airport. This is going to be epic! I'm so proud of you!"

So was I, but there was no time to waste. Getting ready and the drive to the airport were a blur. It was only once I was on the plane and my seatbelt clicked into place that I finally smiled.

Here I come, Fiji. God, please don't let this be a massive mistake.

CHAPTER 4

JAXON

It was barely sunrise when I walked into the local hangar where I helped my friend repair planes when I was in town. Kavan and I had been in the service together, and after he got out, he'd gotten a job there.

The owner didn't have a problem with me coming in to help—as long as I didn't expect payment for any work I did. Which I didn't, considering that it was a hobby for me and not one with many opportunities available to practice it. It wasn't like I could walk into any old junkyard and find a plane to fix up.

Going over to the machine I'd been busy with before I left for my last haul, I found it exactly as I'd left it and grinned. This was another reason why I loved the place so much. Only Kavan and one other guy worked there, and both of them knew to leave my shit alone.

I got right back into it and was wiping sweat off my brow a little before eight when I saw Kavan coming in. He shook his head when he spotted me, walking up to give me a back-thumping, one-armed hug.

"Only you would get to my job before it's even time for me to start work. When did you get in?"

"Yesterday. I woke up early and got bored at home." I smacked him on the shoulder. "We're not all slackers who sleep in, you know."

He narrowed his blue eyes to slits in a mocking glare and dragged a hand over the top of his blond faux-hawk. "We're not all perpetual bachelors who can sleep whenever we want."

I smirked. "Hey, I was there when you married the lovely Mrs. Roberts, remember? You were of sober mind and senses when you said yes. You could still be sleeping whenever you want too. How's she doing anyway?"

"She's fucking pregnant, man."

"Yeah, I know. That's part of why I was asking."

"I know, and that's my answer. She's *fucking* pregnant now. The baby's kicking the shit out of her, she can't really sleep much anymore, and as a result, neither can I. She keeps tossing and turning, and seven seconds after she falls asleep, she wakes up again because she needs to pee."

"You knew all this before you knocked her up though, didn't you?" I arched a brow at him in an attempt to stop myself from laughing. "As far as I know, it comes with the territory."

"No. You think you know what comes with the territory. You fucking don't, man. Thinking you know and living it are two very different things." He patted his stomach. "I'm even picking up weight. Apparently, it's a sympathy thing."

"A sympathy thing or an excuse thing?" It was meant to be a joke, but Kavan flipped me off and punched me in the bicep with his other hand. I rubbed the spot. "You may be picking up weight but at least your fists can still do some damage."

This time, he was the one who smirked. "We're having a little girl. Now is not the time for me to ease up on my fighting skills. I need to hone them more than ever. Who knows when the first potential suitors will start showing up at my door? I need to be ready for those little fuckers."

"Uh, I think you've probably got a few years yet."

He shrugged. "Who knows with kids these days? The youngest girl I've ever even held was eighteen. I have no idea what to expect from having a kid, but especially not from a girl."

"Tutus, tiaras, and tea parties?" I suggested and dodged his fist when he swung it at me again. "I'm not even trying to give you shit. That's honestly what I expect you're in for with a daughter. Besides, at least you'll have Shira around to help you."

"Shira's brain has turned to mush." He scrubbed his hands along the stubble on his jaw, his mouth hanging half open. "I don't know how long it'll be before she's back online either. We're taking it day by day for now. At least we're almost ready for the baby to come."

"By which you mean you've been spending your salary on diapers instead of beer?"

He nodded, grimacing. "Whenever I even look at a beer, Shira reminds me we have better things to spend our money on. I can't even remember the last time I tasted alcohol."

I took a step back in case he would be tempted to try hit me again, then laughed. "I never thought I'd see the day any of this happened in your life. Weren't you always the one who said you'd never let a woman rule you or have kids running around? Look at you now, bro."

"We were in our early twenties when I said that shit, Jaxon. We could've taken down Zeus back then in our minds. Times change."

"You mean you don't think we can take down Zeus anymore?" I smacked a hand over my chest. "That's insulting, man. And discouraging. I had a beatdown scheduled with the king of the gods for this afternoon. Think I should cancel?"

"Yeah, I think you should fucking cancel." He laughed as he pushed past me. "At our age, the only thing we should have a beatdown scheduled with is some or other joint disease."

"Speak for yourself. I'm still healthy and fit as a fucking fiddle." I curled my arms to show off my biceps and he snorted in response.

"I've known you, what, almost twenty years now?" He eyeballed me with amusement in his gaze. "Trust me. I've seen you look much more ready to take on the king of the gods than you do right now. Sorry, bro."

"I think I look pretty good for my age." I lifted the hem of my T-shirt to smack my abs before dropping the act and walking to the breakroom with him to get coffee. "All joking aside, you really ready for this kid?"

"Ready or not, she's coming." He sighed as he pushed through the door and flipped on the ancient coffeemaker. "I think we're as ready as we're ever going to be. We've got everything the books say we need and we've been to the classes. What about you? What's going on in your life?"

"I've actually been thinking about taking a trip to Fiji," I said as I grabbed two mugs from the drying rack beside the rusted sink. "I probably won't do it, but we just flew over there, and I got to talking to a guy who'd visited. Sounds fucking chill."

"I've seen some pictures." He scratched his jaw while he thought. "Why don't you think you'll go? I would. You don't have any ties here holding you back."

"Yeah, that's why I've been playing with the idea. I haven't taken a real break in years. It'll be nice to cut loose a little."

"So go." He lifted the pot when the coffee was ready and filled the mugs I'd set down. Cocking his head at me as he picked his up, he flashed me a smile. "Maybe you'll meet the future Mrs. Scott on faraway shores. Fair warning, if you do, all the shit you've ever given me is coming back at you tenfold."

"I wouldn't expect anything different." I cracked my neck before wagging my eyebrows at him. "Why don't you come with me? Isn't there a name for a break before the baby is born?"

"Yeah, it's called a babymoon and it's taken by the parents." He waved a finger between our chests. "Shira would never agree to you and me going on a babymoon and leaving her behind."

"I could always talk to your baby momma. Shira loves me." I took a sip of my coffee just as Kavan nearly sprayed the one he had just taken all over me.

Once he swallowed, he coughed a few times before he had his laughter under control. "She doesn't love you that much. Fuck, I don't even think she loves *me* that much. Letting us take off to go on vacation in Fiji when she's due in less than eight weeks? There's more of a chance that all the profit made from every oil reserve in the world will be donated to charity than there is of Shira agreeing to that."

"She's been making you watch documentaries about the importance of conserving nature and marine life again, hasn't she?"

He nodded, a heavy sigh parting his lips. "It's the baby animals, man. They get to her."

I hummed a sympathetic noise at the back of my throat. "You have less than eight weeks to go. You'll make it. Just hang in there. It'll all be worth it in the end."

"I think so." He smiled and gave himself a visible shake. "Worrying isn't going to help anyway. So, Fiji? You going?"

"I think so," I said, echoing him. "Fuck it. Why not, right?"

"You only live once. Or whatever it is the cool kids are saying these days." We walked out of the break room and to our respective workstations.

When I got to mine, I took my phone out of my pocket and pulled up the airline's website. There was no harm in knowing when the next flights out were.

As if fate itself was giving me the nod on this plan, there was a crew seat available on a plane leaving in just a few hours. I hovered with my thumb above the reserve button for all of thirty seconds before I made my final decision.

Kavan and the cool kids were right. We only lived once. If even fate wanted me to go to Fiji, I sure as fuck wasn't saying no.

CHAPTER 5

LINDSAY

A wall of thick humidity hit me as soon as we disembarked from the plane. From my quick view of my surroundings before I got whisked away in the crowd, it was green there. Green and lush and lively.

Not that any of the liveliness extended to me.

I felt like I'd been hit by a water balloon filled with vapor and my lungs were mildly protesting with every breath I drew in. As my fellow travelers swept me up in their wake, everyone seemed to know where they wanted to go.

I followed willingly, feeling like a fish out of water and as uncomfortable as a cat with tape stuck beneath my paws. Rock anthems blared in my earbuds, and I was tempted to scream out the lyrics as I tried to find the carousel with my bag on it.

I couldn't hear the announcements in the airport, but when I lifted the earbuds out and heard that none of what the airport management was saying was in English, I realized they wouldn't help me much anyway.

Hoisting the strap of my backpack on my shoulder, I looked around and hoped to find out where to go. A flickering screen on a pillar to my left displayed flight information coupled with the number of the belt where passengers' luggage had to be collected, but Houston wasn't on it yet.

My fellow travelers were nowhere to be seen—none that I recognized anyway. People swarmed past me like ants on a mission to get to a fallen cube of sugar, but no one stopped when I tried to speak to them.

It didn't help that there was a whole contingent of honeymooners arriving, acting as a constant reminder that I should've been there with my husband as well. Will might not have knocked my feet out from under me, but I really had been looking forward to being married to him. We'd been friends for years before he finally asked me out on our first date. Transitioning from friendship to a romantic relationship had been as easy as breathing, even if it wouldn't have qualified as the most epic of love stories. Without him being there with me, I felt empty and lost in more ways than one. I'd lost my friend and my fiancé in one fell swoop, and now I couldn't even find my luggage.

Houston finally snuck onto the board with the collection information, but when I got to the carousal corresponding with the number displayed on it, there was nothing and no one there. I shut my eyes and sucked in a breath in an attempt to keep the tears threatening to fall at bay.

"Excuse me, miss?" a chirpy voice behind me said. "Have you arrived on the flight from Houston?"

Opening my eyes, I spun around to see a young woman dressed in an official-looking uniform smiling at me. "I have. Do you know where I can collect my luggage?"

"This carousel is giving us problems today. Please proceed to number six. Everything is being offloaded there."

I nodded my thanks and made my way through the crowd of people, searching for the number six above each belt as I went. Silently fuming about why they would've put up a different number on the display screen just minutes ago, I almost missed the other people from my flight clamoring around a carousel on my right.

A relieved sigh escaped me as I joined their ranks with my trolley, waiting patiently for my suitcase to come around. The same cases appeared time and again, until they were all gone and the people around me had dispersed.

Eventually, the belt stopped and the screen above it switched off. I frowned up at it, dread already pooling in my stomach.

"Is there a problem here, miss?"

The same woman from before came to stand beside me, smiling as politely as before. It seemed she was the official dealing with this flight.

I sighed as I turned to face her yet again. "Yes, there's a problem. You just directed me to this carousel a little while ago. It was supposed to be the one for the flight that came in from Houston, but my baggage never came out."

She nodded briskly while I spoke, asked for my boarding pass to check the baggage tag on it, barked something into the handheld radio she carried with her, then gave me an apologetic smile when a reply came through.

"I'm so sorry. It seems your luggage has been misplaced. Rest assured that it is our priority to return it to you safely. We will deliver it to your hotel tomorrow. I just need you to sign some forms for me."

Rage, frustration, annoyance, and immense sadness swelled inside me and battled for dominance. In the end, all that came out was a soft grunt and a half sob.

"Fine. Just tell me where to go."

Arguing with her wouldn't get me anywhere. She was only doing her job. It wasn't her fault my bag was missing, and making a scene wouldn't make it miraculously get here faster. The only thing I could speed up was how soon I could get out of the airport, and cooperating seemed like the best way to get that done.

What felt like a whole ream of paper later, I was finally on my way out with nothing except for the backpack I'd had with me on the flight. At least I had my toothbrush and some other basic toiletries in there.

Once I got to the resort, I'd have to wash the simple tank top and shorts combo I was wearing. At least it would dry overnight, considering the airy fabric it was made of.

Trying to keep my emotions in check and my spirits up, I reminded myself that I was in freaking Fiji—without Will—but I would have to get used to doing things without him anyway. Being alone had never bothered me before and I was determined to get back to that frame of mind.

When I walked out of the terminal, I focused on the vivid colors and the beautiful scenery instead of the gaping hole beside me where my husband should've been. Bustling roads surrounded the airport, but beyond them were mountains covered in lush greenery and palm trees reaching up toward the bright blue sky.

A slight smile was on my lips when I spotted my resort's counter. Unfortunately, the parking bay behind it was empty. The smile dropped, and once again, I got the distinct feeling that something else was about to go wrong.

"I'm sorry," the man manning the desk said. "The shuttle service left about fifteen minutes ago. There will be another shuttle, but it is only arriving in time for this evening's flight."

I rubbed my hands over my cheeks and brought my palms together underneath my chin. Maybe coming here had been a colossal mistake after all. It was becoming increasingly clear that the universe or fate or whatever just didn't want me there.

"Is there any other transportation available to the hotel?" I was on the verge of tears again, and he must've heard it in my voice because his features suddenly pinched in sympathy. *And there's the pity I don't want. Half a world away and it's still fucking there.*

"There are taxis going out that way, ma'am, but the line for them is about an hour long."

He nodded toward a snake of people lining up not far from where we stood. "The next bus leaves in fifteen minutes, but the tickets might be sold out."

After explaining to me where the bus terminal was, he wished me luck and I hurried to the ticket counter. The giggling couple in front of me snagged the last seats on the next bus, leaving me misty eyed when I joined the others waiting for a taxi.

When I finally got into the backseat of my transportation, I was exhausted and blind to the landscape as we zipped past. The driver quickly realized I was in no mood to make small talk, and the cab soon filled with upbeat, island-style music that accompanied the worst ride of my life so far.

I was in such a stupor that I hardly noticed when we stopped and the man had to all but jostle me to get out. Paying him in American currency because I didn't even have local dollars yet, I gathered my backpack and went in search of the front desk.

A long bath, blackout curtains, and a fluffy hotel robe while my clothes dried were just what the doctor ordered. There were colorful flowers in vases on glass tables, marble floors, and a glorious view of the ocean from the lobby, but I just couldn't bring myself to take any of it in.

All I wanted was a bath, my bed, and for it to be tomorrow.

Even that, it seemed, was too much to ask. A kind-eyed woman with a wreath of flowers around her neck grimaced after typing my information into her computer.

"I'm so sorry, Ms. Flinn. It appears we've had a double booking for your room. Our other guests checked into it over an hour ago."

Hysteria welled up like a tidal wave in my chest. "Are you kidding me?"

She glanced at her screen again, shaking her head. "I'm afraid not. We're fully booked for the week, but perhaps we can arrange a voucher at a different—"

I waved my hand, unable to stand listening to even another word out of her mouth. Rationally, I knew this wasn't her fault either, but I'd had it up to my eyeballs with this shitty day.

Marching away from the front desk, I sagged into the closest chair I could find and frantically searched for my phone in my backpack. Tears spilled out of my eyes and rushed down my cheeks, even if I was doing a good job of not turning into a screeching mess.

There were too many people around and I didn't want anyone bearing witness to the breakdown I felt coming.

Ember answered on the first ring. "How're the cocktails on the beach?"

"I should never have come here." I hiccupped, fighting back sobs while trying to keep my voice low. My volume rose as I picked up speed, though, despite my best efforts. "I got stood up at the altar, don't have my supposed-to-be husband with me, my luggage got lost, I missed the shuttle, and now I don't have a room."

"Fuck." My poor best friend spent the next few minutes trying her best to talk me off the ledge and out of jumping on the first flight home. "Okay, now that you're breathing again, this is what you're going to do. Wipe your eyes. Take a deep breath. Then you go right back to that receptionist and demand a room. Don't leave until she gives you a goddamn bed."

"Right." I wasn't exactly feeling it, but I had no other choices at the moment. "I'll call you later."

"Go get 'em, girl!" she cheered before hanging up.

Squaring my shoulders, I followed her instructions before getting back to my feet. Instead of rejoining the crowd waiting to be checked in, I went right back to the same lady at the front desk.

"I'm sorry, ma'am, but there's nothing I can do," she said once she'd finished up with the clients she was busy helping. "We don't have any rooms available and—"

A man's voice spoke up from behind me just as a heavy, muscular arm draped itself over my shoulders. "I don't think you understand. My wife and I have reserved a room for our honeymoon and we'll get one. The double booking must've happened at your end, which means it's your responsibility to make it right."

The body suddenly pressed up to mine was as hard as a rock and a faint spicy scent came off it. The cologne smelled amazing, and I wondered what it was. My mind immediately drifted to whether Will would like it. Then I remembered it wasn't my problem what he liked anymore.

I turned toward the stranger, having to tip my head back to get a good look at him. He was taller than I expected. The top of my head only reached his cheek.

I nearly stumbled backward when I saw what he looked like. His features were as chiseled as his body felt against mine, his jaw angular and dusted with light brown stubble. High cheekbones looked like they could cut glass and would make a model jealous, yet there was no mistaking the masculine ruggedness he exuded.

Glancing down, he caught me gaping up at him and winked a melted-honey-colored eye at me. Technically, I supposed his eyes would be classified as brown, but there was an amber ring around his iris and bolts of it shooting from his pupil to the outer edge.

A small smirk lifted the corner of his mouth before he turned his attention back to the receptionist and took charge of the situation when she repeated her excuses to him. "We'd like to see your manager. This is our honeymoon and we're not taking no for an answer. You can go get him now, thanks. Much appreciated."

She stared at him for a beat before she turned around and disappeared behind a door in the paneling of the wall. The guy didn't loosen the grip he had on my shoulders, but he did turn slightly into me, that same mischievous smirk still in place.

"Hi, it's nice to meet you. Play along, okay? We'll get a room, but only if they believe us."

There was so much light in those eyes when they met mine that I could only nod my agreement.

"Okay then, darling wifey, let's get ourselves a room." He smiled, and my heart skipped a beat. There were some people in this world who had absolutely dazzling smiles. This mysterious stranger was certainly one of them.

Which begs the question, who is he and why is he helping me? Beautiful strangers don't usually go out of their way to help borderline hysterical dumpees, do they? I had no idea. Nothing even remotely like this had ever happened to me.

I still didn't even really know what *was* happening to me. It was confusing as all get-out, and I hated being confused. But under the circumstances, I wasn't about to smack his arm off me and demand answers.

I wanted a room, and he seemed confident he could get one for me. *Have it your way, kind stranger. Just get me my damned bath. Then I'll worry about getting answers.*

CHAPTER 6

JAXON

The woman stared at me like I was crazy. Maybe I was, but I didn't really care. Even though her face was stained with tears and her cheeks were mottled with red blotches, she was hot as hell. Thick, jet-black hair was piled into a high ponytail at the back of her head and she gave me that look through the deepest, clearest blue eyes I'd ever seen.

Droplets still clung to the long lashes framing those eyes, but that didn't detract from their beauty. In fact, all the tears really served to confirm was that she wasn't wearing any makeup because nothing was smudging.

So she was naturally beautiful. I liked that. There was nothing worse than all those layers of warpaint so many women covered themselves in daily.

This woman wasn't dressed to impress either, but considering what I already knew about her, that wasn't surprising. Her navy linen shorts and simple white tank top had been paired with brown leather sandals. I had to give it to her. She looked good—especially if what I'd overheard her saying was true. She definitely wasn't trying to impress, but somehow, she still did.

A throat clearing behind us yanked my gaze away from her. It landed on a beefy man wearing a suit and a nametag that read, Bobby. "What can I help you with today?"

"Well, Bobby, it seems your lovely establishment has made a mistake. My wife and I have just arrived for our honeymoon and we've been told there's no room available for us. There's been a double booking."

A defensive, arrogant gleam entered his dark eyes. "Yes, so I've been told. I've also been informed that you've been offered a voucher for a different hotel in order to correct the situation but that you're refusing it."

"Yeah, see, that's because we booked here for a reason. This is supposed to be one of the nicest hotels around, and we'd really rather stay here."

"We have no more rooms available for the week, as you've been told." He folded his arms across his wide chest and lifted his chin, narrowing his eyes slightly on mine. "There is only a suite available here and it's more expensive than the garden-view room you've paid for."

"That's a shame for you," I replied, tugging the woman into my side and sliding my free hand under her chin to let her know I wanted her to look at me.

Staring into those expressive eyes that might as well have been screaming at me to tell her what the fuck I was doing, I fixed a dopey expression to my face and didn't break eye contact with her as I addressed the manager.

"We'll take the suite, but we're not going to pay more for it than we already have. We will have a place to consummate our marriage tonight, and if we don't get to those keys very soon, that place will be those couches at the entrance."

Her nostrils flared, but she didn't argue. She just took another deep breath, nodding at him before turning her face into my shoulder. Clearly, she wasn't comfortable with my threat of public sex.

I would've laughed if I wasn't trying to convince the rude ass-wipe that I was serious. Personally, if it were with a woman who looked like her, I wouldn't have a problem getting it up even if there was a rather large audience gaping at us and the very real possibility of being arrested.

It would be so worth it.

But I was trying to convince him I was serious, so I leaned down and ran my nose along the length of hers, closing my eyes to breathe her in. "I'm not kidding, dude. Keys or couches. Your choice, but make it fast."

I felt her shaking against me. When I opened my eyes, it became clear that she was laughing. That was why she was hiding her face, not because she was embarrassed. Or maybe it was a little bit of both.

Knowing she was laughing about it made it that much harder to keep myself from doing it. The manager sputtered a few times, but eventually, he made the right decision and held a key card out to me.

"Please enjoy your stay, sir."

"We will." I plucked the card from his hand between two fingers, slid it into the back pocket of my shorts, and tugged on her. "Come on, baby. Let's go get this party started."

We walked away with her still tucked under my arm, and I heard him whispering to the receptionist furiously about how tourists had no shame. Chuckling under my breath, I only let her go when we reached the elevators.

"Where is the suite?" she asked, taking a step away from me and angling her head back to look into my eyes. "My room was supposed to be on the third floor."

I checked the card before returning it to my pocket. "Beachfront bungalow seven."

Glancing at the map of the resort mounted on the wall next to the elevators, I jabbed the button to go down. "Seems it's right on the beach. I'm Jaxon, by the way."

"Lindsay." She held out her hand to shake mine, but I enveloped her in a hug instead. We'd be fucked if that manager saw us shaking hands and exchanging names.

She tensed in my arms but let me hold her for a second before pushing me away. "Why did you do that?"

"I overheard you on the phone," I admitted. A low ding signaled the arrival of our elevator. I ushered her in with a hand to her lower back. "Maybe this room will make it better for you."

She turned away from me, but not before I saw the flush creeping up her cheeks. Three walls of the elevator were made of glass, and she braced her hands against the copper railing inside, her gaze firmly fixed on the ocean beyond before we dipped beneath the greenery surrounding the main building of the hotel.

"I'm sorry you had to hear all that," she said as the doors slid open again, depositing us on the ground level of the impressive resort.

I shrugged and held a hand in front of the doors to keep them open while she walked out first. "Don't be sorry. I'm just glad we got the room. Sounds like you've had a rough go of things the last couple of days."

She snorted in the most adorable way and rolled her eyes as she looked back at me over her shoulder. "That's one way of putting it. Another—and this is the one I prefer—is that it's been a clusterfuck of epic proportions that not even the most sadistic of scriptwriters would've put the beloved characters of their movie through."

I barked out a laugh. "I like that description better too."

Checking the room numbers and arrows on the wall, I pointed down toward a pathway that wound through the garden. "I'm pretty sure it's that way."

Adjusting the strap of my duffel bag on my shoulder, I stayed half a step behind her while navigating us in what I hoped was the direction of the bungalow. We'd only gone a few yards when the path opened up behind a cluster of palm trees.

A thin stretch of bright green grass separated a row of free-standing, reed-roofed bungalows from the beach. Hedges created the perimeter between the garden and the sand, but there was a walkway cut into each patch of greenery leading from the entrance of every bungalow.

Hammocks were stung between the trees in front of each room as well, giving the impression that everyone had their own private place to hang around and watch the sun set. I let out a low whistle and arched a brow at Lindsay.

"This is pretty awesome, huh?"

Her eyes were wide when she brought them back to mine. "It's definitely better than a garden-view room on the third story."

We located the number on our key and I swiped it in front of the reader before swinging the door open and motioning her in. She grinned until she noticed I wasn't stepping back.

"What are you doing?" The grin morphed into a frown. "Why aren't you leaving?"

"I couldn't get a room here either, so maybe we can help each other out."

Blinking rapidly, she lifted her hands and took a step back. "Oh. No. No. No. No. No. I'm not sleeping in the same room as some stranger. Look, thanks for your help, but no."

"There's a conference on the island," I said. "All the hotels are fully booked for the next few days. You're not going to leave me on the street, are you?"

"That's exactly what I'm going to do." She crossed her arms and moved into the doorway. "Thanks again for your help. I hope you find someplace to sleep."

I peered over her shoulder and spotted a couch I was pretty sure rolled out into a bed. There were telltale bars visible at the bottom from this angle.

"I already have found a place to sleep." I inclined my head and jerked a thumb toward the sofa. "Right there. You won't even know I'm here."

She turned slowly, eyeing my proposed sleeping quarters before moving farther into the bungalow. I let her have a look around but dropped the duffel at my feet. I had no intention of leaving there without a bed for the night.

Getting a flight hadn't been a problem at all. Accommodations, however, was proving to be a challenge. I was perfectly happy to couch surf in shared spaces too, but not even that was available.

When Lindsay came back, her arms were crossed and she glared daggers at me. "There's a door between the bedroom and the couch. The bathroom is accessible from both sides, but all the doors can lock.

If I catch you fiddling with any of the doors when they're locked, you're out."

"You got it. I only need a place to sleep anyway. I'll grab a shower when you're out. No worries."

"*No worries,* he says," she muttered, blue eyes dark with disbelief. "Trust me. I'm worried."

She sighed and turned around without saying anything else. Taking it as my cue, I stepped into the room and stripped out of my sweat-soaked shirt immediately.

Her eyes narrowed again when she reached the door to the bedroom and turned to see me half naked. "What are you doing?"

"Getting comfortable." I smirked. "It's been a long-ass day, and have you felt how hot it is out there?"

Releasing another sigh, a heavier one this time, she shook her head and slammed the bedroom door behind her like she was aggravated with me. I couldn't help chuckling and shaking my head right back at her.

She wouldn't even have been in the suite if it wasn't for me. I had no idea why she was acting so hostile and uptight all of a sudden, but I wasn't letting her ruin this for me.

Fucking Fiji, baby. I'd actually done it. I was there.

One anxious roommate wasn't going to fuck up my vacation. I'd been prepared to live with tons of roommates in hostels or someone sleeping on the couch next to mine. I could deal with one emotional woman in the next bedroom.

This suite was more than big enough for the both of us.

CHAPTER 7

LINDSAY

The mattress I lay on was firm, the sheets were as soft as silk, and the comforter was quite fluffy. I'd only switched on the air conditioning minutes ago when I entered, but I had an idea of why the bedding was so plush despite the heat outside.

"He moved in with you?" Ember laughed.

I lifted the phone away from my ear until the cackling stopped. "Are you done? It's not funny."

"You're right. It's not funny. It's hilarious."

I rolled over on the bed and watched the waves lapping at the shore while listening to my best friend's attempts at making light of the situation. "What's not funny about it? A smoking-hot guy gets you a suite at one of the nicest hotels in Fiji, pretends to be your husband, and then decides to shack up with you? It's the stuff movies are made of."

"Horror movies maybe," I said. "His name is Jaxon. If anyone finds my body carved up like pieces on a sushi buffet, point the authorities in his direction."

"Did you get a funny vibe off him?"

"Did any of Jeffry Dahmer's victim's get a funny vibe off him until it was too late?"

I could practically hear her eyes rolling all the way from home. "Don't assume the worst in him. This could be the best thing that could've happened to you. You were worried about being alone and having people pity you. Now you won't be and they'll be envious if he's as good looking as you say he is. You didn't happen to snap a picture, did you?"

"No." I sat up and stared at the door, trying to develop X-ray vision. Not because he'd been well on his way to getting naked when I'd left, but because I wanted to see what he was unpacking from that massive black duffel bag of his. "Maybe I should try to later, though. It might help when you have to send the cops after him."

"I'm pretty sure that hotel has cameras everywhere. They'll be sure to have a good shot of his face. I don't want a picture so they can track him. I want to see what your new roomie looks like."

"He's not my roomie." Theoretically, he was my *bungalowie*, but he wasn't stepping a single foot in my room. "I didn't come here to deal with the what-ifs of a guy I don't even know, Em. I came to relax and enjoy my me-moon."

"Maybe your me is in for a new moon," she joked, and I scoffed at her.

"That doesn't even make any sense."

"It makes sense to *me*," she sang. "Go out there and get to know this Jaxon. He sounds like quite a character."

"He could be a serial killer for all we know. Aren't they known to be charming and good looking?"

"I'm going to the beach if you want to join me," he called from the other side of the door.

I froze, mortified while trying to figure out if he could've been listening in on my conversation.

"I'm not going to find any opportune victims for my serial killing," he said. "I'm just going for a light swim."

Blood rushed to my cheeks when I realized he'd probably heard every word.

Ember cracked up over the phone, obviously having heard him

too. "Dude, he has a sense of humor. You have to go to the beach with him."

I groaned into my pillow, thrashing about on my bed and wondering how exactly I was supposed to get over this latest embarrassment. She wouldn't let me stew, though.

"Can you see the beach from your window? Has he left?"

"I think so." My voice was muffled by the pillow I still held over my face, but then I got genuinely curious about whether I would be able to see him.

Slowly dropping the pillow to the side, I got off the bed and moved stealthily, as if he had that X-ray vision I'd tried to develop and would be watching my every move. "Hang on. I'm going to the window. I'll tell you in a second."

"Why are you whispering?" She kept her own voice low, though I could hear the laughter threatening to break free.

"Because he was listening to us a minute ago," I hissed. "He might still be there."

"Nothing you say now will be as humiliating as what he's already heard." She giggled. "Hurry your ass up and check if you can see him. Then describe what you see in fine, fine detail."

"I'm not about to check him out and report back to you, you perve. The only reason I even agreed to let him stay is because without him, we'd both have been without a room for the night. Possibly even the week."

"You say potato. I say *potahto*." There was a definite shrug present in her voice. "I know you're not planning on having hot rebound sex with him, but would it hurt to get to know the guy and spend some time with him this week? You're fake married to him, remember?"

"Don't remind me. I'm already regretting playing along with his charade." I wasn't really, though. The sound of the waves against the sand and the magnificent view of the ocean from my bedroom window were enough to convince me that he'd done us both a favor. "I know I have to try and make the best of this whole situation. I just don't know how."

Guys like Will were the only ones I'd ever been friends with. They

41

played video games for fun, argued about philosophy over Pinot Noir on nights out, and still thought of the gym as the place where the jocks who beat them up at school hung out.

They were my kind of people. Hence why I was only friends with people like them.

Ember was an exception. She was the epitome of the bad-ass girl with all her tattoos and piercings, devil-may-care attitude, and lack of faith in humanity. The gym was her hunting ground and the men who thought they were the predators, her prey.

We hit it off because we were opposites. She was the yin to my yang, and it worked that way. I didn't need another yang. No one needed two yangs to their yin.

She exhaled into the receiver. "You don't need to know how, my dearest friend. He invited you to the beach, so you go. Didn't you say he completely took charge in the lobby?"

"I did say that." Much to my chagrin right then.

"Then let him take charge," she said like it was obvious. "If you end up having cocktails on the beach with him instead of alone, who cares? You sure as hell shouldn't."

"I'm not exactly the kind of girl who lets a guy take charge." I very much preferred to be in control of my own life. "Who even does that anymore? You know women are allowed to vote now, right?"

She made a gagging noise. "Spare me the feminist speech. There's a big difference between letting him befriend you and show you a good time, and him dominating every aspect of your life while expecting you to have dinner cooked and on the table at seven."

"Point taken." I scrunched up my nose as I walked to the window. "That wasn't really what I meant anyway. I just... I feel so lost."

"I get that, babe." Her voice turned gentle. "It's completely understandable. Your world turned upside down a few days ago. Will tossed your precious planner out the window and now it's time to make new plans. All I'm suggesting is rolling with what fate has pushed into your path."

"So what am I supposed to do?" I pushed my face almost all the way up to the glass, craning my neck to be able to see the beach in front of our bungalow.

Jaxon was standing up to his knees in the water, his wide back muscular and all inked up. I was too far away to make out any details of the artwork covering his skin, but it was etched from hip to hip, extending all the way up to and across his shoulder blades.

There were splotches of ink on his upper arms too, which I'd missed before when I'd barely caught a glimpse of his bare skin before retreating into my room. He did a half turn when a wave rolled at him, displaying more color on his chest as well.

None of it would show when he was wearing clothes, but it'd obviously been well positioned. Almost every inch of skin that would be hidden beneath a shirt was tattooed.

Although the lines beside his eyes and on his forehead made him appear older than I was, it was obvious he kept his body in great shape. Distance again hampered the details, but the V between his hips and the definition of his shoulders, arms, and torso would've been visible from outer space.

A wave smacked into his back, and he turned a second later and dragged both hands through his hair to slick it back. He grinned when he turned back, like he was having the time of his life and was just soaking it in.

That grin made me feel slightly jealous of him. He seemed to have everything in life perfectly under control, content with every fucking thing that happened to him. Like he knew the universe would cater to his every whim and he simply trusted it to do so.

My tongue stuck to the roof of my mouth. *What would it be like to live like him?*

"What do you do?" Ember repeated my question through the phone. "You be yourself and you—" She stopped talking, sighed, and changed direction. "Actually, you don't be yourself. You be someone else. Just for this week. You live someone else's life and you see where it takes you."

"That sounds like a horrible idea," I said, but I nodded my agreement with her plan anyway. "I'll let you know how it goes."

"You do that."

We ended the call shortly after that, and I thought about what she'd said. Jaxon didn't know me and neither did anyone else on this island.

If there was ever a time to cut loose and just go with it, this was it. My one and only opportunity.

Ember was right about the resort having cameras. If I suddenly disappeared, they would know to start with him. He hadn't been wearing a cap or anything, so he should be easy to identify.

Besides, going out to the beach with him seemed like a minuscule thing in comparison to agreeing to share a room. Since I didn't have a suitcase or any other clothes than what I was wearing, I went to splash some water on my face before making my way out to the beach.

Jaxon broke into a huge grin as I padded onto the soft, warm sand. "Come hang out with me, roomie. It'll be fun."

I ground my teeth but sat down at the edge of the water, praying that this time I was actually making the right decision.

CHAPTER 8

JAXON

Lindsay had obviously washed the tears off her face, and she looked even fiercer than she had before. Her eyes tracked my every movement, the blue in them reflecting the darker parts of the horizon she was pretending to stare off into.

Even though she'd agreed to sit with me, it seemed she was averse to making eye contact. She sat in the sand just beyond where the water could reach her but stretched out her legs so the surf touched her toes when it came in.

She was skittish, but I couldn't blame her. She was obviously still pissed I was sharing her room with her, and she didn't quite know what to make of me.

Can't fault her for that either. "Do you really think I'm a serial killer?"

Breaking the ice felt like the right thing to do. I couldn't really make conversation with the girl if she was convinced I was going to gut her.

She brought her gaze to mine as she folded her arms around her knees. "Are you?"

"No." A wave crashed into the backs of my knees, but I took a step forward to avoid toppling onto my face just in time. "I'm here for the same reason you are."

"You got stood up on your wedding day and decided to go on your honeymoon anyway?"

I chuckled. "Maybe not the exact same reason. I'm assuming you wanted to get away from it all. So did I."

She shrugged. "Everything had already been paid for. It seemed like a waste to not make use of it. I don't know. Coming here was a spur of the moment decision."

"You don't make a lot of those, do you?" It didn't take a genius to see that she was uncomfortable, and it wasn't just because I was rooming with her.

She dipped her head in acknowledgment. "I prefer plans as opposed to spontaneity."

"You can't plan for everything." I smirked and pointed a thumb at my chest. "There's no way you could've planned for meeting me, for example."

"That's because you might be a psycho. Who goes around hotel lobbies eavesdropping on private conversations and then inserting themselves into that person's life?"

"Me. I didn't plan it either, if that makes you feel any better. I just walked in there hoping to get a room, and I ended up standing near the chair you were sitting on. When I heard what you said, I thought maybe we could solve both our problems."

"How much did you hear?" She planted her hands in the sand behind her and leaned back on her palms.

"Enough." I walked forward a few steps and saw her gaze trailing down the length of my body before she snapped it back up. She was doing a lot of that—checking me out before she caught herself doing it.

I didn't mind. I just didn't know why she felt like she had to stop. I was doing the same thing to her, minus the stopping part.

She tilted her head and lifted a hand to shield her eyes from the sun. "What do you do for a living if you're not a serial killer?"

"I think even they have day jobs," I joked. "I'm a pilot. My hobbies do not include homicide, mayhem, or any of the other colorful thoughts you've had."

"What are your hobbies?" she asked.

I shook my head. "You first. What do you do for a living?"

"I'm in Human Resources." There was a hint of pride in her voice. "Senior consultant."

I trailed my gaze across her face again. "Senior, huh? You don't look like you should be a senior anything."

"I worked hard." She jutted her chin out. "Youngest in the department to ever get promoted to senior status."

"How old are you?"

She shook her head and motioned to me. "Your turn."

"What do you want to know?" I walked the rest of the way out of the water and went to sit next to her.

As much as I enjoyed looking at Lindsay, the way she kept looking at me was getting my blood flowing, and in my wet shorts, there would be no hiding it. The last thing I needed was her thinking that I was going to try to get into her pants.

I very much would've liked to get into her pants, but I doubted she would be interested. Despite her thinking I was hot and her undressing me with her eyes, she hardly seemed to be the type to fuck what had happened out of her system.

"My hobbies?" I focused on the question she'd asked me instead of letting my brain wander to speculating over how I might be able to help her if she *was* interested in fucking it out of her system. "Working on old planes, hiking, scuba diving. A bunch of stuff really. A lot of physical activity."

She slanted her gaze at me, once again running it over my body even though I was now seated. "Well, at least that's one thing about you that adds up."

"Everything about me adds up," I said. "I haven't lied once since I met you."

"You haven't?" She lifted her brows. "Did you and I get married in some ceremony I don't remember then?"

"I haven't lied to *you*." I propped my elbows on my knees and admired the view while we talked. Whoever thought the ocean was just the ocean no matter where you went clearly hadn't been here before. "Don't pretend like you minded me lying to that manager. It got us the room, didn't it?"

"Are you ever going to let me forget that?"

"Nope." I grinned. "It's true. Now answer the question. You didn't mind me lying to him about us. I saw you laughing. There's no point trying to deny it."

"I was laughing because what you were threatening to do was ridiculous." She rolled her eyes when I glanced at her. "I still can't believe he thought you were being serious."

"Hey, if this was our honeymoon and they didn't have a room for us, I would've done exactly what I threatened him with. In that context, I was being serious. If I thought you'd have been willing to take the act that far, I'd have done it anyway if he'd refused us a room."

"There's no way you'd have gotten intimate with that many people around."

I laughed. "Who said anything about getting intimate? I was talking about fucking. And yes, I would have done it with that many people around. I don't know them."

"Maybe not, but they would've gotten to know you pretty damn well during the ensuing criminal trial."

"Do you really think any cop would've arrested me for simply wanting to consummate my marriage to my beautiful bride? Lack of self-control isn't a crime."

"It is when the failure to control yourself results in you committing a crime. Having sex in the lobby of a hotel is definitely a crime."

"I'm a man in love. No one would blame me. In fact, I'm pretty sure I'd have been able to spin it against the hotel for not having a room for us."

"Not being able to get a room at a hotel doesn't constitute a justifiable excuse to escape criminal charges for sex in public. Can you imagine the consequences if it did? People would be banging all over every lobby of every nice hotel. Especially over holiday weekends. It would be a disaster."

"Wow. You really don't like sex in public, do you?"

She shrugged. "I wouldn't know and we're not discussing this anymore. I just really can't believe the manager took you seriously. That's the point of this conversation."

"Nah, the point is he was right to take me seriously because if I was married to you and I'd already been forced to keep my hands off you for the entire flight, you better believe I'd have made good on my threat if they didn't give us a room."

"The flight is less than fourteen hours long. It's hardly as punishing as you're making it out to be."

"That's fourteen fucking hours of sitting next to you and keeping my hands to myself. It's way more punishing than I'm making it out to be."

She turned her head to give me a look, but our gazes caught and held for longer than either of us intended for them to. There was incredulity in her deep blue depths, but there was some heat there too. It seemed talking about this was turning her on.

I didn't have to know her well to know she'd never admit it, but I wasn't about to ask anyway. She wasn't the only one getting turned on, and I still didn't want her to know I was attracted to her at all.

If I did, I wouldn't put it past her to kick my ass out of the bungalow.

Her tongue darted out and she swiped it across her lips before giving her head a little shake. "Not being able to have sex for fourteen hours is hardly anything. Let's just leave it at that."

"Fine. As long you know we're agreeing to disagree on your final statement."

She rolled her eyes. "How old are you anyway? Aren't we both a few years past being dominated by our sexual urges?"

"Thirty-eight. I'm not dominated *by* my sexual urges. I simply dominate my sexual urges." I wagged my brows at her and grinned. "How old are you? Aren't you a few years past being so repressed and judgmental about sex?"

"I'm not repressed or judgmental." She dropped her gaze to the sand and sighed, dipping her head between her shoulders. "Okay, maybe I am a little bit of both of those things, but that's not any of your business."

I was burning to delve into that little nugget, but when she kept her eyes down, I realized it was time to let it go. "Tell me about your ex. Who leaves a woman like you at the altar?"

"Why would I talk to you about that? I hardly know you and that's highly personal."

"Who better to talk to than a stranger?" I asked. "At least you know you'd get an unbiased opinion."

She didn't say anything for a few beats. Then she sighed and pulled her knees up to her chest. Forming a bridge with her arms between them, she laid her chin down in the crook of one elbow and stared out at the azure blue swells rising and falling in the distance.

"Will and I were good friends for a long time. I should've seen it coming, but I really didn't. When I called him and he said he couldn't do it and that we both knew it was for the best, I was honestly shocked."

"Shocked but not heartbroken?" Her voice hadn't wobbled at all as she spoke. She sounded strangely detached, like she was talking about someone else's wedding falling apart.

"Why would you say that?" she asked.

"Just from the way you said that. It doesn't sound like you were all too interested in this guy. Unless you're still in shock?"

She scowled at the horizon before climbing to her feet and dusting the sand off her ass. "You know what? I tried to talk to you, but it's pointless. I think it's best for me to just go."

Storming off without another word, she left me wondering what the fuck had just happened. On the other hand, she'd been stood up mere days ago from what I could tell. It made sense that she'd be a bit volatile.

Her emotions were probably all over the place. She really didn't seem all that torn up about the breakup, though. But maybe pointing it out was somewhat tactless.

I headed back into the ocean and swam until my muscles felt it before I decided to hit the shower. As I made my way back up to the room, I caught a glimpse of Lindsay sitting alone in the dining room at the end of the row of bungalows.

It was an outdoor dining area with a kitchen under the sky and a simple thatched roof over a concrete floor. Strings of light wrapped around the beams were just starting to blink on, but she didn't seem to notice any of it as she stared out into the distance again.

I didn't stop to watch her or to wonder what she was thinking. As far as everyone at this resort was concerned, that was my wife sitting there all by herself. That was *not* a good way to spend the first night of a honeymoon, and I wouldn't let it stand.

CHAPTER 9

LINDSAY

A man who had to weigh at least four hundred pounds grinned as he came up to my table. He wore an apron with the words "If a cook ain't fat, don't eat the food" emblazoned on it, and he carried two menus in his hands.

"You're my new arrivals, right?" he asked, his big brown eyes latching on mine. "I'm Big Mac. The chef down here."

"It's nice to meet you." I smiled back at him. "I'm Lindsay."

He set the menus down on the table. "Your waitress will be coming around soon, but can I order you a drink?"

"No, I'm fine. Thanks." I pulled one of the menus closer and studied my options. "What's good here?"

All I wanted to do was eat and go to bed. I'd had a quick shower after getting back from the beach, but I hadn't had a chance yet to wash my clothes. Everything that had happened was weighing heavily on me, and I was more than ready for sleep.

Big Mac's grin widened. "Anything I make is good, but I'll whip you up something special. Take care of whatever pain you're in."

My head jerked back and I frowned up at him. "Why do you think I'm in pain?"

He shrugged. "I've met a lot of people. I know pain when I see it."

His pitch-black curls bounced as he nodded. "I think I've got just the right thing in mind for you and your new husband."

I was confused for all of about three seconds before I remembered about Jaxon. "I'm not sure if he'll be joining me this evening."

We were also going to have to figure out what to tell people if everyone at the resort knew their guests as well as Big Mac seemed to. His dark eyes lifted toward the entrance. "Oh, he is. Look over there. He's already here."

He introduced himself to my supposed husband, and the two of them hit it off immediately. While they talked about the seafood platter Big Mac suggested he would bring us, I took a minute to study Jaxon.

His hair was damp and he was wearing different clothes, so presumably he'd had a shower as well. It looked like he'd run his fingers through his hair because it was slicked back, but it was still too messy to have been brushed.

The light blue T-shirt he had on clung to his tattooed body like a second skin, stretching over his abdomen and biceps. Now that I knew what was underneath the fabric, it was a little more difficult to ignore the way he filled it out.

The guy might be a possible serial killer and thought he knew much more than he actually did, but I couldn't deny how attractive he was physically. Everything about him just worked. There wasn't a single feature out of place or anything about him that could've been better.

He smirked when he caught me staring at him again, and I narrowed my eyes, seriously considering flipping him off. The ass had overheard my conversation with Ember. He knew I thought he was good looking, but he really was. It was an objective fact. He didn't have to look so damn pleased about it every time he caught me in the act.

An act I shouldn't have been committing, sure, but I couldn't help it. He really was just that gorgeous. So what if I needed a minute to get used to being around someone who looked like him?

By the end of the week, I probably wouldn't even notice him anymore. This was just an adjustment period.

"No allergies. That sounds great, man. Thanks." He grinned at Big Mac before lowering himself into the seat across from me. The smugness from a minute before had evaporated from his eyes, leaving an unexpected warmth in them when they met mine. "You don't have any allergies, right?"

"Isn't that a question you should've asked before you ordered whatever you just did?"

"Nope. If I'd asked you in front of him, it would've been pretty fucking obvious that I don't know very much about you. Who marries someone if they don't even know about their allergies?"

"I could've been a mail-order bride," I suggested.

He smirked. "That's not really my style. Call me old fashioned, but I'd at least like to know if shellfish is going to kill a person before promising to spend the rest of my life with them."

"Would that be a deal breaker for you?" I asked. "Being allergic to shellfish?"

"Absolutely." He grinned again and there was a hint of a dimple in his left cheek.

Damn it. Because that makes it better. Fucking dimples.

"I don't have any allergies." I focused on the sun setting over the ocean instead of the stupidly sexy man sitting with me. "Do we have to eat together? I was just going to grab a bite before going to bed."

"You can still do that," he said, folding his arms on the table and leaning forward. "I'm not going to keep you here against your will. I'm not a kidnapper either."

"Good to know." I kept my eyes on the water and the gorgeous streaks of crimson and amber in the sky.

Jaxon reached over and touched my hand to get my attention. It was nothing more than a brush before he withdrew again, but it still felt like I'd been zapped with awareness of how good his skin felt against mine.

"Okay, look, I'm sorry about earlier. I shouldn't have pried." He sounded so genuine that I actually believed his apology. "I won't ask you any other questions about your relationship or your wedding. Deal?"

"Why did you?" He didn't exactly seem the type of guy who offered women a shoulder to cry on and a tub of ice cream. Then again, I didn't know whether he was that kind of guy. I didn't know much about him at all.

He cocked his head, lifting one of his shoulders as he kept those beautiful eyes on mine. "I was curious. I'm sorry if my comment offended you. I have a habit of calling things like I see them and I often forget that my observations aren't always welcome."

"Thank you. I appreciate the apology." I couldn't blame him for being curious, but I hoped to the highest of heavens that he kept his promise. "But we already have to live together. Do we really have to eat together too?"

Sitting back, he wagged his eyebrows at me. "Married people usually do, don't they?"

"Yes, but you're forgetting the fact that we're not actually married."

He lifted his hand slightly and pointed a finger before circling it. "You're forgetting the fact that everyone here thinks we are."

"The staff sure do seem to know everyone." A waitress who greeted us as Mr. and Mrs. Flinn proved my point when she came to get our drinks order. As she left, I caught Jaxon's gaze and smiled. "So, Mr. Flinn, what are we going to do about our little conundrum?"

"I'd really have preferred it if you were Mrs. Scott." He pursed his lips into a mocking pout. At least I thought it was a mocking one. If it was real, the dude had issues.

"Next time, you can make the reservations then," I said. "Since I made this booking, we're the Flinns."

"Fine." He sighed but I didn't miss the humor shining in his eyes. "I guess I could be the new-age guy who took his wife's last name."

"Look at you, being all progressive."

He winked. "As long as I get to call the shots in our marital bedroom, you can call me whatever you want."

"You just have to have the last word, don't you?"

"Yep."

The waitress delivered our drinks, and I laughed when I realized Jaxon's was a cocktail served in a massive pineapple, complete with pink umbrellas and a purple bendy straw.

"That drink kind of stole your thunder there," I said.

"When in Fiji." He shrugged and stirred the bright red liquid inside the carved-out fruit. After sticking the straw between his teeth and taking a sip, he let out a low groan. "I'll definitely be having a lot more of those. Want to try it?"

I eyed the drink and tried to ignore the effect hearing that sound from him had on me. My body had never turned on me this way before, and I didn't like it very much. "Sure. Why not?"

As soon as I wrapped my lips around the same straw his had just been around, I realized I should've insisted on getting my own. Who knew what germs this guy had, and here I was sharing a straw with him?

Why don't I care more?

I parked the thought for later consideration when the tart liquid filled my mouth. After swallowing, I licked my lips and pushed the drink back to him. "You're right. I'll definitely be having a lot more of those too."

His gaze was resting on my mouth when I looked up at him. He didn't seem to be in any hurry to move it either. When he finally lifted it to mine, I knew I wasn't imagining the smoldering heat in it.

"Why are you looking at me like that?"

"Because I was just thinking about kissing you." He didn't look away, complete confidence in his gaze. "I won't, so you don't have to worry about it. But I told you I hadn't lied to you and I didn't want to start now."

"How can you just say stuff like that?" I didn't think I'd ever met anyone quite like him.

"Why shouldn't I? Would you have preferred if I lied to you?"

"No, I just..." I trailed off. "I'm not used to people just saying whatever is on their minds, is all."

"You'd better get used to it if we're going to be spending this week together."

"Are we, though? Spending the week together? We could just pretend like we had a fight and that's why we're not doing everything together."

"I don't know anyone else here and I'm sure you don't either. No one is going to buy a couple on their honeymoon spending all their time apart. So why don't we just go with it? It'll be a nice break from the real world, and neither of us will have to keep trying to keep track of a bunch of made-up bullshit about why we're fighting."

I studied him for a long minute, taking in everything from the serious set of his jaw to the caramel-colored warmth in his eyes. "You're right. I suppose it will be easier if we just do some stuff together as opposed to having to make up excuses all the time. That sounds exhausting."

His full lips spread into a smile. "I knew you'd make the right decision. I hope you're hungry, wifey dear. That platter is huge."

Twisting around in my chair, I spotted Big Mac carrying a tray laden with all kinds of seafood and fries so big they looked like they were half a potato each. The smells wafting from it were divine when he set it down between us with a lopsided grin.

"Dig in, my friends. Please enjoy your meal."

We thanked him, and he winked at us before walking away. I smiled at the wide expanse of his back before turning back to Jaxon. "I like him. He's interesting."

"Yeah, I like him too. He reminds me of a guy I used to serve with. Alex was a Pacific Islander as well, and it just so happens he also cooked like a machine."

"You were in the service?" I probably should've guessed he had been, but I honestly hadn't gotten quite that far yet. "Is that how you became a pilot?"

"Yep. Air Force. I never would have left if I hadn't been medically discharged."

"What happened?" I asked before realizing I was now the one

delving into deeply personal territory. "Sorry. You don't have to tell me if you don't want to."

"I fucked up my knee." He moved his right leg to the side and extended it. "Tendon damage. It doesn't bother me so much anymore, but it still disqualified me from active duty."

"I'm sorry you got hurt," I said, surprised by how much I meant it. "It must've been a really difficult time for you."

"It was, but it was also years ago." He looked into my eyes. "I don't mind talking about it now. You'll get there too, you know? One day."

"What happened to me was just humiliating. I don't really think you can compare the two at all. You were a real-life superhero who wanted to keep fighting for his country, and I got dumped."

"Maybe, but it'll still get easier to talk about it."

"My brother is in the military too. I haven't seen him or heard from him in years." I didn't really know why I'd just told him that.

"Really?" Jaxon sat up straighter. "What's his name? Maybe I know him. Where is he based?"

Fuck. I'd opened the door to his questions, so I knew he wasn't just trying to pry again. I really didn't want to talk about my brother, though.

Grabbing a bite of calamari, I popped it into my mouth and widened my eyes at my fake husband. "You really have to try that. It's great. Tell me about your time in the service instead. I'd much rather hear about that."

I could practically see the gears turning in his head. He knew I'd changed the subject intentionally, but he plucked up a piece of the calamari anyway and didn't push me for answers.

We spent the rest of our dinner stuffing our faces with Big Mac's incredible food, and Jaxon told me several hilarious stories of things he'd gotten up to in the Air Force.

By the time my stomach was so full that I doubted I'd even have space to fit ice cream, I realized I may have judged him too harshly earlier. Under the circumstances, I could've spent the evening in far worse company than his.

So he'd made an insensitive comment about my previous relationship? He hadn't been wrong. I wasn't ready to talk about that particular topic with him yet, but I had a feeling that when I was, that unbiased opinion he'd offered me earlier might actually just be helpful.

CHAPTER 10

JAXON

I woke up to the smell of coffee and the sound of cabinets opening and closing. Cracking open an eye, I lifted my arm to check the watch on my wrist.

Five o'clock in the morning? What the fuck is going on?

"What are you doing?" I asked, sitting up with a groan. "It's five a.m. We're on vacation. Why are we awake?"

She turned where she was standing in the small kitchenette that was really more of a counter with a basket of fruit and a coffeemaker on it. There was a tiny sink that was probably only there so one could rinse the fruit and a few cabinets underneath with the basic cutlery and crockery.

I'd heard Lindsay washing her clothes in the bathroom after we'd gotten back from dinner, and then I'd spent an hour trying not to think about the fact that she was sleeping naked only feet away from me before I'd eventually drifted off. That felt like it'd only happened five minutes ago.

Her clothes had obviously dried overnight because she was wearing them again, clutching a mug as she stared at me with wide eyes. "I didn't mean to wake you. Sorry. Go back to sleep."

I rubbed my eyes, shaking my head before stretching and letting out a yawn worthy of a lion. "I'm up now. Again, though, why exactly is that?"

"I have a whole list of things I want to do today. I want to get the most out of this trip, see everything I'd planned on seeing, and that won't happen if I spend all day in bed."

"It's five a.m.," I repeated. "Sleeping for another hour or two would hardly count as spending all day in bed."

She shrugged, lifting the spoon out of her mug and rinsing it in the sink before setting it down on a plate. "If I get an early start today, I'll fit in more of the sights I want to see."

"You do realize that nothing is going to be open at this hour, right? You're going to have wait until the attractions open before you can actually see them anyway."

"Some of the things I want to see aren't the ordinary run-of-the-mill tourists' attractions. I'm sure I'll be able to find a taxi and I'll ask the driver to take me where I want to go. Simple."

She smiled.

I slammed my back down on the sofa-bed and grabbed a pillow, covering my face with it while I yawned again. "It's unnatural to be awake this early in the morning when you're not working, wifey dear. Go back to bed and I'll get you a taxi myself in a few hours. Just relax a little, would you?"

"Nope. I didn't come here to relax."

I frowned and yanked the pillow away, rolling over to face her and propping myself up on my elbow. "What are you talking about? You came here on your honeymoon. What else were you planning on doing?"

Her smile turned into a smirk. "Do you really have to ask?"

"When you decided to come by yourself, I meant." I cleared my throat and thanked my lucky fucking stars the sheet was still covering me from the hips down. "Didn't you come here to rest and relax?"

Why is the word come *coming up so damn much in this conversation?* It was way too early for this shit.

Lindsay's eyes were trained on mine, like she was also trying to force herself not to look anywhere she shouldn't be looking—or thought she shouldn't be looking anyway.

"I chose Fiji because there were so many things I wanted to see and do here. I would still like to see and do it all. Rest and relaxation can happen later."

Our gazes remained locked. "Are you sure I can't coax you into staying in bed a little bit longer?"

"I have a schedule and I'm sticking to it. Plus, I've already showered. There's no way I'd be able to fall asleep again now, and if I'm awake anyway, I might as well make productive use of my time."

It was clear she wasn't going to cave, so I gave in. "Fine. I'm ready then. Just give me a minute to brush my teeth and grab a clean shirt."

"I wasn't trying to get you to come with me. You're more than welcome to stay in bed."

"No, you've convinced me. Let's have a proper sightseeing adventure."

She rolled her eyes. "You've got five minutes, and if you're not ready to go by then, I'm leaving without you."

I climbed out of bed, stretching again, and nodded. "You got it, boss lady."

"You're going to make an excellent husband to some lucky lady someday. So well trained already."

Wadding up the T-shirt I'd worn last night, I tossed it at her head and walked into the bathroom to the sound of her laughter ringing out as she pulled it off. "What? You know it's true, husband dearest. Now, chop chop."

"Is this what people mean when they talk about how much wives nag? Just let me have a shower. I'll be out in a minute." I closed the door behind me, but I could still hear her through it.

"First, it was just brushing your teeth. Now it's a shower. What's next? Shaving?" She laughed again. "Don't make me come in there and drag you out."

"You can come in here anytime, but consider this your only warning. I'm already naked." I pushed off my sweatpants and grinned when she didn't reply. "What? Cat got your tongue?"

"Yeah. Nope. I mean—" I chuckled softly as she stammered. "Just hurry up."

I did what had to be done before I realized I hadn't brought clean clothes into the bathroom with me. Knotting a towel around my waist, I wondered what her reaction was going to be. Unfortunately, it seemed like she'd decided to wait outside.

After getting dressed and grabbing my stuff, I found her standing at the hedge separating the garden from the beach. She turned around when she heard me shutting the door. She glanced down at her watch when I stepped onto the grass.

"That wasn't bad timing actually. Ready to go?"

"The sun hasn't even risen yet." The sky was awash in navy blue but was no longer the starry, inky black of night.

"That's part of the point. I want to watch the sun rise from the Tavuni Hill Fort. We don't have much time to get there, so you're going to have to move that lazy butt."

"This lazy butt only wakes up after two cups of coffee," I grumbled but fell into step beside her. There were very few people around at this time of the morning, but I took Lindsay's hand anyway as we made our way through the lobby and greeted the few staff members around.

She tensed when I wound my fingers around hers but quickly caught on to what I was doing and wrapped her arm around my waist as she leaned into me. Once we were out of the hotel, there was no need to keep up the charade but neither of us let go.

I flagged down a taxi a few minutes after we walked out of the lobby, and the driver happily agreed to be our guide for the day. Once we were on our way, I turned to the woman nestled into my side on the backseat.

"Have you always been such a planner?" I'd seen her list while we were on our way out, and it was meticulous.

She nodded, pulling back to look up at me. "I'm a big fan of structure. I like knowing what's going to happen and when."

"Don't you ever just let things happen?" I frowned. "Structure is fine and all, but it can also be pretty damn boring."

"You should meet my friend. Ember keeps telling me exactly that. I'd have thought you'd be better at structure, considering your time in the service."

I laughed at her comment. "I can do structure perfectly well when I have to. When I'm on my time, I just prefer to do what I want, when I want."

"That sounds terrifying." A visible shudder ran through her. "I'd be lost without a plan for the day."

"It's not so bad. You should try it sometime." I peered into her eyes, curious to see how she would react to the suggestion I was about to make. "In fact, let's do it tomorrow. Today can be your structure day, but tomorrow, you have to do what I want."

She hesitated before nodding, taking in a deep breath through her nose. "Okay. Fine, but you better move it when we get to the fort. We're five minutes behind schedule already."

CHAPTER 11

LINDSAY

Jaxon stayed true to his word about sticking to my schedule, not even complaining once. We hauled ass up the hill from where the taxi dropped us off, making it to the top just in time to watch the sky lighten and take in the breathtaking views of the sun rising over the ocean, forest, and town below.

He sucked in a breath as we stood in the stillness of the early morning, his hands in his pockets and his gaze glued to the horizon. "I've seen a lot of sunrises, but this one rivals all of them."

"Beautiful, huh?" I bumped his firm bicep with my shoulder. "Worth getting up at five a.m. for if you ask me."

"It was a good call." A low chuckle rumbled in his chest, and I couldn't help noticing how much more relaxed and carefree it made him look—younger even. "Let's not plan on making it a habit, though. Not while we're here."

I shrugged, refraining from giving him an answer because I didn't know how to agree to sleeping in when we were in this exotic place. I also didn't feel like having an argument about it, so saying nothing seemed like a better idea.

Confrontation wasn't something I necessarily steered clear of, but the morning was too peaceful and the view was too beautiful to bother with an argument about wakeup times. We stayed on the hill until the sun had cleared the horizon, taking the pastel shades in the sky with it, before slowly winding our way back down to our driver.

"What's next, Cruise Director Flinn?" He grinned as he held the door of the taxi open for me.

I rolled my eyes at the nickname, but I also kind of liked it. "The Kula Wild Adventure Park."

"Sounds like the sort of place I'll enjoy." He lowered himself onto the backseat after I climbed in.

While he wasn't looking, I took a few seconds to admire the strength in his muscles and the intentional way in which he moved. There was nothing clumsy or floppy in the way he did anything. He was in complete control of his movements at all times.

Thick ropes of muscle rippled beneath his skin even when he did something as simple as leaning over to close the door or lift his arm to hold on to the "oh shit" handle above the window. He smirked when he saw where my eyes had gone.

"I'm not a backseat driver, but I far prefer being the one in control of the vehicle."

"Says the guy who doesn't like structure even if it means control," I said, but there was nothing snide or sharp in my tone. "How does that work? You seem like a natural leader. Taking charge obviously comes easily to you, yet you don't find comfort in planning or setting things out."

"Like I said, I can adhere to structure perfectly when I want to. There are certain aspects of my life I exercise strict control in at all times, but I can also deal with day-to-day shit without feeling the need to know what's going to happen next. In that respect, I enjoy the unknown."

I was deeply curious to know all about those aspects that he exercised strict control in, but I didn't ask. I was pretty sure he only meant work anyway, not the darker, dirtier places my mind had flung itself into.

What is it about him that activates that part of my brain? I'd never met anyone that made me think about sex as often as he did. It was like he was drenched in pheromones and I was chemically incapable of resisting.

Strangely enough, I didn't think I would resist even if I could. It was nice to know that my libido was still intact after everything that had happened, but it was even better to know there was this hidden part of myself I could still discover.

Ember had been right when she'd said this gave me the chance to be someone else, but it turned out there was this whole other part of myself left unexplored. I could simply let out that part of me for a bit.

Leaning back against the sun-warmed leather seat, I shifted so I could look at him. The bare skin of our knees brushed when I moved, and tingles raced from the point of contact and settled firmly between my legs.

Jaxon glanced down at our legs when I didn't immediately remove mine from being pressed to his. Then he brought his eyes up to mine. "If you want to touch me, go ahead. I don't mind."

My cheeks heated under the intensity of his gaze. It didn't leave mine for a second, but he still seemed to take in my flush and the way my nipples peaked beneath the thin fabric of my top.

"I didn't do it on purpose." I scooted back an inch to separate from him before crossing my arms over my breasts. "And was that an attempt at flirting?"

He shrugged but an amused lightness crept into his eyes. "Yes. It's been a while since I've tried it, so I'm probably a little rusty. How am I doing?"

"You're very direct." I liked it, though. "Want to know more about the adventure park?"

If we didn't change the topic, I was going to end up squirming in my seat just from the way he was looking at me and how charged the air in the cab suddenly felt between us. This guy definitely had a magnetism to him.

"Sure." There was a knowing gleam in his eyes, but again, he didn't call me on it. "What's this park all about and how do you feel about rides?"

"It's not really that kind of park. There are a few rides, but it's more about getting to experience the wild side of Fiji in a safe and comfortable environment. Walk-through enclosures allow tourists to see the habitat of different kinds of species from the inside. There are marine displays too, so we can get a glimpse of what it's like under the ocean around here."

"Sounds pretty cool. Not the safe and comfortable part of it so much, but I suppose we'd get to see creatures we wouldn't necessarily see if we just went for a walk."

"Exactly. Plus, there are wooden walkways and bridges leading through the valleys the property is set on. It's supposed to be a pretty unique experience. I wanted to get there early so we can get ahead of the crowds."

"Good idea. Those places are usually packed as far as I know."

I nodded. "If you want to be able to go on the Rollercoaster Zip Rail or the Jungle Water slide, which are the rides there are, it wouldn't help to get there too late."

"I'm definitely down for those." He cracked his neck, grinning as he took me in. "Am I going to be on them alone?"

"Just because I like to plan things doesn't mean I'm opposed to fun." I raised my chin, holding his gaze firmly. "Depending on how wet we get on the water slide, I might need to borrow a shirt from you later. My suitcase is supposed to be arriving today, but I don't know what time it'll be there."

He scratched his jaw. "I guess I could loan you one when we get back, or we could buy matching ones from the souvenir shop. They should have one of those at a place like that, and it seems like a quintessential *honeymooney* thing to do."

"You'd wear matching T-shirts?" I nearly gaped at him.

A light brown brow arched at me, but I didn't miss the laughter in his eyes. "Of course, I would. If my dearest wife wanted me to, I'd do just about anything."

"Wait. Don't tell me you're a romantic at heart?"

He laughed out loud this time. "No one has ever accused me of that before, but yeah, I guess I am if you consider that kind of thing to be romantic."

The gift shop was located near the entrance of the park, and after he paid for our tickets—which he insisted on doing despite my protests—he dragged me into it first. Picking out two pink T-shirts with brightly colored parrots and a collage of other animals on them, he carried them to the cashier and paid for those too.

Five minutes later, we both emerged from the bathrooms wearing our newly acquired tourist gear. The color accentuated how tanned his skin was and managed to bring out the brightness in his eyes at the same time.

Despite it being a decidedly girly color, he pulled it off really well. Opening his arms when he saw me walking toward him, he turned in a slow circle. "Well? What do you think?"

"Gorgeous." A smile played at the corners of my lips. "I think we should get you a whole collection before we leave."

"Done," he said cheerfully before bowing and offering me his arm with a goofy grin on his face. "Shall we, wifey dear? So many ziplines to take, so little time before this place is swarmed with fellow sightseers."

I linked my elbow with his, again feeling tingles running through me at having his skin against mine. Putting the obvious chemistry between us aside for the moment, I turned my attention to our surroundings.

The humidity was higher in the forest, but the dense greenery and the earthy smell more than made up for it. Even though we were barely through the gates, I could already see multicolored parrots sitting on thick branches in the nearest enclosure and a house of reptiles on our left.

Jaxon eyed the signpost for interactions with a Boa Constrictor and turned to me. "We're doing that. Come on."

He dragged me off before I could answer, but while I wasn't the largest fan of snakes, I also wasn't afraid of them. After greeting the woman in charge of the encounter, he lifted the heavy constrictor and carefully draped it over my shoulders.

"You okay?" he asked, watching my expression before stepping away, still balancing some of the weight on his palms.

"Perfect." I pulled my phone out of my back pocket and held it up to him. "The passcode is 67890. Take a picture for me, will you?"

"Trusting me with your passcode already, huh? That was fast." He waggled his eyebrows as he tapped in the code. "Smile, darling. The family is going to be so proud of you for not running away from that thing screaming."

I smiled. "It's okay, honey. They'll all understand why you made me go first. It's such a large, scary animal. No one will blame you if you'd prefer to run away screaming."

Humor lit his eyes as he held up my phone to snap the photograph. "I won't. You're here to protect me. I can do anything with you by my side, even wrestle a magnificent, powerful snake into submission. Trust me. I've been doing it since the minute I first laid eyes on you."

He winked and my jaw nearly dropped. Again.

Blood rushed to my cheeks as I widened my eyes at him. "Jaxon!"

Shrugging at the snake-trainer lady, he fought a grin when he looked into my eyes. "What? It's true."

Even the snake lady turned a shade darker than she had been when we'd gotten to her. Shaking my head at my roommate, I motioned to the constrictor and turned my gaze to her.

"What's his name?" I asked.

"Fred."

Jaxon laughed and came to stand in front of me again. "Hand Fred over, baby. Remember to take a picture of me *not* running away screaming because I'm used to handling things his size."

"Really? You're going to keep that going?" Sliding my hands beneath Fred's scaly belly, I began the process of gently lifting him off me and transferring him over. "Also, what's with all the nicknames?"

"It's our honeymoon. Aren't we supposed to use goofy nicknames and stare lovingly at each other all the time?"

"I think you've been misinformed about what honeymoons are all about." Once he had the snake safely in his hands, I took a few steps away to put some distance between us. Being so close to him was defi-nitely not good for my oxygen supply or my heart rate.

He smirked when he caught my eye. "I'm not the one who keeps blushing when any reference is made to what honeymoons are all about. Plus, what happens outside the bedroom is important too. Don't you think?"

He aimed his question at the snake lady, who'd turned her back and who—I was pretty sure she was pretending—was talking on her phone.

False hurt entered his eyes as he pouted. "Maybe it's just me who cares about what happens outside of the bedroom. I think goofy nicknames and staring lovingly at each other is important too."

"Sure, big guy. Let's get that photo and leave the nice lady in peace, shall we?"

Blinking away the pained expression on his face, he laughed and handed my phone back to me. "Just use yours. Unless you want to go digging in my pocket."

"Nope. I'm good. I can just message it to you later."

We took the picture, thanked the poor woman, and let her be.

Hours later when we were headed back to the hotel after a jampacked day, I was a little sunburned and had aching feet, but I was also relaxed and happier than I had been in a while.

It was like someone had lifted a giant weight off my shoulders that I hadn't even realized I was carrying. While I still didn't really know what to make of Jaxon, he was fun to be around and made me laugh much more than I was used to.

Somehow, he managed to challenge me but be a comfort all at the same time. He didn't pretend to be someone he wasn't, and he didn't want me to either.

A straightshooter with a good sense of humor and a talent for give and take. I liked all that about him.

"What's on the schedule for dinner?" he asked just before the driver dropped us off outside the lobby.

I leaned my head back on the rest and shook it. "I didn't have a plan for dinner. Do you want to go back to Big Mac's restaurant downstairs? It was the best meal I've had in ages."

"Agreed." He took my hand once he'd paid the driver—again

insisting—and tugged me into his side as we made our way to the elevators.

We walked back to our room in a comfortable silence, our hands swinging between us as I leaned just a little into his side. No doubt we looked like a real couple right then, and the weird thing was that we'd both just gravitated into the position. It hadn't felt unnatural at all.

When we got to the bungalow, my suitcase was waiting on the made bed and I let out a whoop of joy to see it.

Jaxon laughed from the lounge. "I'm assuming you want to shower and change before we go out?"

"Yes, please," I called before closing the door and getting cleaned up.

Choosing a light yellow casual dress and sandals I'd bought specifically to match it, I was in such a good mood to have clean clothes that I even sprayed on some perfume after I got out of the shower.

Jaxon came out of the bathroom shortly after I emerged from the bedroom, stopping in his tracks when he saw me. He wore a pair of faded jeans and a black T-shirt that hugged his muscled frame perfectly once again, but this time, I wasn't the one caught staring.

I also didn't blush this time when *I* caught *him* staring. Propping my hands on my hips instead, I copied his move earlier and turned in slow circle. "Well?"

He swallowed heavily. "You clean up nicely."

"Is that your way of saying you didn't like my outfit before?" I teased.

"Nope, it's my way of saying you look nice." Moving past me to deposit his dirty clothes in his bag, I noticed how he folded them and tucked them into one side before zipping it up again.

So some of that famous military structure and discipline are left inside him after all.

He took my hand again when we left, tugging me against him and slinging his arm around my shoulders. We were still in that position when we walked into the dining area.

Big Mac spotted us immediately, coming over and starting to chat up a storm to us while also barking orders at people about what he wanted for our dinner.

He sat with us for a while, telling us about his time at the hotel and insisting we try everything he ordered for us. We got back to the room much later than I'd thought we would, and I was dead on my feet.

Jaxon released my hand once the door closed behind us, staggering to his bed to pull off his shoes. "Good night, honey bunch."

"That one sucks. It's not sticking." I pulled a face at him. "Good night, pumpkin."

He was still laughing when I shut the bedroom door. "That one's not sticking either."

"We'll see," I called in reply.

I got settled in bed after changing into the lacy pajamas I'd bought to try spicing things up on my honeymoon. I found my thoughts quickly drifting to Jaxon. I wondered what he'd think if he saw me in them. What would come out of his apparently shameless mouth if I walked out there right that very second?

I didn't do it, though. I liked that he was still sleeping on the couch, even though he could've been a dick about it and insisted we take turns.

Also, I needed to take a minute to think about the insane chemistry I had with him. I'd parked the thought earlier, but it needed my attention before I drifted off.

It felt like it was way too soon to feel anything like this with another man, and yet it wasn't something I'd felt before. Not with Will and certainly not with anyone before him. I was drawn to Jaxon— certainly attracted to him on a completely different level.

Why hadn't I felt this with Will? Is it okay for me to feel it with Jaxon? Why do I even care? Will left me at the altar. I was single again, and just because it was fast didn't make what I felt any less real.

Nor did it dampen the excitement for tomorrow. That was new too, and I really fucking liked it.

CHAPTER 12

JAXON

When I woke up the next morning, it was with the feeling that someone was looking at me. I opened my eyes to slits, finding Lindsay sitting awake and dressed in the chair next to my couch.

"I'm ready for the day," she said when she noticed me stirring. "Tick tock. We're burning daylight."

"What time is it?"

She checked her watch. "Six a.m."

I groaned and turned over so my back was to her, pulling my blanket over my head. "It's my day, and we're sleeping for at least another thirty minutes."

A soft sigh sounded in the room, and it sure as fuck hadn't come from me. I could practically hear her impatient thoughts, but she didn't say anything or go anywhere.

It didn't take me long to realize she wasn't going to go back to sleep. I rolled my eyes at her as I sat up. "You do realize the sun is only rising now, right?"

"Yes, but we talked about this yesterday." She leaned forward, giving me a way too tempting view down the front of her loose, flowing top thing. "I like getting an early start because it allows me to make the most of the day."

"Go get dressed for the beach then. It's a shame we haven't spent much time out there and I'm definitely going to need a dip to wake up properly." And to cool down, but she didn't need to know that.

With her reacting the way she did to mere comments, I shuddered to think what she would do if she had to see the serious morning wood I was sporting. Probably try to drown me in sterilizer or holy water.

Just as she got to the doorway to the bedroom, she turned around and fixed me with a serious expression. "What are we going to do on the beach? Obviously if we're taking an early-morning dip, I need a bathing suit but are we going to be walking and keeping active, or lounging? As in, do I need a towel and a book?"

"We're flying by the seat of our pants today. If you want a towel and book later, I'll come get it for you."

She frowned, looking like she wanted to argue before she lifted a shoulder. "It's your day. If you want to spend it running up and down to get things we could've just taken with us to begin with, that's your business."

Disappearing into her room, she gave me all of three minutes before she came out wearing a very skimpy white bikini and a sheer black coverlet. I sighed internally, convinced that I was being punished for something to have to live with a woman who looked like her without being able to touch her.

What was more was that I actually liked her despite her more compulsive tendencies. Maybe because of them. She was an enigma with her easy smile. She was willing to try just about anything—even having Fijian iguanas crawling all over her—while still not being at all carefree.

She planted her hands on her hips and stared at me. "Why are you still in bed?"

Because I need a fucking minute before I can get up. "I sleep in my underwear. You might want to wait for me outside. I'll be right there."

Her gaze dropped automatically to the sheet covering me,

lingering there for a second before she jerked it away. "Don't take too long."

Swiping the blackout drapes away from the window with her arm, she didn't look back before practically running from the room. Once it was safe to get up without showing off my raging fucking hard-on, I scrubbed my hands over my cheeks and willed my body to get over it.

Thankfully, after thinking about nothing but sea urchins and the severe injuries they can cause while brushing my teeth and changing into swimming trunks, I was finally ready to go. Lindsay was standing on the small patio outside the bungalow, facing the ocean and leaning with her shoulder against a pillar.

Her arms were crossed loosely over her chest and her expression was thoughtful. Intentionally not taking the time to check her out in that ridiculous fucking scrap of a bikini, I strode past her and tossed her a grin over my shoulder.

"You're burning daylight, Flinn. Swim now. Think later."

She pushed off the wall and rolled her eyes when she caught up to me. "As if I'm the one burning daylight. What are our plans for the day anyway? You couldn't seriously have meant it when you said we're flying by the seat of our pants."

"Oh, I meant it." We passed the hedges to the beach, the sand soft and still cool beneath our feet. "Whenever we see an opportunity, we're going to take it. Until something comes up, we're just going to do whatever we feel like. Right now, I feel like a swim in the ocean."

"What if I feel like coffee?"

I glanced at her when she stopped walking. "If you feel like coffee, go get some coffee. The dining room does breakfast as well. I'm sure they're open by now."

"Want anything?" she asked after chewing on her lip for a few beats. "Breakfast is included and we haven't really made use of it so far. We might as well eat before we get stuck doing nothing on an empty stomach."

"We're not going to do nothing. I'm going for a swim and you're going to get breakfast. That's something, right?"

"I guess." She released her lip and gave me a cheeky smile. "I have some ideas for later in the day if you need any help. In the meantime, do you want anything for breakfast?"

"If they let you take food away, I'll have a ton of bacon and a coffee. Thanks."

"Coming right up." She started to turn away from me, pausing at the last second to add, "I'll put something healthy on the plate too. I wouldn't want you having a heart attack on our honeymoon, baby bear."

"Baby bear, huh?" I rubbed the stubble underneath my chin. "I don't like that one either, but I can live with it."

Melodic laughter rang out after her when she completed her turn and headed off to the restaurant. She took her time before coming back juggling a plate piled high with crispy bacon, one piece of lettuce on the side, and two takeout cups of coffee.

When I saw her walking back to the beach, I swam to the shore to meet her and took the plate and a mug off her hands. She eyed my wet trunks before sitting down. "You're going to be covered in sand. You should've just let me bring a towel."

I dragged my hands through my hair to slick it back and keep it from dripping into my food while I ate. I lowered myself down beside her without a second thought. "I'll be okay. It's just sand. It'll come off when it dries. Where did you find the lettuce?"

"It was garnish on one of the platters of cold meats. Told you I'd bring you something healthy." Her eyes shone with amusement. "I'm all about taking good care of my husband."

"You're the best, angel face." I grinned and popped a piece of bacon into my mouth, chewing while she moved her lips from side to side.

"I can live with that one if you can live with baby bear." She flicked a hand up and pointed at the signs of life starting up all around the beach. "Should we have a look around at the available activities?"

I looked over in the direction of the cabanas she gestured toward. My gaze snagged on the nearest one. "No need. That sign says parasailing, so we'll start with that and see what happens after."

"Parasailing?" Her brows jumped all the way up. "Uh, no. I'm not great with heights."

"Just *not great* with heights or do you have a genuine fear?" I cocked my head while chewing the next bite of my breakfast. "There's a big difference."

"If I say I'm just not great with it but not genuinely afraid, you're going to make me do it, aren't you?"

"Yep."

She sighed, her head shaking as she burrowed her toes into the sand. "I'm not deathly afraid. I just prefer to keep my feet on the ground."

"Well, I'd prefer to sweep you off them, so we're doing it." I grinned. "I've done it a million times. We'll go tandem. I'll keep you safe. I promise."

Her blue eyes were filled with doubt when they met mine, searching for something that she must've found because eventually she nodded. "Okay, but if I want to, I'm keeping my eyes closed the entire time."

"I'll even keep them closed for you. If that's what you want, I'll keep one hand clamped over your face until we get back to the beach."

"I really might take you up on that." She motioned to my almost empty plate. "Eat up. We've got parachutes to fly and drowning to get to."

"I won't let you drown." I polished off the last of the bacon, stood up, and offered her my clean hand to help her up. "Trust me, okay? We're both going to be just fine."

She slid her hand into mine, not letting it go once she was standing next to me. "Can I? Trust you, I mean."

"You can." I held her gaze for a beat, letting her see the resolute determination in mine. "I won't let anything happen to you, Linds."

"You used my actual nickname there." She squeezed my hand. "I'm guessing that means you're serious."

"I am." We walked to the parasailing booth where we talked to a guy with dreadlocks who got us geared up. Lindsay's eyes were wide with fear as the boat took off, contrary to her expectation of keeping them shut.

I wrapped my arms around her waist and held her to me even

though her harness was also fastened to mine. Bringing my head forward, I spoke into her ear once we were in the air.

"You're doing fine. Just breathe. Take a look around. It's fucking beautiful up here."

I felt her chest expanding as she followed my instruction, then heard her gasp when she noticed what I was talking about. Floating above the crystalline blue waters with the sun only just starting to warm us up and the gentle breeze, we had a view only seabirds used to get. It was absolutely majestic, and her breathing evening out told me Lindsay thought so too.

"This is incredible." She whooped, relaxing against me as she took it all in. "Doing what you want to do might not end up being so bad after all."

"Just wait and see. The day is only beginning now. By the end of it, I think I'll have converted you."

She laughed before starting to point out landmarks on the hill behind the resort. Our ten-minute trip flew by, and when we landed, my supposed wife was smiling wider than I'd ever seen her smile before.

Throwing her arms around me when we landed safely on the beach and returned the gear, she pressed her body to mine and let out an exhilarated laugh. "That was amazing. What are we doing next?"

I hugged her back, holding her tight for a long minute before stepping away and taking her hand. "Follow me, young thrill-seeker. I think I know exactly what we're doing next."

CHAPTER 13

LINDSAY

Jaxon led me back into the main part of the hotel, not even bothering to go to the room to get a shirt. Although there were a lot of shirtless people moving around between the various pools and the beach all the time, he still garnered stares on our way to the lobby.

Mostly from women, but some from men as well.

He didn't even seem to notice it, but I sure as heck did. Jealousy reared up inside me when I caught other people looking at him like they wanted to climb on top of him.

He might not really be mine, but I straightened my spine and gave them all "back off" glares anyway, tightening my grip on his hand. I'd never thought of myself as a jealous person before, but Jaxon was bringing a lot of different things out in me.

Besides, he wasn't really mine, but they didn't know that. It was rude to look at another woman's husband like he was a lollipop to be licked. Not that I would've minded licking him either, but that wasn't really the point.

Lifting our joined hands, I slung his arm over my shoulder and cuddled deeper into his side when one woman actually swiped her tongue across her lips when we walked past. Jaxon didn't even hesitate when I wound my arm his waist.

As if it were a natural action he'd done a hundred times before, he adjusted his stride to mine now that we had to walk so close to one another, angled his body slightly toward mine, and held me to him.

An amused smirk appeared on his lips when he glanced into my eyes. "You're getting mighty comfortable there, aren't you?"

"Yep." I wasn't about to make any excuses about it either. "No one's eye-screwing my husband on my watch."

"No one except you, you mean." He laughed but dipped his head so his cheek was resting on top of my hair. "Don't worry, baby. There's no one for me but you. I wouldn't have bound myself to you for the rest of our lives if there was any doubt about it."

I knew he was joking, but it didn't change the fact that I got a tiny little thrill when he said it. A smile tugged at the corners of my lips until he grabbed a flyer for activities around the resort and held it up to me.

"Stick out your finger, close your eyes, and touch the flyer," he said. "Whatever you touch on is what we're doing next."

"This is what you meant when you said you knew what we were going to do?" My heart fluttered in my chest as nerves took hold of my insides. "There's river rafting and scuba diving on there. Why did you pick up the flyer for adventure activities? Why can't we choose from the cultural-experiences one?"

"You enjoyed the parasailing, didn't you?" His amber-gold eyes bore into mine, and I nodded. "Then you'll enjoy these too. Just pick one."

I captured his gaze, again only seeing patience and a strange calmness there. It was the same thing I'd seen earlier. He was so damn confident that he could keep me safe and he wasn't in the least bit worried about it.

I had to admit though, parasailing was one of the best experiences I'd had in my life so far. It was better than any memory I would've been able to make at a fort or in a market, and one that would stay with me forever.

So I closed my eyes and jabbed at the pamphlet because I wanted more experiences like that. More of the thrilling activities that Houston Lindsay would never even have considered but Fijian Lindsay was loving.

Until I opened my eyes and saw what my finger had landed on. I felt the blood draining from my face but Jaxon still didn't look worried. If anything, he looked more excited than I'd ever seen him.

"I've always wanted to swim with sharks," he said, pulling the flyer away and turning it to inspect the address. "This is going to be awesome. Let's go."

"No." My feet stayed planted exactly where they were. "There's no way I'm swimming with sharks. Bring the activities back. I'll pick again."

"That's not how this works, princess. You picked swimming with sharks, so that's what we're doing."

"No fucking way am I swimming with sharks." Parasailing was one thing and Fijian Lindsay might be a bit more of an adrenaline junkie than Houston Lindsay, but not by that much. "That's a hard no. Fuck no."

"I haven't heard you cuss very often until right then." He grinned, winding his arm around my shoulders again and tugging me toward the activity counter. "We've got to do it. It must be fate. Otherwise, you would've picked something different."

I was still refusing when he started making the necessary arrangements with the woman behind the desk. "We could be there in twenty minutes."

She relayed the message into the phone, so transfixed by my bastard of a fake husband that she didn't even look at me before telling whoever was at the other end that the couple was on their way. She smiled when she put the phone down. "They will be ready when you get there. Have fun."

"I highly doubt it." I narrowed my eyes at her, wondering whether the concept of sisterly solidarity was completely lost in the face of a gorgeous man. She just kept smiling as if she didn't have a care in the world.

Because she doesn't have to go swimming with the fucking sharks. I huffed out a breath while Jaxon organized a ride to take us to the killer fish.

"I'm not doing it," I repeated when we climbed into the air-conditioned cab of one of the hotel's cars. "I've already been stood up at the altar. I really don't think this month has to get any worse, and getting ripped to pieces by razor-sharp teeth feels like a surefire way for that to happen."

"Relax, sugar plum. It's one hundred percent safe. Nothing's going to happen to you."

I tucked my hands into my elbows and slammed my back into the seat. "If it's so safe, why is the guy so available? Because people don't actually want to do it."

"Thousands of people go diving every day. All over the world. They're all fine. Mostly." He reached for my hand, but for the first time since I'd met him, I yanked mine away.

"I really don't think this is a good idea."

He shrugged. "Fate wants us to do it, so we're doing it. It's a great idea."

"Only because you've always wanted to do it." I gave him my most piercing stare. "What's something you're afraid of?"

"Me?" His brows lifted and he shook his head. "Nothing really. I don't have a problem with heights, spiders, or sharks. I don't even mind clowns."

"There's something wrong with you." I turned away to watch the landscape going by as we were driven to our doom.

A gentle hand sneaked onto my leg, his long fingers curling around the bare flesh on my thigh and flexing. "I'll take care of you, Lindsay. Same deal as before, okay? Please trust me."

"Tell me something you're afraid of then." I refused to look at him. I really didn't want to do this, and yet his smooth voice and tenderly murmured words were already softening me toward the idea.

If I looked into those eyes too, I would be getting in that fucking water without any more questions asked.

He kept silent for a long minute. "The only thing that I'm really terrified of is losing the people I love."

And there I go melting into a puddle of goo. "How is it that you always know exactly what to say to me to get me to do what you want?"

"Just being honest," he said as the car slowed. "So, are we doing this? Because I think we've arrived."

"It hasn't been twenty minutes yet."

"Nope, but there's no line, so it shouldn't be a problem." He sounded way too cheerful for my liking.

"There's a reason why there's no line." I only just got the words out before his hand wrapped around mine and he dragged me out of the car with him.

The guy operating the diving charter welcomed Jaxon like a long-lost brother, thumping him on the back as they clasped hands and exchanged greetings. If he was this friendly to his customers, it was clear he didn't have a lot of them.

To my surprise, it turned out that he was always fully booked in advance. He told Jaxon about a group booking that had gotten canceled this morning because their flight had been delayed. When the two men started untying the boat and talking about the different species of sharks we could expect to see, I realized there was no getting out of it.

I should have just stayed in the taxi.

With my heart thundering, I dropped my hands to the hem of my cover-up and yanked it over my head. Jaxon stopped talking in the middle of his sentence, his gaze drinking me in like I was a goddess he'd always believed in but had never seen in the flesh before.

I didn't understand what the big deal was, considering that my cover-up was sheer anyway, but I liked having him looking at me like that too much to question it. When the guide glanced my way, a muscle ticked in Jaxon's jaw and he stepped into his line of sight.

"What are you doing?" he asked.

"Swimming with sharks apparently. Where's the cage? Let's get this over with."

"There's no need for a cage in Fiji," the guide said around Jaxon. "We go snorkeling on the reef with them."

My pulse spiked and my mind went completely blank. "What?"

"That's awesome." Jaxon grinned at the guide but kept his body as a shield in front of me.

Now who's jealous?

The smug thought snapped me out of my momentary shocked stupor. "I'm not doing that."

"Yes, we are." He moved to a seat at the front of the boat when the guide went to stand behind the steering column in the middle. Then he reached for my hand and pulled me into his lap. "You're going to be fine, Lindsay. I won't let anything happen to you, remember?"

"I remember," I muttered, trying not to sink back into his warm, broad chest when he wrapped his arms around my waist again.

We kept touching each other in this intimate way, even when we weren't anywhere near the hotel. Not that it was even strictly necessary there anymore. No one was paying us much attention at this stage, except for Big Mac who came over to talk to us every night.

In spite of all that, I stayed put right where I was. Later on when we got in the water, I clung to him like a toddler without her water wings and didn't let him go for a single minute.

The sleek, powerful predators lazily swimming beneath us hardly even seemed to notice us, simply gliding past and going about their days. I was fucking terrified, but having Jaxon next to me definitely made it much easier. Enjoyable even.

And that was why I was still hanging onto him after the dive when we got back on the boat. At least, that was what I told myself.

He turned to look at me once we were out of the water, his eyes wide and bright on mine. "You just swam with fucking sharks."

"I just swam with fucking sharks," I repeated, feeling the same sense of freedom and exhilaration as I had after the parasailing. It drew me to him, and for the second time in one morning, I pulled him into my arms and hugged him like I wouldn't ever let him go. "Thank you, Jaxon. You have no idea how much I needed to meet someone exactly like you."

CHAPTER 14

JAXON

After our encounter with the sharks, I figured it was time to dial the day down a notch. Lindsay was ecstatic about everything we'd done and kept telling me how much it meant to her that I'd pushed her out of her comfort zone, but I doubted we needed any more excitement today.

We spent the afternoon strolling through local markets, examining handcrafted trinkets, and ended up walking past an ice-cream shop on our way back to the resort.

"We have to get some," she insisted. "There's nothing that rounds off a perfect day like a good ice cream."

"Perfect day, huh?" I smirked as I followed her into the shop. "What about plans and scheduling? Have I converted you yet?"

"Nope. I'll just have to broaden my horizons when it comes to activities to include in my plans."

I laughed as the bell above the door signaled our arrival. An older woman came walking out the back, clasping her hands in front of her as she eyed us.

"Ah, young love." She smiled softly. "How would you like to try my Salted Caramel? It's a new recipe and honeymooners are always so forgiving because they're so happy."

"We'd love to try it," I said before I could give too much thought about why she'd made the assumption she had when we weren't even touching each other at the moment. "Anything else you'd like us to sample? We're very willing guinea pigs."

Her smile spread wider. "Excellent. I haven't had enough of those recently."

She ushered us into one of the small booths, promising she'd be back in a minute with a tasting plate for us. Lindsay looked at me with excitement shining in her eyes as she clapped her hands.

"I didn't think this day could get any better, but clearly, I was wrong. We're about to be treated with an entire tray of different kinds of ice cream. Stuff like that never happens to me by chance."

"That's because you've got to give fate the opportunity to let stuff like this happen to you. If we were on a strict schedule today, we never would've stumbled across this place, which means we never would've been told to sit down and eat."

"You may have a point there." She tilted her head after getting settled on her side of the table. "Maybe I'll think about leaving some space open in my planner for spontaneity."

"Planning for spontaneity might not work so well." I stretched my legs out under the table, not moving them when I felt her calf brushing against mine. "Maybe just try letting go every once in a while. You might be surprised what you find out about yourself in the process."

"How did you get to be so wise?" she asked in a teasing tone, the corners of her eyes crinkling even as she tried to hide her smile. "You're not that much older than I am, yet I feel a little bit like you're my spirit guide or something today."

"I could be your spirit guide," I said. "But only if you keep doing what I tell you to. No more schedules for the rest of the trip, for starters"

She laughed. "No deal, but we can have another planless day sometime. It really wasn't as bad as I thought it would be. Have you always been like this?"

I nodded. "My mother has always told me to follow what my heart tells me and so I have."

"Seems like a good thing to have been taught. My parents were a bit lackadaisical in their approach to life. I think that's why I'm such a stickler for rules and planning."

"You got annoyed with them being scatter-brained?" Even just knowing what little I did about her, it made perfect sense that she'd have tailored all her own habits around what had irritated her as a child.

"Exactly. I don't think either of them ever owned a diary, a planner, or a calendar of any nature. It used to drive me nuts that we were always late—and that was when we didn't entirely miss an event."

"I can imagine how that must've gotten to you."

"It really did." We thanked the owner when she brought our ice cream and tucked in without hesitating. "I took over the family planning duties just after I became a teenager. I went out and bought a calendar, hung it next to our front door, and marked everything on it."

She licked her spoon clean after taking her first bite, and my dick started hardening at the sight of her pink tongue wrapping around the silver. The entire day had been a struggle, but no more so than that very minute.

Even when she'd finally removed the cover-up on the boat and I got my first good look at her luscious curves without any obstructions to the view, it'd been easier to tear my eyes off her then because I'd been supremely aware of the other man on the boat also looking at her.

I'd wanted to stab his eyes out with the wrong side of a fork for getting to see her body, but I couldn't blame him for looking. Lord knew it'd been impossible not to take notice when she stripped down.

The more time I spent with her, the more I wanted her. But I couldn't think about how much I wanted her and all the things I wanted to do to her while sitting half naked in front of her.

Luckily, since it was an island, lots of people walked around in beachwear and I wasn't even the only shirtless man in the ice-cream shop, never mind on the street. I probably wasn't even the only one fighting against an imminent erection, but just that thought was enough for me to get it under control.

"It sucks you had to get your parents organized when you were still so young," I said. "My mother still buys me a planner every Christmas. She says she'll never stop trying to get me to keep one."

"I thought she wants you to follow your heart."

"She does, but she also wants me to start remembering people's birthdays. Apparently, she raised me better than being a forgetful idiot."

Lindsay chuckled. "She sounds like quite a woman if she's the one who raised you."

"She's formidable all right. I've told her that I keep my work stuff on my phone and that I have all the important birthdays on there too, but she won't have it. Ink and paper are the only way to go in her opinion."

"Smart woman. I completely agree." She popped another heaped spoon of ice cream in her mouth, and this time, I kept my fucking eyes off her lips when she did. "Do you have any brothers or sisters?"

"Nope. I'm an only child. It was just my mom and me growing up."

"Are you close to her?" she asked. "My brother and I used to be close to each other even when we weren't close to our parents, but that ship seems to have sailed."

Again, I wanted to ask about her brother, but I didn't. We were still in the process of getting to know each other and she volunteered information easily if it wasn't a difficult subject for her to talk about. Obviously, her brother wasn't an easy subject.

"Mom and I are very close. Always have been and we always will be." My mother was my rock of stability growing up, and that had never changed. "She was the one who encouraged me to come on this trip. Her only condition was that I wasn't allowed to fall in love with a local. She claims she's not moving here to be close to me, but I think she'd love it if she gave it a chance."

"Anyone would." Lindsay smiled as she turned her gaze to the window and the forest covering the hill in the distance. "It's gorgeous, but the heat might get to her."

"She lives in Houston. If she can manage that humidity, she can manage any heat."

Her eyebrows went up. "You're from Houston?"

"Yep."

"Me too." She grinned. "Think we've ever walked past each other on the street and not known about it?"

"Maybe, but probably not." I had a feeling I would've remembered someone who looked like her, but that was a really douchey thing to say, so I kept it to myself. "I haven't been around much for the last two decades or so."

She snapped her fingers. "That's right. I suppose we could've run into each other when you were there, though. It would be interesting if we were able to go back and see how many run-ins or almost run-ins we've had."

We talked a little about home while finishing up with our ice cream, then headed back to the hotel. As I was unlocking the bungalow door, I heard my phone ringing inside.

Kavan's name came up on the screen when I finally located the device in our kitchenette, and I held it up to Lindsay. "I have to take this. Think about what you'd like to do for dinner in the meantime. I'll be back in a minute."

"What's up?" I asked my friend when I picked up, closing the bungalow door behind me. "You should've come with me, man. If you could see the view I'm looking at right now, you'd hop on the next flight out."

"I'm assuming the trip is going well then?"

"Very well." I laughed and rubbed the back of my head as I walked down to the hedges. "It was almost a disaster that would've ended with me on the streets, but then I met this woman, and with her help, I managed to get us a suite for free."

"Us?" He scoffed. "Do you honestly expect me to believe you're sharing a room with a woman you met while trying to find someplace to stay?"

"You don't have to believe it, but it's true. The hotel was trying to tell her they had a double booking. She would've been shit out of luck too. I threatened to fuck my brand new wife right there in the lobby, and lo and behold, they have a room available for us."

"You're unbelievable."

"Thank you." A smirk formed on my lips. "I really appreciate the compliment."

"It wasn't a compliment," he said, sounding like he was biting back laughter. "Who is she? Is she hot?"

I groaned. "You have no idea. Her name is Lindsay and she looks like my walking wet dream."

"Dark hair, blue eyes, curves for days?" He didn't have to guess. There wasn't much we hadn't shared over the years. He whistled under his breath. "You hook up with her yet?"

"No. She's going through some stuff. I definitely wouldn't object if she was down for it, but I'm not sure where her head's at."

"Jesus, I wasn't suggesting you ask the girl to marry you. Have a little holiday fun. It'll be good for you. You don't have to do anything with her after. Just enjoy your time together."

"You're suggesting a fling?"

"Why not?" I could almost hear him shrugging. "It's not like you'd be doing anything wrong. I really think it'd be good for you."

"So do I." I would definitely make it good for her, but I wouldn't make a move unless I got a clear sign that she wanted me to. She'd been through way too much, and even I wasn't that much of an asshole.

Kavan and I talked a few more minutes about the island and his daughter's arrival in a few weeks. When we hung up, the sun had almost set completely and I was looking forward to getting something to eat from Big Mac.

Walking into the hotel room, I noticed the bedroom door was closed. I hadn't moved far away from the bungalow and I hadn't seen Lindsay leaving to go to dinner yet, so she had to still be changing.

"I'm proud of you for today, you know?" I called, knowing she could hear me through the door. "Maybe tomorrow we should look into quad biking in the forest. Have you thought about what you feel like for dinner?"

I rummaged through my bag, searching for a shirt when I heard the bedroom door opening. She didn't answer my question, so I looked at her, wondering if maybe she hadn't heard me after all.

My breath froze in my fucking lungs at the sight that greeted me when I slid my gaze to her. She was standing in the bedroom door wearing nothing but powder-blue lingerie.

The lace bra plunged between her creamy breasts while the panties were so small I could see she was completely bare. Swollen too.

All my blood rushed south, leaving me instantly hard as a fucking rock as I straightened up slowly. "Lindsay?"

She lifted her hands to free her hair from a tie, sending it tumbling down past her shoulders as she shot me a sensual look. "I've thought about what I want for dinner. You."

I would've pinched myself if there weren't far more pleasurable ways to make sure I wasn't dreaming. Closing the distance between us in two purposeful strides, I cupped her face in my hands and slammed my lips down on hers.

No. Nope. This is definitely not a dream. It's really happening.

Sliding my arms around her without hesitation, I lifted her off her feet and carried her into the bedroom. I kicked the door shut behind me because I suddenly couldn't even remember if I'd closed the outer door.

I interrupted our kiss only to whisper with my lips still against hers. "I want you too, baby. Let me show you how much."

CHAPTER 15

LINDSAY

Books often described first kisses as so incredible, so earth shattering and mind blowing that the world ceased to exist around the characters. I'd never experienced a kiss like that so, as I'd done with so many other things, I'd chalked it up to being impossible in real life.

It turned out to be yet another belief that Jaxon blew out of the water completely. Kissing him was all that and so much more.

My knees went weak, my brain went blank, and my core turned to liquid heat. And all of that happened in the space of one heartbeat.

I sagged against him, but he held me up and then went one step further by literally sweeping me off my feet. He tasted like the sweet ice cream we'd had just a little bit earlier, and the scents of ocean, sunscreen, and barely there clean sweat met my nostrils.

His lips were soft but firm and his body was just as hard as I would've expected if I'd planned this at all. It was a dizzying combination that was as intoxicating as it was unbelievable.

After he'd taken his call and I walked into my bedroom, I noticed the corner of this set of lingerie peeking out from the mesh insert at the top of my suitcase. My gaze had snagged on it, and my mind immediately went back to imagining Jaxon's reaction if he saw me in it.

Fighting against the nerves and uncertainty that swirled around inside me like a brewing thunderstorm, I'd decided to throw caution to the wind. We were doing what we wanted today, and I wanted to put on the sexy new underwear and see where we ended up.

My palms had been clammy and my hands trembled when I'd opened the door, but as soon as I looked into his eyes, my nervousness took a backseat. There had been no mistaking the raw lust in his gaze, and he'd acted on it without question.

It was the most wanted I'd ever felt, and when he wrapped those muscled arms around me, it was also the most need I'd ever felt. Obviously, I'd been turned on before. Heck, I'd been horny pretty much since I first felt his body against mine in the lobby.

Yet I'd never felt like I might go up in flames if he didn't touch me. It'd been mild discomfort and the awareness that I wanted to get off more than the burning need waging war with logical thought that I felt right then.

My clit was so hard just from his kisses and the feel of his body against mine that I moaned into his mouth when I pressed up against his stomach as he carried me to the bed. Wrapping my legs around him, I hooked my arms around his neck and brought him down with me when he lowered me to the mattress.

Since he was still in his thin swimming trunks, I could feel every inch of him as his weight settled on top of me—every one of the too many inches hiding beneath the fabric as well.

Writhing when he ground his bulge against me, I shoved my hands into his hair and wrapped my fingers into the silky strands. Pleasured moans spilled out of me unabated, and my entire body was clenched in anticipation.

Jaxon slowed our kiss before lifting his head only an inch or so away from mine, propping himself up on his elbows placed on either side of me. He stared into my eyes with a look so intense and filled with desire that my hips arched against his without any input from my brain.

He hissed out a restrained noise before shaking his head at me. "Just hold up a second."

"Why?" Doubt bloomed deep inside me, and I flicked my gaze to the side, unable to look at him when I realized I'd effectively just thrown myself at him. Maybe I'd completely misjudged what was going on between us. It was entirely possible with my track record. "It's okay if you don't want this."

He let out a dark chuckle and brought his forefinger and thumb up to my chin, pushing my face back up so I was looking into his eyes again. At the same time, he thrust his hips forward and his eyes momentarily rolled back into his head. "Does that feel like I don't want this? I'm only asking for a second to check in with you."

"Why?" I stared up at him, and he must've seen something in my gaze that tipped him off to the conflicting feelings inside me. "I practically threw myself at you. Why would you feel the need to check in with me?"

"You didn't throw yourself at me. You opened the door. I was the one who came to you." He tapped my chin before kissing the tip of my nose. "I feel the need to check in with you because I'm not a total prick. The last thing I want to do is take advantage of you if you're feeling vulnerable. Maybe you just wanted to tease me by coming out in your underwear, or maybe you'd put it on to sleep in and were only coming out to get a glass of water."

"Do you really believe that?"

"Nope." He smirked before tracing the line of my cheekbone with his thumb. "But I'd rather ask before I do something you're going to regret."

"I won't regret it, but if you don't want to..." I closed my eyes, feeling the first stings of rejection when his weight suddenly disappeared from me.

My body still ached for him, but disappointment washed over me until I heard the tell-tale rip of velcro and the faint rustling of clothes. When my eyes flew open, I nearly moaned at the sight I was greeted with.

Jaxon was standing at the foot of the bed naked. His eyes were hooded and almost completely black as he stared at me, lying with my legs still spread on the mattress in front of him.

He had his palm wrapped around his impressive length as his gaze drank me in from head to toe and back again. I watched him stroke himself slowly, noticing the wetness seeping from his tip and how fucking erotic it was to see my inked-up fake husband doing what he was. My teeth sank into my lower lip but I couldn't hold back my moan.

"Does this look like I don't want to?" he ground out when he brought his eyes back to mine. "I've wanted to get inside you since I saw you for the very first time."

"When I was bawling my eyes out?" My brows swept up.

He nodded. "You're gorgeous, Linds. Fucking hot, even when you're crying."

"It's official. You have massive issues." Even so, my core tightened and my clit was begging to be touched.

Jaxon noticed when my hand twitched toward it, a low growl ripping from his chest. "Nope. I just have a massive hard-on for you. Is it safe to say we've settled that we're both sure about this?"

"Yes," I breathed as he released himself and lowered down to his knees before grabbing hold of mine. "What are you doing?"

"What does it look like I'm doing?" Closing his long fingers around my legs, he gave me a firm tug toward the edge of the bed.

He cocked an eyebrow when he looked up at me, amusement dancing with the obvious arousal in his eyes. I frowned when he pushed my knees even farther apart and planted himself between them. "Wouldn't you rather get back on the bed?"

"Not right now." He slid his hands up the length of my thighs, curling his hand around the front panel of my panties and swiftly pulling it aside. The next breath he dragged in was a ragged one, and his eyes shut for a second before he sent a penetrating glare at the roof. "Trust me when I tell you there's nothing I want to do more right now, but you were really tense before. If I've got any chance at not exploding the second I get inside you, I need to know you're a little more relaxed."

"Why?" I frowned again but more at myself than at him. *Why am I asking so many questions?*

Another chuckle came out of him and the look he gave me could only be described as pure sex. "Because if your pussy is as tight as your muscles were right then, I would've been done for."

Before I could process the dirty word he'd used, his mouth descended to my most intimate place and I cried out. His tongue lapped at me while his fingers toyed at my entrance, spreading the wetness he found there and moaning when he tasted it.

My back arched and I felt the most insane need to close my legs. I felt his lips twitch into a grin against my sensitive flesh, but I didn't bother asking any more questions when he reached up to play with my nipples. The lace bra still covering my breasts somehow managed to make it even more of a sensory experience and I was whimpering long before I should've been.

I wasn't embarrassed about how fast he'd gotten me there, though. The guy was either *that* good or I was *that* attracted to him. Regardless of which one it was, I figured it was something to own up to. *Why not?*

He'd made it pretty clear what effect I'd had on him, and it'd been more than I ever could've hoped for. In fact, the sight of him stroking himself was imprinted on the backs of my eyelids and something I wanted to see every single fucking time I closed them. It'd been *that* hot.

If he could be that unashamed and outright about it, I could be the same. I dug my fingernails into his shoulders as overwhelming pleasure raced through me. Tears wet my eyes as I cried his name over and over again.

I was pretty sure I broke the skin where my nails scraped against his back, but I didn't give a damn. He looked like the kind of guy who could take a little pain with his pleasure. I didn't think I could stop anyway, even if I wanted to. I was that far gone and my body was in complete control, my brain turned to mush as my orgasm sent it flying to another galaxy.

Panting in the aftermath, I was surprised when he placed light kisses on the insides of my thighs and didn't remove his fingers from me. He smirked when his eyes met mine, the pad of his thumb gently circling my clit.

"Well, that was fucking hot. Let's see if I can make it happen again." He sounded completely confident in his abilities.

Me? I didn't quite know how to break the news to him. "I'm not like that."

"Like what?"

"I, uh, I can't..." *Damn it.* After what we'd just done, talking to him shouldn't be this hard. "I've never gotten there twice in one, uh, session."

"Oh, well." He still didn't pull away from me. He also sounded definitely cheerful. "I'll take that challenge. Thanks for letting me know."

He planted a loud smacking kiss between my belly button and my mound before lifting himself onto the bed, still moving his thumb in those tantalizing circles. There was a satisfied smile on his face but his eyes burned with resolute determination.

"It's okay," I said when his face got close to mine. "I'll return the favor. Please don't worry about it."

"I'm not worried." He kissed my mouth before trailing his lips along my jaw. "We've got all night. I'm pretty sure I can get you out of your head and make you feel good a few more times."

I snorted, even though the little bursts of need from his ministrations down below made my nipples pebble again. When one of his hands traveled up my side and cupped my breast, yanking the lace down to free it and eventually removing it altogether before he squeezed it a little harder than I was used to, my breath hitched.

"See? Leave it to me, baby. You have no idea how many times I've thought about all the things I want to do to you."

I wanted to argue, but the heat building at the apex of my thighs and my quickening breath told me that my body had different ideas. I wasn't really the type to lie there just letting him do things for me, and since he was within reach now, I wrapped my fingers around his warm, thick shaft.

He moaned when I swiped my thumb over the tip, gathering the wetness there and spreading it out before giving him a few soft pumps. His heart raced where his chest was pressed against my arm, and he nipped my earlobe.

"Harder, baby," he said huskily. "You're not going to break me and you're not going to hurt me."

I tightened my grip, and when he moaned again, shivers skated down my spine. In that moment, I knew I would get there again. If only because I felt like he knew what I needed better than even I did.

With the feel of him hard and ready in my fist and the primal noises he made while we touched each other, I went tumbling over the edge again in no time. I stopped moving my hand as the pleasure started building up in me, but when I tried to start stroking him again once I'd caught my breath, he closed his fingers around my wrist.

There was a tortured expression on his face when his eyes met mine, betraying how close he was and how much he needed his own release, but that smirk was still on his lips. "Let me grab a condom real quick. I'll be right back."

He pressed an almost playful kiss to my forehead before sauntering out of the room like he didn't have a care in the world. When he walked back in, he was already rolling the latex over his length and he wasted no time getting back onto the bed.

He didn't crawl over me like I expected him to, passing me instead to sit with his back against the padded headboard. "Come ride me. I want to look at you while you bury my cock inside you."

My eyes flared wide open but there was no denying the excited spike in my pulse. "Has anyone ever told you that you really have a mouth on you?"

He shrugged, studying my expression as I scooted over to him on my knees. "You like it."

"I do." I smiled as I planted my knees on either side of his hips, positioning his broad head before gripping his shoulders. "I don't know why I expected anything different."

I lowered myself slowly, taking him in and trying to adjust to his size while I was at it. I had no idea how I'd managed to fit him in his entirety by the time he was fully inside, but I'd definitely never been as filled up as I was right then.

It was almost painful, but it turned out it was just on the right side of the pleasure-pain barrier. Jaxon didn't give me time to get used to having him inside me before his hips started moving. His eyes glazed over as he splayed his fingers over my hips and hung on tight.

"Fuck, you feel so damn good," he moaned as he rammed himself up into me. One of his hands came up to my breasts while his mouth descended to my neck.

I didn't know how long it took before his other hand slid from my hip to my aching bundle of nerves. He was buried so deeply inside me, touching places I didn't even know I had while his fingers performed yet another miracle.

I came again before he lifted me off him and flipped me onto my front, tucking my legs in beneath me before slamming inside again. I was really going to feel it tomorrow, but I didn't give a damn. I was too drugged up with lust, too lost in the intense sensations he was causing. I'd really thought I was done after that last time, but he was hitting me at a totally different angle now.

His hand sneaked around to circle my clit again and his big body folded over my back as he told me what I did to him in harsh whispers. My core clenched again, and when I felt his stomach muscles dip against my lower back and he just about roared that he couldn't hold back anymore, I found myself coming apart around him one last time.

When it was over, my limbs were numb and my throat was parched. I only just managed to climb underneath the covers and flip the bedside lamp off before my eyes were closing. Feeling the mattress shift, I reached for his hand but hit his thigh instead.

No matter. The movement from his side of the bed still stopped.

"Sleep here tonight," I muttered, barely recognizing my own voice.

My eyes fluttered open to see him smiling at me in the soft moonlight filtering in through the window. He nodded when he saw me looking, joined me in the bed, and rearranged me so he was the big spoon to my little spoon.

The last thing I remembered before sleep dragged me under was him sweeping my hair to the side and placing a gentle kiss at the top of my spine.

"Sleep tight, baby," he murmured, and I was gone, feeling more sated, comfortable, and protected than I ever had in my life.

CHAPTER 16

JAXON

When I woke up, Lindsay was—unfortunately—already showered and getting dressed for the day. She smiled when she saw me opening my eyes, her hair tied up as she pulled the straps of a soft cotton dress over her shoulders.

"Good morning, husband dearest."

I grinned and opened my arms. "Is that any way to greet your new husband in the morning? Get over here."

She rolled her eyes but gasped when she settled in my lap to hug me and felt what was going on underneath the covers. "Are you always hard?"

"Only for you." I smirked before lifting a hand to cup her neck and pulling her closer for a lingering kiss.

She smacked my chest playfully, her cute nose wrinkling when we finally came up for air. "Have you ever heard of morning breath?"

"Have you ever heard of morning wood?" I countered, shrugging while she planted another little kiss on my jaw before clambering off me.

Her eyes met mine once she was standing next to the bed again. I didn't miss the flush on her cheeks or how dilated her pupils were, but she was obviously not a morning-sex person. She probably already had something planned and refused to be late.

"Of course, I've heard about it." She pursed her lips and gave me a look. "Just not after a night like that night."

"Last night is not today." I waggled my brows at her. "It's a brand-new day and I vote for spending it in bed."

"It's my day," she said, running her brush through her long ponytail before twisting it up in a knot on top of her head. "I don't want to make things awkward between us, but I booked a couple's spa day for today. Ages ago, obviously, but when I woke up, there was a gift basket from the spa at the door. I totally forgot about it."

"Why would it be awkward?" I pushed the covers off and stood up, ignoring the way her eyes turned dark again when her gaze devoured me in my birthday suit. "I'm more than ready to pretend to be Mr. Lindsay Flinn again."

"You'd better get dressed then," she said with a dazed look in her eyes when she yanked them back up to mine. "We're going to be late if you don't hurry."

"Wouldn't want that," I teased and gave her a light slap on the butt as I walked past her into the bathroom. "I just need a few minutes."

"Evidently, you might need longer than that," she muttered under her breath, her voice a little raspy.

I doubted she meant for me to hear it, but I paused in the doorway to look back at her anyway. "Only when I'm trying to hold back, but don't worry. I'm saving myself for my sexy wife. I just need to brush my teeth since my morning breath was just pointed out to me."

She laughed and ducked out of the room. I'd never been to a spa before, but I was definitely curious about why so many people attended the places religiously. Once Lindsay and I walked into the treatment center at the resort, I totally understood it.

"They built this place on a plateau known to the villagers as Heavenly Hill," she informed me as we made our way to the front desk. "It's called Bebe Spa, which is the Fijian word for butterfly, but it also means 'your cocoon' or 'your sanctuary.'"

"It looks like a sanctuary," I said.

It offered gorgeous views of the ocean from everywhere I could see, but when we were led to our private treatment room, I nearly swallowed my fucking tongue.

"Your open-air balcony has panoramic views of the coast," the white-coated massage therapist guiding us said. "You also have an outdoor rain shower on it, as well as a hydrotherapy tub for sublime relaxation."

She wasn't joking either. The building was surrounded by lush, undulating landscape, and at the altitude the spa was at, there was no doubt that I would spending the day in that tub being sublimely relaxed.

"Thank you," I said after clearing my throat. "My wife and I have really been looking forward to this."

The therapist inclined her head, but I saw how Lindsay rolled her eyes at my roleplaying. "I'll be here to start your first treatment in thirty minutes. Please enjoy the fresh fruit and pastries we've set out on the balcony for you."

"We definitely will. Thank you." I bopped my head. "I'm sure it will be lovely. I'm so glad my wonderful wife insisted on this."

Once she shut the door behind her, my wonderful yet fake wife elbowed me in the ribs. "You don't need to lay it on that thick."

"Of course, I do. I really am glad you dragged me out of bed for this." I eyed the tub before reaching for her and tugging her closer to me until her chest was pressed up against mine. "Although, they won't be here for another thirty minutes, and I don't know about you, but I'm not that hungry for breakfast all of a sudden."

"Cool your jets, stud. We didn't eat last night either." She pushed me away gently, reluctantly almost.

"I did." I grinned and earned myself another smack even though she was smiling again, her blue eyes coy on mine. "Fine. Have it your way, but at some point today, I'm getting my hands on you in that thing."

"Give it your best shot." She blew me a kiss before heading out to the balcony.

I pulled her chair out for her, then shrugged when she shot me a questioning look. "What? I'm giving it my best shot."

She laughed when I rounded the table to take my own seat, then piled our plates high with the food that had been left for us. In the end, it was a good thing she'd turned me down.

Our half hour for breakfast was over before I'd even taken my last bite, and two therapists walked in right on time for our couples' massage. At first, it was a little uncomfortable having another woman's hands all over me and only a small towel covering my ass, but when I saw the serene smile on Lindsay's face and realized she'd dozed off, I relaxed too.

Warm towels were applied to our backs to draw out our tension after a light massage, and I nearly moaned out loud over how good it felt. Seriously. I was definitely going to start frequenting spas if it was always like this.

The massage was followed by time in a sauna, and the lazy smile was still on Lindsay's face when we entered. The hot air and thick humidity made it hard to breathe, but it also made me feel more languid than I ever remembered feeling before.

"Enjoying yourself?" she asked as she gave me a sidelong glance, sitting down next to me on the heated wood.

She was only wearing a short robe, which elongated her legs when she kicked them out in front of her and crossed them at the ankles. I couldn't tear my eyes off them, but I still answered her question. "Definitely. This has to be the best part of having a wife so far."

"Really?" She kicked my ankle to dislodge my heated gaze. "The best? Better than last night?"

"Second best," I corrected before letting out a sigh when I looked into her eyes. "Last night wins, hands down. But this is fucking awesome."

"I'm guessing none of your previous wives dragged you to a spa?" she joked.

"Nope. Clearly, none of them loved me enough to expose me to this kind of experience."

She tilted her head slightly to the side, leaning back but keeping her eyes on mine. "Seriously, though. You've never had a girlfriend bring you with her or booked a spa day for an anniversary or something?"

"I've been light on the girlfriend front," I admitted after a brief pause. "Back when I was still in the service, there just never seemed to be enough time for anything meaningful to develop. Now, I'm still away more often than I'm at home. It makes it difficult to get to know me and for me to really get to know someone else."

"Are you saying that you've never been in a relationship?" Her eyes stretched wide open, the blue filled with shock and disbelief.

"I've been in relationships. They've just never lasted very long. What about you? Other than your last relationship, obviously."

She chuckled, not tensing or clamming up like she had the last time her ex had come up. "I was too busy focusing on my career to spend much time bothering with love and relationships. I had a few before Will, but they also never got serious. I spent far too much time in the office for it to get that far. I guess we've got that in common."

"I know you don't really want to talk about Will," I said cautiously, "but why would he leave you? Did you ever take him to a spa? If you did, he was fucking crazy to run out on you."

"Are you really that impressed by all this?" She flicked her hand in the air. "I mean, it's nice, but it's not really the kind of thing that would inspire someone to stay with you."

I scoffed. "I wasn't only talking about the spa, but I could be convinced to stay with you forever if you keep bringing me to places like this."

Laughing as she shook her head at me, she dropped her gaze to her lap when it turned sad. "I don't really have a good answer for you about why he left me. And yes, we did spa days together all the time."

"If it counts for anything, I think he was an idiot for leaving you." Truth rang out clear as a bell in my voice, and Lindsay shot me a small smile.

"Does that mean you think I'm cool?" she asked.

"Not cool... but all right." I winked as I wound my arm around her waist and pulled her closer to me despite the intense heat in there. "You're definitely one of the cooler planners I've ever met."

She rested her head against my shoulder. "You're one of the cooler impulsive people I've met."

We talked for a while longer until the therapist came to get us again. Exfoliation and detoxification treatments were on the menu for the afternoon, and we emerged smelling vaguely of the papaya and pineapple lotions they'd applied to rejuvenate our skin.

As we were saying goodbye, one of the therapists handed us a neon flyer for a beach party the resort was hosting that night. She smiled when Lindsay took it from her. "We hope to see you there. You can't leave here before you've experienced a party beneath our star-filled skies."

Lindsay's eyes darted up to mine, and I saw the hesitation in them. "I don't know. I'm pretty ready to just fall into bed after how relaxing this day has been."

A minute ago, I'd felt the same way. But now, all I could think about was dancing with her curves pressed against my body underneath that star-filled sky the therapist had just mentioned.

Giving her my very best puppy-dog eyes, I wrapped my hand around hers and brought it to my mouth to brush a gentle kiss against each of her knuckles, interspersing the kisses with words.

"I think we go should, baby. It's a beach party. I love beach parties."

A soft smile lifted the corners of her lips as she sighed, then nodded. "Yeah. Okay. I'm down to go if it means that much to you."

"It does." I bent over and kissed the top of her head. "It really does."

CHAPTER 17

LINDSAY

The night was clear when Jaxon and I walked out of our bungalow after cleaning up and having a drink together on our patio. Stars glittered in the sky above us, and the scent of a bonfire and grilling meat drifted in the air.

He took my hand when we stepped onto the beach, spotting the festivities just a little ways away and located farther down the private stretch of sand. Although we'd been holding hands a lot, I still felt a tingle whenever he first pressed his skin against mine.

Now that I knew what else he could do with those hands, the tingle was accompanied by a healthy dose of lust. It'd taken everything I had to turn him down this morning, but I knew that he would make good on his promise of keeping me in bed all day and I'd really wanted to go to the spa.

As for turning him down again once we'd gotten there, that'd purely been my inhibitions talking. The treatment rooms were private in terms of the fact that one was shielded from view of the occupants of the neighboring rooms, but they were definitely *not* soundproofed. We'd heard other couples laughing and talking while on our balcony, and I knew there was no way they wouldn't hear us if we did anything on ours.

I wasn't a prude. I just really didn't want to have to look people in the eye after if he made me scream and moan the way he had last night. And none of those noises had been fake or exaggerated.

Jaxon squeezed my hand, peering down at me as we walked along the moonlit beach with the waves crashing gently to the shore. "What's got your mind all busy?"

"Nothing much." I bit my lip, averting my gaze to stare at the luminous, glowing white ball as it hung just above the horizon. "Just about how this trip has turned out really differently from what I'd expected."

"You're starting to realize meeting me was a happy accident, aren't you?" He didn't smirk. His expression was filled with genuine warmth as he walked beside me.

I nodded. "Maybe I am, but the same can be said about you meeting me."

"True, but I never thought otherwise." He bumped his side gently into mine. "I realized what a happy accident meeting you was as soon as I saw you laughing into my shoulder when I threatened the manager."

"Jeez. I can't believe that was only days ago. It feels like I've known you for years." It was true, even though it was a truth that scared me a little.

"What can I say? I'm an easy guy to get to know." He licked his lips, his eyes narrowing as he brought our joined hands up to drape his arm over my shoulders again without letting go of my hand. "Actually, that's a lie. I'm really not that easy to get to know. I feel the same way about you, though. It seems almost impossible that it's been less than a week."

"Well, I suppose we're already living together," I joked, trying to lighten the mood. "If you count the cumulative amount of hours we've spent together so far, I think it'll probably be the equivalent to having dated for at least a couple of months back in the real world."

"How do you figure?"

"Think about the average length of dates and how many times a week you see that person." I got comfortable in the crook of his shoulder and pressed a kiss to the top of his arm. "We've barely left each other's sight in—what is it now—probably just over a hundred hours?"

"What do you think the average length of a date is?" he asked. "About three or four hours?"

"If it's going well, yes. It's probably around there somewhere." I rocked my head from side to side while I thought. "That's either thirty-three or twenty-five dates worth of time we've spent together."

"How many times a week do you think regular couples go on dates?" He grinned down at me. "Two or three nights a week?"

I shrugged. "Seems fair enough. We'd have to look it up to be sure."

"I don't really give a fuck, but let's accept for the sake of argument that we're right. That means we've spent as much time together as people who have been dating for anywhere between two to four months."

"Wow." I blinked back my surprise. "A lot of people who've been dating for that length of time are either engaged or married for real."

"See, baby bear?" He gave me another of the fake, dopey looks he seemed to love so much. "We're meant to be."

I checked his hip with my own but couldn't hide my smile. "Yeah, it's got to be that. You're actually becoming less annoying with time. I haven't found one of your socks in the bathroom in all this time."

"Does that mean I can start leaving my socks in the bathroom now?"

I shook my head and punched his side gently. "Don't you dare. The fact that you fold up your clothes and pack them away so neatly is one of the most endearing things about you."

"Here I thought it was my good looks and my banging body."

"Banging body?" I laughed as I rolled my head back on his arm to look into his eyes. "You just gave away your age, buddy."

He opened his mouth to reply, but we'd reached the party. The smell of the fire and the roasting meat was even stronger there, and I also caught a whiff of the sweet-smelling, tropical flowers decorating the tables.

The event looked very much like what I imagined a luau did, with tables laden with food, local music being played by a live band, and fires everywhere. People danced to the sultry sounds of the guitars, and a singer was swaying with her eyes closed on the makeshift stage.

Jaxon grinned when he saw Big Mac ambling up with his arms open and a flowery necklace in each meaty hand. "Welcome, my friends. I'm so happy to see a real couple decided to join us. I can't stand all these touristy, fake, 'I love you' couples."

"What do you mean?" I asked, suddenly super aware of the real status of my relationship with Jaxon. Even though it was starting to feel real, it wasn't. *Not by any stretch of the imagination.*

Big Mac shrugged a dark shoulder, the skin revealed since the shirt he was wearing had no sleeves. It was like a vest that had started out as a T-shirt, and the print of the front was faded. He draped the flowers around each of our necks while he replied.

"You know what I'm talking about. Those couples who think they need to prove to everyone just how in love they are by constantly kissing and being on each other's laps."

I opened my mouth to say something, but Jaxon beat me to it. "Thank you for recognizing the depth of our relationship."

He glanced down at me with another simperingly sweet look on his face, and I rolled my eyes at him. "Sure. Yeah. That's what it's all about."

One corner of his mouth twitched up at my response, and he buried his face in my hair to hide his laughter.

"Come and meet everyone," Big Mac said when my fake husband had regained his composure. "I've been telling them all about the only couple on the island I can stand being around."

"Why do you work at a resort catering mostly to honeymooners if you can't stand the couples?" I asked curiously as we fell into step beside him.

He grinned and shared a look with Jaxon over the top of my head. "The pay, the perks, and the bikinis. In case you haven't noticed, there are a lot of barely clothed people around here."

Jaxon laughed, tucking me closer to his side. Warmth bloomed inside me at the possessive gesture. There was no way he could be threatened by Big Mac, whether the man had checked me out in my bikini or not, but it was like these things came instinctively to him. Like he just couldn't help himself because he didn't even always realize he was doing it.

Back home and in my career, I was no shrinking violet. I was the head of my department and dealt with a bunch of egotistical jerks all the time. Being a ball-buster was only one of the ways in which I'd progressed as fast and as far as I had.

Will had known me that way, and he'd been perfectly happy to let me wear the proverbial pants. If there was a problem at a restaurant, I was the one to have to sort it out. When he caught another man making eyes at me, he'd trusted me to deal with it.

While I was more than capable of handling everything myself, I couldn't deny that I enjoyed the whole dominant, possessive thing Jaxon had going on. Alpha-male bad boys had never really been my thing, but now I was starting to wonder why.

Not that he was a bad boy—at least not to me—but he definitely gave off that vibe with other people. And the way he had sex? Well, he definitely wasn't a *good* boy. *That's for sure.*

On the other hand, he wasn't a boy at all. There was nothing even remotely boyish about him. He was a man, and a pretty darn sexy one to boot. It wasn't just his body or his looks that made him sexy. He just was.

While I didn't need the white knight galloping in on his horse to save me, it was nice to know someone really had my back for a change. That I didn't always have to do everything myself. In the short time I'd known him, he'd made me feel more like a part of a team than always having to be the one leading from the front.

"Where do you keep disappearing off to?" He whispered into my ear as we walked, his lips moving against the shell and his warm breath fanning across my cheek.

Turning my head into him to be able to speak without being overheard, I decided to take another risk. "I was just having a girly moment and thinking about how sexy my new husband is."

He squeezed my hip and lowered his head, a lock of his light brown hair that shone almost gold in the firelight falling across his forehead as heat crept into his eyes. He brushed his lips against mine in the faintest of kisses but it still managed to feel like it held so many promises.

"Funny. I've been having the same thoughts about my beautiful new wife." He said it without lifting his mouth all the way off mine, his hard body pressing into me. He was so close that I could smell his delicious, clean scent, and I couldn't help but take a breath that was just a touch deeper than normal.

Everything—the way he looked, sounded, and smelled—got to me so badly that I rubbed my thighs together to ease the sudden tension between them, and he must've noticed something shift in my expression because he suddenly kissed me much more fervently.

"I promise you I feel the same way," he said. "Let's meet all of Big Mac's friends, have something to eat, dance a little, and then blow this joint. What do you say?"

"Yes." It was a whispered word, but he obviously heard it above the music.

He kept me close to him all night, his fingers wandering along my sides and my arms while he talked and joked with the locals. They were innocent touches, but they sure didn't feel that way.

When we danced later on and he slid his leg between my knees, moving his hips in a way that nearly drove me out of my mind, I shook my head and moved to step away. "I can't do this. It's too much."

He held me in his firm grip but eased up on the sensual dancing in favor of simply taking me into his arms and dropping a sweet kiss on top of my head. "Better?"

"Much." I sighed and wrapped my arms around his neck. "Where did you learn how to dance like this anyway? I didn't know dancing was a requirement for the Air Force."

"For the Air Force?" He let out a low chuckle, eyes filled with amusement as they held mine. "No. The Air Force didn't require dancing, but getting a date with this chick I had a thing for in high school did."

I threaded my fingers into his soft hair, smiling as I tried not to get lost in the melted honey of his gaze. "Oh? Did you end up getting your date?"

Rolling his hips in some kind of fancy move I thought I might've seen in Latin dancing at a club once, he grinned and lifted a shoulder. "What do you think?"

"I think you're not the guy who's going to let a bit of dancing stand in his way."

"You know me so well already." He ran his hand up my arm to remove mine from his shoulder, pushing me away from his body as he spun me around. Bringing me back to him once I'd completed the turn and was a second away from swooning as he dropped me into a quick dip, he held me with his front molded to my back, his lips brushing against my ear. "I should probably mention that the date I got wasn't with the girl I joined the class for."

I rolled my eyes—something I seemed to do a lot of with him—and tossed him a look over my shoulder. "Why doesn't it surprise me that you were a player?"

"Player? Me? No. That doesn't sound like me at all."

When he turned me back to face him, he held me tighter to his chest and peered down at me through his long lashes. "Not now that I've met my wife anyway. You still hungry?"

"Nah. I had enough of the canapes they were passing around to last me the next week." I rested my head on his chest and wound my hands around to my back to take his. "I'm ready to call it a night."

I wasn't sure if he'd heard me, but when his fingers curled around mine and he pulled me to his side, I knew he must have. We waved goodbye to Big Mac, who watched us go with a knowing expression on his face and a quick salute with his beer, then turned back to the group of friends he was talking to.

The walk back to our room was made in comfortable silence. After opening the door, Jaxon followed me inside and made for the sofa-bed and his bag.

It was cute that he thought I was going to make him sleep there alone. I went into the bedroom and changed into a tank top and sleep shorts before going back to the doorway, beckoning to him when he looked up at me.

"Do you really want to sleep out here?" I asked.

He got off the bed immediately, coming over to wrap his arms around me. "Not if there's another option available."

"I think there just might be. The bed is big enough for both of us, wouldn't you agree?"

"Yes." Without saying another word, we walked to the same sides of the bed we'd woken up on and pulled back the covers.

The only light on in the room was the one on Jaxon's side of the bed, and he flipped it off once we were both comfortable. He didn't stay on his side of the bed much longer though, moving over and holding me the same way he had the night before.

"I'm ready for another day without an itinerary," I said softly.

I felt his answering smile, even in the dark, before he pressed another one of his sweet kisses to the back of my neck. "So am I. Let's get some sleep. No waking up before at least noon."

A groan escaped me, and he chuckled before giving me another kiss. "Joking, sweet cheeks. Now go to sleep. There's no knowing what tomorrow will bring."

Despite how worked up I'd been earlier, I fell asleep without feeling sorry that we hadn't done anything. The massages earlier really had exhausted me, and our late night last night certainly hadn't helped things.

Besides, knowing Jaxon, there would definitely be a chance to have my other needs tended to tomorrow. *Thoroughly.*

With that thought in mind, I succumbed to sleep, smiling and holding the hand draped over my middle.

CHAPTER 18

JAXON

I hadn't slept next to a woman in years. Yet I'd slept next to Lindsay for two nights in a row, and one of them hadn't even been in a post-coital haze.

For once, I was awake before her and had already showered by the time she opened her gorgeous eyes. She frowned when she saw me dressed and ready for the day, her gaze flicking to the window before she brought it back to mine.

"What's the time?"

"Hey, that's my line," I teased, leaning over to kiss her cheek before motioning to the coffee I'd already made her. "It's only seven, so you can relax. I was planning on waking you up soon anyway. I didn't want you having a cardiac event if you only came to mid-morning."

Groaning as she rolled over and pulled the covers over her head, she lifted her arms out from underneath them and stretched. Her back arched as she did, pushing her breasts up as if she was offering them to me.

My dick stirred, but I ignored it and focused on her instead. "Come on, sleepyhead. We've got places to go and things to see. Chop chop."

I grinned when I repeated her words from earlier in the week back to her, and her head popped out from under the covers just enough to show me her eyes as she glared at me. "Very funny. Keep the coffee for me. I'll be right out."

Taking that as my cue to give her some privacy for her morning routine, I left the bedroom and heard the shower starting to run just a few seconds later. It was ridiculous how refreshed I felt, considering how early it still was, but sleeping next to her seemed to do that to me.

I heard her humming when she got out of the shower and smiled, seriously thinking about going back in there while she was still naked. It was a day without a plan, my day, and spending it in bed with her still seemed like a really good idea to me.

Too bad she'd never go for it. I let out a sigh, but I couldn't really say I was disappointed. So far, every day on this island had been incredible. Loathe as I was to admit it, she had a point about getting an early start and making use of every hour of the day.

There was no beach party tonight as far as I knew, so perhaps we could spend the night in bed instead of the day and order some room service instead of going out for dinner. *Win-win.*

Lindsay finished up and came out of the bedroom dressed in another pair of linen shorts, a black, low-cut tank top, and sneakers. She gestured down the length of her perfect fucking body with a crease appearing between her eyebrows.

"Since I don't know what we're doing, I didn't know what to wear. Is this okay?"

I nodded, clenching my fingers into fists around the sheets of the sofa bed until my knuckles were white. There was nothing I wanted more than to drag her back into that bedroom to discover for myself what she was wearing underneath those clothes, but I held myself back.

Because I also wanted to just fucking spend time with her. It was exhausting constantly having to fight against such strong, conflicting urges. *It's no wonder there are so many bachelors in the world.*

"I'm assuming you noticed I was wearing sneakers too?" I asked instead of insisting she get back inside the bedroom and wait for me —naked.

"Yeah." She smiled. "I figured I couldn't go wrong if I wore something similar to you. Care to fill me in on what we're doing?"

"Nope." I relaxed my hands and got to my feet, jerking my head toward the door. "You ready?"

"I guess so." Nerves skittered across her eyes, and I knew she was thinking back to parasailing and swimming with sharks. But then she blinked and there was nothing but excitement staring back at me. "Let's go do this thing."

I chuckled as I led her to the door, then locked it once we were outside. The air was already hot and thick, but I was getting used to the humidity, and it really didn't bother me much anymore.

"The first thing on our program for the day isn't massively exciting," I warned as we walked toward the outdoor dining area, "but we're going to need our strength. Strenuous physical activity in this heat without eating would be a terrible idea."

"Are you telling me we're just going to breakfast?"

"Yep." I whistled under my breath as we walked, and she shot me an incredulous look.

"I won't argue because the food the other day was divine and the breakfast they served at the spa yesterday was delicious, but I won't lie about the fact that I'm a little surprised. I thought maybe you'd insist on grabbing local cuisine from a cart on the street or something."

"That's not a bad idea. Let's keep it in mind for another day. I think I'm in love with the way this place cooks their bacon. I just can't get enough."

"How do you look the way you do with the way you eat?"

I gave her a one-shouldered shrug. "We're on vacation. Cutting loose is kind of the point, isn't it? Besides, I think we've been plenty active enough to burn it all off. Someone wouldn't just let me laze around all day."

"Someone who obviously cares about your health." She batted her eyelashes innocently at me.

I laughed and hugged her from the side. "Aww. I knew you cared about me."

our hotel room to pick up a backpack with our supplies, we got into the taxi I'd ordered for us earlier.

The trail was unlike anything I'd ever seen before. The dense forest it was cut into made it impossible to see much beyond the path, but the towering trees, the birdsong, and the views as we ascended made it a truly unique experience.

Unlike some other hikes, there wasn't only one way up this mountain. Several different paths branched off from the main one, and Lindsay and I chose one of the quieter ones. It was well enough signposted that we wouldn't have to worry about getting lost.

Signs of civilization had made it up here too, but the small information huts also carried medical kits and were built entirely of natural materials. It made them unobtrusive, and since we could also refill our water bottles there, they came in real handy real soon.

Sweat glistened on Lindsay's brow, but whenever she looked at me, her eyes were alive and she very much had a bounce in her step. About halfway up, we came across a little girl standing in the middle of the path, tears gushing from her eyes as she looked around.

Lindsay and I exchanged a glance before we both rushed to her side. I got to her first, dropping into a crouch and discreetly checking her for injuries while I spoke. "Hey, sweetheart. Do you speak English? What happened? Are you okay?"

She shook her head, her lower lip trembling as she answered Lindsay instead of me. "I got lost. I can't find my mom or dad anywhere."

Her voice was heavily accented with an Australian lilt, but at least she understood us. Lindsay gave me a worried look before lowering to her haunches next to me. "Where did you last see them?"

"They were asking about the waterfalls at one of the kiosks. I didn't mean to go so far away from them."

"Can you remember which way you came from?" I asked. "Were you going uphill or downhill?"

"Down." Her lip trembled again. "But there's a fork just up there and I can't remember which way to go."

"That's okay," Lindsay said soothingly. "This is Jaxon and I'm Lindsay. You did the right thing by just standing still when you realized you were that lost."

"We'll help you find your parents," I said. "What's your name?"

"Tammy." Her voice shook. "I'm not supposed to speak to strangers."

"I understand," I said. "We're not going to hurt you, okay? There are a lot of people out here even though we seem pretty alone at the moment. Neither of us will lay a hand on you, and if you feel unsafe with us at all, you can scream and scream. Someone will definitely hear you and come help."

"How do I know you won't stop me from screaming?" she asked.

Smart kid.

Shifting on my heels, I extracted my phone from my pocket. "Do you know your parents' cell number?"

She nodded and I handed the device over after unlocking it. "Call them and ask them where they are. You can talk to them while we walk. How does that sound?"

"Good." She sniffed, already dialing a foreign number.

When her parents answered and heard her voice, they were so frantic that I could hear them from a couple of feet away. Tammy explained what had happened and whose phone she was using, then gave us the name of the hut they'd returned to when they couldn't find her.

Apparently, they'd already called for help.

Unzipping the backpack, I found the map we'd gotten at the bottom of the trail and quickly located the hut. I couldn't pinpoint our exact location, but I gave Tammy the name of the trail we were on, and she relayed the information.

Five minutes later as we were heading up the hill, a tear-streaked couple came running around the corner and swept the little girl up in their arms. They thanked us profusely for taking care of their daughter and left shortly after to call off the help they'd summoned from the authorities and search-and-rescue.

"You're actually quite good with children," Lindsay commented once we were alone on the path again.

"I don't like seeing people looking lost or hurt." I raised my shoulders and pushed my hair off my face. "It was nothing really. Just coming up with a plan to let her know she was safe with us until we could find her parents."

"It might have been nothing to you, but it meant everything to them." A thoughtful expression came onto her face before she looked up at me with a mischievous smile forming on her lips. "Come with me."

"Where are we going?" I asked, following her when she disappeared off the trail and wound her way through the wide trunks of the trees surrounding it.

"I want to do something spontaneous," she called.

When I walked around the tree her voice had come from, she was topless and in the process of shimmying out of her pants. My jaw slackened as I drank her in, raking my gaze over her nearly naked chest and all the curves on display.

My dick stirred again, and this time, I didn't ignore it. A grin spread on my lips as I took the step separating us and pushed her up against the tree. "I thought you weren't a fan of sex in public."

"So did I." She smirked as she pushed her hands under my shirt, her fingertips trailing along my abdomen. "But seeing you in white-knight mode was seriously hot. I didn't think you'd object to me having a change of heart about it."

"Keep your sneakers on," I growled as I bent my head to nip and lick at her neck. "You never know what might be lurking around here."

She moaned when I sucked at an apparently sensitive spot below her jaw, and I pulled back to look into her eyes. "Keep it down, baby. We're not very far away from the trail and we wouldn't want to get arrested, now would we?"

CHAPTER 19

LINDSAY

Holy. Shit.

H I didn't know who this girl was that had brazenly taken off her shirt in the middle of a tropical forest with people all over the mountain, but I liked her. Being her was so thrilling that my panties were soaked even before Jaxon's body pressed me up against the rough bark of the tree.

Although it wasn't just the liberation of acting on what I wanted that had gotten me that way. I'd been pretty much raring to go since I woke up, and getting my blood flowing on the hike hadn't helped.

I'd gotten distracted by the beauty of our surroundings, but every so often, my mind strayed to what it would be like to slip off the beaten track and then have Jaxon slipping into me. Seeing him once again taking complete charge of a situation and then helping that little girl had inspired me to take charge of my own situation.

There was no denying that I wanted him, and I suddenly couldn't think of a reason why not to act on it. As his lips pressed to my jaw and he shoved his hand into my panties a little more roughly than before, I mentally patted myself on the back for having had the courage to take what I wanted.

Jaxon groaned into my ear when he found me slick between my

legs, and his tongue darted out to suck the lobe between his teeth. "Are you always this fucking wet?"

"Never." I gave him complete honesty. "It usually takes me a while to get into it."

"Not in my experience, but I fucking love it," he mumbled, sliding his fingers lower and pushing my legs apart with one of his. "You're going to be good and keep it down for me, right? I promise I'll make it up to you later. You'll be lifting the roof when we get back to the bungalow."

I nodded, sucking both lips into my mouth to keep quiet when he pressed down on my throbbing clit. He spoke with his lips still next to my ear, his breath causing goosebumps to rise on my flesh as it ghosted over my heated skin.

"Good. Let me know if you need any help keeping it down." Without any further warning, he plunged a thick finger inside me while he started playing with me.

He freed my breasts from my bra with his other hand, pinching my nipple before dipping his head to soothe the hardened nub with lavish kisses. I pressed up against him, wanting more of what he was doing —everywhere.

I felt his hard length against my hip, suddenly more desperate to touch him than I'd ever been. Reaching down between us, I skimmed my fingers past the waistband of his jogging shorts and relished the rumble of his groan against my chest when I brushed against his tip.

His erection was firm but his skin was as soft as satin in my grip. I ran my fingers over his length, all the way down to his taut balls before scraping my fingernails gently against his skin on my way back up. He let out that hissing noise again, then slammed his mouth down onto mine to swallow the moans slipping from my lips as he curled his fingers inside me.

My inner muscles pulsed around his fingers, and it was my turn to absorb the noises he made. This kiss was different to any of the ones we'd shared the other night. Deeper, faster, and more carnal.

It spoke to the fact that we weren't there to take our time and explore one another. We were there to fuck. *Hard and fast.*

Not that the other night hadn't been hard, but it surely hadn't been fast. I'd felt him between my legs the whole of the next day, and I frankly couldn't wait to feel him there again.

Adding a second finger, he pumped into me faster while also strumming me with his thumb. A pleasurable shiver ran through me, and he rammed me into the tree with his hips, using them and the rough bark to keep me upright.

"I've never done this standing up before," I confessed between passionate kisses.

"I won't let you fall," he promised, his voice rough as he moved his pelvis farther forward as if trying to reassure me.

It made stroking him a little more difficult, but I was losing speed as my climax crept up on me anyway. It didn't seem to bother him. If anything, he was just getting more into it.

"Come for me, Linds. Just remember to keep quiet." His voice was a harsh whisper.

I buried my head in the crook of his neck, biting his shoulder to keep any sounds from escaping as heat spread through my veins and that euphoric precipice was so close my toes were already curling. A retort about how bossy he was in the bedroom—or the forest for that matter—died on my lips when I went tumbling headfirst over the edge with another flick of his thumb.

My body tensed against his, but I didn't feel like he was about to let me fall. Somehow in the midst of everything that we'd done together, I had come to trust him. Really trust him.

The realization sent powerful aftershocks ripping through me before I finally went all but limp in his arms. Looking up at the savage expression on his face as he watched me in the aftermath of coming apart, I knew he wasn't done with me yet.

Despite him following through on his promises the first time we were together, I felt so sated that I really doubted I'd get there again. Seeing that look on his handsome face made my insides involuntarily clench again, though.

How? How does this guy have such an intense effect on me? I didn't know, but this was hardly the time to question him. Not that I thought he knew, but at least I was pretty darn confident it was the same for him.

"You okay?" he asked, his voice almost tender even while he was pulling a condom out of his wallet and shoving his pants and underwear down over his large cock.

I nodded before dropping my head back to kiss his lips while hooking one leg around his hip. "How are we going to do this?"

He kissed me, fast and demanding, before he brought his palms to my thighs and lifted me against him. "How's that bark against your back?"

I didn't even have time to answer him before he released one of my legs to yank his shirt off over his head. He blanketed it over my shoulders before resting me against the tree again. Instead of answering him with words, I offered my mouth again and he took it as he lined himself up.

Concern clouded his gaze when he glanced down at me again. "This is going to be hard and fast. You okay with that?"

"It's like you read my mind." I looped my arms around his shoulders and burrowed my hands into his hair, kissing him again as he thrust into me.

I would've cried out if his mouth hadn't already been on mine, but it came out as a muffled moan instead. He withdrew as far as he could before returning to me like he just couldn't help himself.

His hips set a brutal pace, but I loved every minute of it. I worked to meet his thrusts, but it was almost impossible to do much in this position.

Leveraging my arms on his shoulders and calling on muscles I didn't even know I had, I managed to roll into him instead of thrusting, but my efforts felt pretty amazing to me. From the concentration on his features when I opened my eyes to sneak a peek at him, I'd say he felt the same way.

At this angle, with him filling me up and hitting me in all kinds of places as a result of my own actions, it didn't take me long before I was fluttering around him again. Pleasure swelled up from deep inside me, cascading out in an almost violent wave when the dam walls burst and I let him have it all.

He moaned right along with me, his rhythm finally breaking as he slammed into me three more times before finding his own release. I felt him expand deep inside me, his powerful muscles quivering as he rode out his climax.

When he was done, he dropped his forehead against my shoulder, breathing heavily as he placed kisses on my bare skin and whispered between them. "Fuck, Linds. That was incredible, but we need to get dressed."

"Could you give me a minute?" I held on to him, unable to feel my extremities but also more than hesitant to let him go in such an intimate moment.

He nodded without removing his head, waiting until I wriggled before pulling back to look at me. "You okay now?"

"I think so." I flexed my fingers to be sure, then nodded. "Yeah. I'm okay. The rest of the walk might be a little interesting, though."

He chuckled, keeping a careful eye on me as he let me down. "I could carry you, but I'm guessing you wouldn't let me."

"You guess correctly." My feet touched the ground and Jaxon stepped away when he was satisfied that my legs were stable enough to hold me up. "I've never been like this, you know? I've never done anything like that before."

My limbs still felt like jelly, but I managed to get my clothes back on once I shook the leaves out of them. One or two stuck to me, but I picked them off with one hand while Jaxon wrapped the other up in his and guided us back to the path.

He looked sexy as all hell with his hair tousled from my fingers, his lips swollen, and his eyes still dark when he looked at me. "I'm sure you say that to all the guys you have sex with in a Fijian forest."

I hit his shoulder, but it lacked the intention to actually harm him in any way. "Is that any way to speak to your wife, baby bear? I think not. You've obviously been a bad influence on me."

Light came back to his eyes when he laughed, kissing me again just before we rejoined the rest of the tourists sticking to the trails. "I've always wanted to be one of those. Thanks for the compliment, princess."

"I'm no princess," I said against his lips, tossing my ponytail over my shoulder as I pulled away from him. "I'm a queen. Don't ever forget it."

He laughed and gave me a playful smack on the ass before slinging his arm around my shoulders as we made our way to the nearest waterfall. "Trust me. There's absolutely no way I'd ever forget that. You have a permanent spot carved into my memories, my queen. I'll always remember every minute that we've spent together."

For the first time, it dawned on me that our holiday—and by extension, our fake marriage—was quickly coming to an end. My heart flipped over at the thought, which was surprising because it wasn't supposed to be involved at all.

As I settled in against his side, where I really had become just as comfortable as he'd teased me about the other day, I felt tears pricking at the backs of my eyes. I wasn't ready to let him go, and yet it wasn't like we could stay.

Well, this is an unexpected turn of events.

CHAPTER 20

JAXON

I reached for Lindsay before I even opened my eyes, but my fingers didn't touch anything other than air and bedding. A frown tugged at my brows when I realized she wasn't there.

Worry punched me in the gut, but then I remembered where we were, and I figured she probably just needed to be alone for a while. She'd probably gone for a walk on the beach, not wanting to wake me up after all my complaining about early mornings.

Glancing at the windows, I saw that the sun was already up but it didn't look like it'd been that way for very long. The light was still too soft and it had that definite early morning haziness to it.

Flopping back on the mattress, I yawned and let a smile break free as I thought about our hike. And after.

Sex in the woods had been fucking hot, but I hated that she had to keep quiet. I wasn't exactly a stranger to fucking in public or semi-public places, but I'd never been as greedy for a woman's moans as I was for hers.

At least I'd kept my promise about making her raise the roof later. We'd had a picnic near a stream when we reached the waterfall. The afternoon had been spent talking, exploring a few of the shallower caves, and having an early dinner at a small local restaurant on our way back to the hotel.

When we'd reached our bungalow, I'd hauled her into the bedroom and kept her there for the rest of the night. At around midnight, we'd ordered grilled cheese and ice cream for a snack along with a bottle of champagne, eaten in bed, and then I'd guzzled the drink from her bare flesh before we finally fell asleep at some godforsaken hour of the morning.

At times, between rounds of enjoying our time together, I'd noticed her drifting off into her head. Knowing that she probably had a lot to work out was why I wasn't upset about her leaving me alone after all the time we'd been spending together.

Despite what it'd felt like this week, she wasn't mine. She didn't owe me a text or a note. After she'd sent me the pictures of us with Fred the Constrictor, she had my number. If she needed me, she'd call.

I wouldn't have been surprised if she'd left so she could speak to Ember privately. They'd been texting on and off throughout the trip, and since I'd heard the conversation the last time they spoke, it seemed likely that she'd gone off to speak to her where I wouldn't be privy to every word said to her friend.

Wherever she was, she wasn't mine to worry about. I didn't own her, wouldn't even if we really were married, and yet, I couldn't deny that I was a little worried, if only because I hoped she wasn't freaking out over us hooking up.

I got out of bed to make some coffee, but before I even got to the kitchenette, the outer door opened and Lindsay walked in carrying a tray. She looked gorgeous as always.

A yellow sundress covered those curves I'd come to love touching so much, and her hair was down and still damp. It hung to her waist, tumbling in waves over her shoulders. Simple white flip-flops adorned her feet, but she kicked them off as soon as she walked in.

She started when she saw me, obviously having expected to find me still in bed, but smiled when we made eye contact. "Morning, hubs. I got some breakfast from Big Mac himself."

There was something sad in her gaze. She was trying to hide it, but her smile lacked some of its usual luster, and her eyes weren't quite as bright.

Walking over to her, I took the tray and set it down on the small round dining table beside the door before opening my arms and pulling her into them. It came as naturally as breathing to me to hold her now. *Whatever the fuck that means.*

"You okay?"

"I'm fine. I've just realized that it's time to go back to reality soon. One more day and this will all be a distant memory."

I held her tighter, something dark forming a pit in my stomach. "Going back is going to suck. This place really is paradise."

She hummed her agreement, staying in my embrace for only a couple of beats longer before releasing me. "We should eat. The big man made our eggs fresh and he warned me about not letting them cool. Apparently, the chickens that could've lived if it weren't for his Eggs Benedict weep in his dreams if people try eating them cold."

"That's gruesome." I chuckled as I went to pull out her chair, waiting for her to sit down before pushing it back in and circling the table to take my own. "I'm going to miss him when we leave here, and not just his food."

"I know what you mean." She cut open her egg, and the yolk was cooked perfectly from where I was sitting. "He really has become like a friend. Although I'll definitely miss his food too."

"Maybe we could keep in touch," I suggested, and hope sparked in her eyes until I finished my sentence. "I'm not sure if the hotel has a policy against that kind of thing, but we could ask. When are you heading out?"

"Tomorrow." She didn't look at me, choosing to admire the view of the ocean beyond our window instead.

Can't blame her. A strange twisting happened inside me when I realized she'd meant it literally when she'd said she only had one more day. "That soon, huh?"

"Yep. Will you be okay? Do you think they'll kick you out of the bungalow when they realize I've gone?"

"It's fine. I'm not sure if they would, but I'll have to head home soon too anyway. I'm sure my job will be calling me back any minute now. It's a little surprising they haven't contacted me already."

In fact, I hadn't had much time to think about it, but I really should've heard from them by now. *Ah, fuck it. I'm not going to look a gift horse in the mouth.*

If they'd called me back earlier, I'd have missed out on at least one of the days with Lindsay, and there honestly hadn't been one I'd have wanted to miss. I would check the flights out later today, though.

Between her leaving anyway, the awkward situation with having to explain why my bride left the honeymoon before I did, and a possible phone call from the airline demanding to know when I'd be back, it was about time for me to look into options for getting home.

The knowledge that my time with her was so limited that the actual end was coming *tomorrow* settled in that pit of my stomach, joining the yet unnamed darkness and forming a heavy weight I couldn't shake.

She'd told me a little more about her relationship with her ex—the fucknut who'd let her go—in the last few days, but our conversation when she'd mentioned her brother still hovered at the back of my mind.

If we were running out of time, I wanted to know everything I could about her.

"You know, you never told me," she began, but I spoke at the same time.

"So, your brother is in the military too?" I cut myself off and gestured for her to go ahead, but she didn't complete whatever was she'd been about to ask.

The sadness in her eyes grew darker, and for a second, I was afraid I'd pushed her too far by asking. But then she dragged in a deep breath and gave me a slight smile. "Yeah, he's actually in the Air Force too. It's a small world, huh?"

"How old is he? Any chance I knew him?"

She shook her head. "Nah, probably not. It depends on exactly when you left, but he's only twenty-seven. He enlisted about four years ago."

"Ahh, you're probably right then." I reached out and touched her hand, warmth spreading through me when her fingers closed around mine. "I'm sorry I asked. I just kept thinking about it and I was curious."

"It's okay." She tightened her grip on my fingers, spearing another bite of her food with her free hand. She chewed with a thoughtful expression on her beautiful face, swallowing it down with a swig of the orange juice Big Mac had sent along. "Talking about him can just be hard sometimes. We didn't leave things on the best foot."

"You don't have to talk about it if you don't want to." I understood what it was like to have things you'd rather keep to yourself, but I also knew that sometimes bottling it all up made it even worse. "I can listen if you want to, though."

She let out a soft sigh, her eyes darting back to the window as she nodded. "It's been a really long time since I've spoken about him, but he's not some deep, dark secret. I don't want him to seem that way. He was just always a troubled kid, you know?"

"Troubled how?" My voice was cautious.

We'd made a lot of headway this week. I would hate to see it all crumble the day before she fucking left.

Lindsay didn't even hesitate, though. She still didn't meet my gaze and focused on the ocean with a wistful look in hers. "He was my best friend growing up. I loved him more than life itself. It was me and him against the world."

"What happened?" I asked quietly.

She lifted her shoulder. "I don't even really know. We were in our teens when he started growing distant. His school would call all the time to let us know he hadn't shown up. I'd already graduated by then, but I knew some of the kids he'd started running with. They were a bad crowd."

"Drugs?"

She shrugged again. "I think so. There were definitely rumors, but we never found anything on him, and he never seemed that out of it or anything like that."

"You haven't asked him?"

"No." Closing her eyes, she took another deep breath. "He'd pretty much shut me out by then. When he left high school, he took a stab at a few different things but nothing ever panned out. I'm pretty sure my parents sent him off to the military, but they've never admitted it, and I haven't heard from him since."

"I'm sorry, Linds." I stroked her knuckles. "I shouldn't have brought it up. I still have a lot of contacts there if you want me to ask about him."

"No. It's okay. I don't want to pry into his life. I just like to think that he's doing well for himself now. It's better this way. We'd have heard if he'd been discharged. Four years is longer than he's lasted anywhere else, so it must be good for him being there."

I felt her pain all the way down to my bones. There were so many people just like her brother that I'd served with. People who had no more ties to their families and thought it was better like that.

Since I'd always been so close to my mother, I'd never been able to understand it. I always felt for them, though. Not pity but the same immense sadness I felt coming from her now.

I didn't know what I would've done without Mom in my corner. I hoped I didn't ever have to find out. That only compounded the grief I'd felt whenever I'd heard a story like hers, though.

Fuck knows how you survive without family support.

Lindsay swiped her fingers underneath her eyes. "That's enough of my sob story. What are you going to do today?"

"I don't know. It's your day. I figured we'd hang out together again. What's on the cards for us, Cruise Director Flinn?"

She laughed but it didn't quite sound genuine. "I'd actually planned a wrap-up day. Do all the things I hadn't gotten around to doing. I've ditched that idea, though. I'm going shopping for some clothes instead."

"What me to come?" I asked, even though I couldn't think of anything worse than spending possibly my last day here shopping.

"I'm okay," she said, giving my hand a final hug before freeing hers to finish her breakfast. "Enjoy yourself. I'm sure we could both use some time to decompress before we head back home."

I hadn't known her for very long, but that cloudy gleam never left her eyes as she gathered her things and headed out. It clued me in to the fact that she wanted alone time because the vacation was coming to an end, considering she'd been sad about that since coming back from the dining area, but it was also about her brother.

Having already asked her about him, I didn't push the subject any further. I didn't even know the dude's name, but digging deeper would only bring her unnecessary pain to appease my own curiosity. It wasn't right.

She didn't want me finding out about him anyway, so it really didn't make a lick of difference who he was. It killed me to see her hurting so much over him, but I'd extended the offer.

If she ever wanted to take me up on it, she could. For now, I simply kissed her goodbye before she left and then I went down to the beach.

I didn't want to leave without scuba diving, and snorkeling with the sharks didn't really count as that. I knew there was a dive operator on the premises, and I was itching to get wet before my time on the island was done.

Setting my thoughts and worries about Lindsay aside, I headed out to do just that. *Make the most of every moment, right?*

Even the ones that would feel kind of empty now with the Lindsay-shaped hole she'd left at my side.

CHAPTER 21

LINDSAY

The town closest to the resort was situated on the banks of the river after which it had been named. Jaxon and I had done some exploring there before, and I was sorely aware of his absence now.

I wandered around the market selling fresh produce, tropical fruits and vegetables, freshwater mussels, and a whole variety of other things. When I'd told Jaxon I wanted to go shopping for clothes, I hadn't been completely honest.

It was true that I did want to pick up some of the locally made textiles and maybe another T-shirt or two as souvenirs, but I really just needed some time to myself. A bustling market was a strange place to come to so I could be alone, but it allowed me to do some window shopping for trinkets and to get lost in the crowd.

What I couldn't tell Jaxon, nor let him in on, was that I felt miserable over the prospect of having to leave. Talking about my brother this morning had simply made it a little bit worse. I wasn't sorry Jaxon had asked me about him. I'd meant it when I said he wasn't a deep, dark secret. My heart just ached whenever I thought about all the good times we used to have together.

It was an ache I was used to, however. The other ache which was much more intense and completely unfamiliar came whenever I thought about the fact that in less than twenty-four hours, I'd be on my way home.

Without Jaxon.

Sure, he lived in the same city I did, but he'd said in so many words that he was hardly ever there. I also knew that he didn't really do the relationship thing. So there I was, ostensibly on my honeymoon, crushing on my fake husband who I had no chance of ever having anything real with. The whole situation was so absurd that I would've laughed if I wasn't so close to tears.

A handicraft store at the end of the market near the railroad boasted a coffee shop, and I darted inside and ordered the biggest Americano they had. I had to get the pitiful weepiness out of the way and out of my system before I went back to the hotel.

Just because I'd wanted to spend some time by myself today didn't mean I wasn't planning on spending the night with Jaxon. It was our last night together—probably ever—and a herd of wild horses couldn't drag me away.

I wasn't in such a state that I didn't recognize I needed to talk to him about all this, at least hear his thoughts on staying in touch, but that required *me* having a handle on what I felt all this was. Which I didn't.

A friendly barista delivered my coffee to the table I'd chosen near the edge of the property and the river, and I stared off into the middle distance before I realized I was getting nowhere. No matter which way I sliced it, I just kept coming up with the same two conclusions.

The first was that I had a major crush on my fake husband and I'd like to see where it goes, and the second was that I knew for a fact he wouldn't be interested. If there was anything I'd learned from this week though, it was that taking unplanned risks could lead to the most treasured experiences I could ever have.

But before I marched back into the bungalow, sat him down, and confessed that my feelings were more on the real side of the spectrum now, I needed to talk to Ember. My voice of reason had never steered me wrong. Without her, I wouldn't even have met Jaxon to begin with because I'd never have come here if she hadn't encouraged me to do it.

Fiji was seventeen hours ahead of Houston, so I checked the time on my phone to ensure I wouldn't be waking her up with my drama. *Nope. All good. It's still yesterday afternoon there.*

Her voice was chirpy and cheerful when she answered my call. "The prodigal bestie has finally found a moment to speak to me, huh? I'm honored you'd take time away from your hottie so I can actually hear your voice for a change. Unless it's been him texting me all along because he ended up being a serial killer, and Jaxon wearing Lindsay's skin is on the other end of this call. In which case, prepare to lose your dick, mister."

"That's a weirdly specific threat." I laughed when her rambling greeting ending. "And no, it's not Jaxon wearing my skin. It's really me. Total false alarm on the whole serial killer thing."

"That's what I wanted to hear," she said excitedly. "Tell me everything. All I know is that you're okay, spending time with the hot husband you still haven't even sent me a pic of, and that we'll talk about it all later. Texts suck. I can't wait to see you in person."

"Yeah, me either." It was true. I really missed my friend, and having her sitting across from me while I worked all this out would've been the best thing ever. "I'll be home soon, though. You're still picking me up from the airport, right?"

"Of course. I've got that printout of your ticket stuck up on my fridge. You can bet your sexy ass I'll be there."

"Thanks," I said but my voice sounded strained even to my own ears. The pickup we were talking about was rushing at me way too fast, and it felt like I still had too much to get through before I left. It was really only one conversation, but it was one that had the power to make me feel like utter shit.

Unreciprocated crushes are the worst.

Ember obviously noticed my tone, and all the bouncy excitement disappeared from hers. "What did he do? I was being serious about cutting off his dangly bits if he hurt you."

"He didn't hurt me." Not intentionally anyway. "I might've just gotten a touch too attached to him."

"Whoa. That was fast."

"I know." I covered my face with my free hand and hung my head. "I'm a terrible person. It hasn't even been a month—"

"You misunderstood me. I don't give a fuck about Will. He left you on your wedding day without even having the balls to tell you to your face it was over. I'm talking about it being fast for you to have fallen for Jaxon."

"I haven't fallen for him." I scoffed, lifting my head away from my hand to sip on my wonderful caffeine fix. "I'm just crushing a bit. That's all. He's so different than any man I've ever been with, and I think I've gotten a little intoxicated by him. It's nothing serious"

"How is he different? I've never heard you use the word 'intoxicating' in connection with a man before. Actually, I don't think I've ever heard anyone use it that way in real life."

"That's because they haven't met *him*." I groaned. "You don't understand the effect he has on me. Being with him makes me do stuff I'd never even have considered before. He has this presence I can't escape. It draws me to him again and again."

I lowered my voice and whispered furiously into the receiver. "I seduced him on a hiking trail yesterday, for God's sake. There is something wrong with me when I'm with him. How is intoxicating not the perfect way to describe that?"

She let out a whistle between her teeth. "That sounds really intense. Good on him for fucking you in the woods or wherever you were hiking, though. It's about time someone lights that fire in you."

"What am I supposed to do with it now that it's lit?" I shook my head. "I'm leaving tomorrow. I can't even think about saying goodbye to him without getting all emotional."

There was a long pause before she replied. "This is the trip you needed, Linds. Something quick and dirty and without any ties. He's just the rebound guy. The one who shows you everything that the world has to offer and that you don't have to settle for the boring guy unless that's actually what you want."

I dipped my head back and let the sun soak my face, but I still felt cold on the inside at the prospect of leaving behind this little slice of heaven I'd carved out for myself here. "It's not just a rebound crush. I really, really like being around him. It's been unreal and I'm not ready for it to end."

"Listen to me and listen well," she said firmly, letting the steel core of who she was shine through. "Every single person who's ever had an erotic hookup on a tropical island has probably felt the exact same way you're feeling now. It's the kind of relationship you enjoy, but you leave it behind in Fiji. That's where the magic lies, my friend. You don't bring that shit home with you."

"I don't know how to leave it behind," I admitted after hesitating for moment. "I don't want to ruin the magic, but I also don't know how to say goodbye."

"Easy. You have one last wild monkey-sex night with the guy, and then tomorrow morning, you shake his hand and wish him luck as you wave goodbye. Clean break, honey. It's the only way."

Ember drilled me for information about Jaxon for a few more minutes and made me promise to snap some shots of him on the beach. I might do that but I would never show them to anyone. Then we hung up.

Her advice was solid. Logically, I knew that what she'd said was the right thing to do. My head was right there with her. It was my heart, the bastard, that was the problem. It ached painfully every time I tried to imagine a scenario where I shook his hand and waved him off.

Moping about it wouldn't bring me anywhere, though. The only part of her plan that sounded appealing was making the most of the last night I had with him. Regardless of my emotional state, I should never have suggested that we spend this day apart.

Our last day.

Dropping a few notes on the table for my coffee, I hurried into the street and hailed a cab. As I slid into the backseat, I snapped at the poor unsuspecting driver. "Step on it please. I need to get there as soon as I can."

The entire vacation, I'd been harping on about how we had to utilize every moment to its fullest, and yet I'd wasted more than half of my last moments with him wandering around a market feeling sorry for myself. At least I'd purchased a few souvenirs along the way, but that hardly made up for it.

Stupid. Stupid. Stupid.

I raced through the lobby once I'd tipped the driver handsomely for getting us there fast and for having had to put up with my crappy attitude. I knew Jaxon wouldn't be in our room, so I bypassed the bungalow and headed down to the beach.

He wasn't there, though. Brightly colored sails dotted the ocean in front of the activity stands on the other side of the beach, and I suddenly knew where he would've gone. As I jogged along the warm sand, I heard my name being called out from the patch of grass in front of the empty outdoor dining area.

My head jerked to the side at the sound of the familiar voice, and I headed up to Big Mac when he grinned. He seemed to know a lot of what was going on at this hotel. Perhaps he knew where Jaxon had gone.

"Hey, Lindsay. Heard you went shopping." He eyeballed my empty hands. "Need any pointers on where to go?"

"No. I dropped my parcels in the lobby. I'm looking for Jaxon actually. Have you seen him?"

"Ah, so my favorite couple gets separation anxiety after all." He let out a good-natured chuckle and patted the grass beside him. "I saw him much earlier. He was going diving, but that was hours ago."

"You haven't seen him since?"

He shook his head, but his eyes suddenly sparkled as he patted the grass again. "Sit here with me. He's probably still out on the water somewhere. I'll keep you company for a while before you head back to your room."

I sighed, raking a frustrated hand through my hair. *Of course, he's gone off on the water. He lives for that stuff. No way would he just sit around waiting for me to come back.*

Tired of being alone for the day, I plopped down beside the big man and looped my arms around my knees. My eyes were fixed on the ocean, hoping to catch a glimpse of tanned, broad shoulders and that "why, yes, I can do it all" smirk.

Big Mac let out a low chuckle. "I've seen a lot of couples come and go, but the relationship you have with Jaxon is rare."

"What makes you say that?" I asked, splitting my attention between him and the crowds of tourists participating in all manner of water-sports in front of us.

"People come here to get married, on their honeymoons, to have their vows renewed, or to bring their families when they've been together many years. It's not often that I see the kind of friendship combined with electric chemistry that you two have together. It's a beautiful thing to witness."

Guilt settled heavily on my chest. "That's very kind of you to say."

He glanced at me from the corner of his eye, frowning like he had that first day. "Why do you seem like you're in pain again?"

Fuck. Am I really that easy to read? Suddenly, I didn't want to hold the truth back any longer. Big Mac had become our friend, and even if he ratted us out if I told him, what were they going to do?

I'd happily pay the difference in the room rate if it meant getting the opinion of the insightful islander next to me. "It's all a lie. Jaxon and I aren't married. We met in the lobby of this very hotel on the day we arrived. There was a double booking and he couldn't find any last-minute accommodation anywhere. Long story short, we've been pretending to be newlyweds the whole time. We don't even know each other."

To his credit, our new friend didn't seem too shocked. Nor did he jump up and wave his hands around shouting "frauds" at the top of his lungs. "That explains your pain, but it doesn't mean I'm wrong. Are you sure you don't know each other? It might've been true when you arrived, but I'm not so sure it's true anymore."

His words hit me like a sledgehammer to the chest. He was right. Jaxon knew me better than almost anybody except maybe Ember. He certainly knew parts of me she didn't, and he definitely understood me better than Will ever had.

Big Mac smiled. "I thought so."

His voice was so calm and sure that I couldn't do anything but listen. "Something brought you two together here in Fiji. The universe sometimes connects us in strange ways, but those connections are already written in the stars, and they always have been. It's not something we should ever ignore. It's not something *you* should ignore, Lindsay."

Tears welled in my eyes, but he wasn't done yet. "Just because you met in an unconventional way doesn't make your connection any less real. I've seen it with my own eyes. Everyone here has and we consider ourselves experts in these matters."

"I'm leaving tomorrow," I whispered, "but I'm happy I got to meet you. Thank you for telling me all that. I'll keep it in mind."

He reached into his pocket and extracted a plain business card with a number handwritten on it. "It was cheaper that way than having them printed, but that's my private line. Call me if you ever need to talk. The universe might've pushed you together, but that doesn't mean the path will always be an easy one."

Grasping his card in my palm like a lifeline, I flung my arms around him. He chuckled as he rubbed my back in soothing, friendly motions. "Jaxon's in your room by the way. We didn't know what time you would be back, but he was almost done the last I saw him. This little chat should've bought him the time he needed, but every word I said was true."

I gave him another squeeze before pushing to my feet. "I need to speak to him. Thank you again for everything, Big Mac. We're really lucky to have met you."

The man inclined his head in the direction of our room and mouthed the word "go." I didn't wait any longer, practically sprinting back to the bungalow. When I opened the door, there were rose petals on the floor leading to the dining table. Candles were lit on every available surface, and Jaxon was just setting a box of matches down in the kitchenette.

He turned slowly to face me when he heard the door, and those stars Big Mac had been talking about seemed to align when I looked into his golden eyes. There was no way what I was seeing there was fake. He felt something for me too.

The only question is what?

CHAPTER 22

JAXON

Lindsay's blue eyes shone when they met mine. There was a storm brewing behind them, but I hadn't spent most of my day setting this up to have our last night dissolve into a whirlwind of emotion and another fight about me pushing her to talk about things she wasn't ready to.

After my fifty-minute dive early this morning, I'd realized that asking her about her brother had been insensitive. I didn't want that memory overshadowing the time we'd had on this island, so I called in the cavalry and set this up to hopefully wipe that stupid misstep from her mind.

"I know it's our last night here together, and I wanted to make it memorable," I said, taking a step toward her. "No more talk about anything that makes us sad. No talking about how our time in Fiji has come to an end. Tonight, it's just about you and me and making one more memory we can take home with us and look back on wistfully while we're slaving away at work. We'll just be in the moment tonight, agreed?"

She swiped her tongue across her lips, looking like there was something she wanted to say, but then she lifted her hands and gave me a smile. "That sounds amazing. You're remarkable for putting this all together in a few hours."

I shrugged. "I had a little help from our new friends. Go put on what I've laid out for you in the bedroom, and then we'll get this party started."

She laughed softly when she recalled I had said those same words to her in what seemed like an entirely different lifetime on the day we'd met. "If it's lingerie so we can make good on your threat to the manager, you need to know that I'm not that converted to spontaneity just yet."

"It's not that."

"I'll be back in a minute then." Reaching out to brush her hands against mine as she walked past, I saw her chest heave at the same time that I felt the electricity that always seemed to be present when we touched.

I wasn't a big believer in all that shit, but what I felt with her was undeniable. There was no point trying to rationalize away what I knew to be true.

Lindsay disappeared into the bedroom and closed the door behind her, like she'd done those first couple of nights we hadn't spent together. She emerged a few minutes later wearing the red dress I'd picked out for her earlier. It fit like it'd been tailored for her, plummeting into her cleavage without being indecent, hitting at about mid-thigh, and the richness of the color showing off her sun-kissed skin.

I'd known she was going to look fucking good in it, but what I hadn't expected was that it wasn't just my dick showing a definite reaction when she walked out of the room. My heart practically fell over itself at the sight of her in it, and my very blood seemed to thicken in my veins as it pounded in my ears.

"Wow," I breathed. "You look incredible."

"Thanks to you." She lowered her gaze and peered up at me in a way that made her look both flirty and vulnerable at the same time. It made me want to take her into my arms and protect her from anything that might hurt her, while also fucking her six ways from Sunday.

Confusing as balls.

"You might want to stop looking at me like that if you want to get to the early dinner Big Mac has prepared for us," I said in a warning tone.

She laughed softly, nodding as she moved toward the table. "I wouldn't want to pass up the opportunity for his food. You really did all this for me?"

"Well, no, actually. A few of the other fake wives I've spent almost every minute of this week with are coming by later. You might want to clear out before they get here."

Rolling her eyes in that way that had become so familiar it was like I'd been seeing it all my life, she lowered herself into the chair I pulled out for her. "I'll be sure to leave them some leftovers, but I guess I should just be honored that I'm getting served first."

"Only the best for my first wife." I winked as I took my seat, extending my legs to intertwine them with hers. "What did you get up to today? I thought you were going shopping. Didn't find anything you like?"

"Oh, I, uh, I dropped my packages in the lobby. They said they'd have them sent over."

"They're under strict orders not to disturb us tonight, but I'm sure everything will be here first thing in the morning. Get everything you wanted?"

She stared at me for a long time, her head starting to shake before it turned into a nod. "Yeah. Sure. Almost. There's one last thing here I want, but I don't know if I'll get it yet."

"I'm sure you will." I grinned at her while uncorking the champagne from the silver bucket next to the table. "If you really want it, that is. The girl I've come to know doesn't let anything stand in her way if she really wants something."

"Yeah. I guess I have been called tenacious once or twice." She blinked rapidly, like she was trying to clear something out of her mind, and then smiled. My heart stuttered again, and I wondered if maybe I needed to have it checked out when I got back to Houston.

"So," she said, leaning forward across the table and taking both my hands in hers, "if we're being in the moment, what could we possibly talk about?"

"I think we've covered just about everything but the basics this week." I turned my palms up to hers, wagging my brows as I made my suggestion. "What about twenty questions?"

She laughed but nodded her agreement. "Fine, but I go first. What's your favorite place in the world?"

"Right now? Fiji. Before I came here, my mother's house," I said honestly. "Yours?"

"Fiji." There was no hesitation before she answered. "Favorite color?"

"Black." Too easy. "Favorite sexual position?"

Her cheeks flushed. "Any of the ones I've done with you."

I hardened behind my zipper as they replayed on a loop in my mind, but that wasn't what tonight was about. Clearing my throat, I motioned to her. "Your turn."

"What do you hate the most?"

"Waking up early on vacation."

"That explains a few things." She chuckled and took a sip of champagne. "Mine is waking up late on vacation."

I shook my head at her, pursing my lips like I was terribly disappointed. "I guess we're just not meant to be."

It was meant as a joke, but there was a flash of something in her eyes that I was curious to know about. Since I'd made the rule of just being in the moment though, I let it go. *For now.*

"Would you go back into the service if they asked you right now?" Her voice was a little flat, but she was clearly not eager to discuss whatever had caused it either.

"In a heartbeat." I tilted my head as I watched her. "What is the quality you admire most in other people?"

"Hmm, interesting. Honesty, I think, but there are many others that seem just as important. If you could be anything, what would you be?"

"That guy who runs the adventure sports counter on the beach outside." I chuckled and lifted my shoulders when she gave me a disbelieving look. "What could possibly be better than that?"

After thinking about it for a second, she rolled her lips into her mouth and released them slowly. "I actually don't know. He gets to be on the beach here every day. He obviously lives nearby. The people he works with at the resort seem pretty great and I guess he has to have some kind of passion for the activities he offers. He's always very enthusiastic."

"My thoughts exactly." A knock at the door interrupted us, and I knew it had to be our food.

Big Mac had sent us the same seafood platter he'd prepared for us that first night, but he'd added extra delicacies that he'd picked up on us liking over the course of the week.

Lindsay eyes widened when she saw the sheer amount of food being set down on the table between us. "You were joking about all your other wives coming by later, weren't you? How on earth are we supposed to eat all that?"

"Whatever doesn't get eaten at the resort gets donated. It's actually a pretty cool system they've got going on. Big Mac explained it to me earlier."

"I like the idea of getting more involved with charities, but there never seems be enough time," Lindsay said once the server left. "I think that's something I need to work on going forward."

"I volunteer at a couple of places that involve flying. One is an organization that arranges for kids who dream about going on an airplane to take a flight, and the other is one to teach children about how to go about getting into a career in aviation. It's pretty rewarding."

I could've sworn I saw her jaw loosen, but she caught herself before it dropped. "Is there anything you don't do? I mean, come on."

"Mom taught me from an early age about the importance of giving back. Besides, like you pointed out, I'm good with children. I like 'em."

"Do you want any?" she asked.

"I wouldn't have minded, but it just never happened, and I'm not sure it ever will."

"That wasn't my question."

I chuckled. "Right. Do I want any? Yeah. I do. You?"

She narrowed her eyes in thought and blew out a breath through her nose. "I was going to give you a similar answer to the first one you gave me, but then I realized that wouldn't be fair. My answer is yes."

We ate our dinner while we continued asking each other questions and just talking. After polishing off more of the food than I would've expected over the next few hours, Lindsay pushed her chair back and stood up. "I think we should take a walk. I'm stuffed."

"A walk, it is."

We took another moonlit stroll barefoot on the beach and murmured quietly to one another for no good reason other than not wanting to interrupt the peacefulness of the dark night.

Once we got back to the bungalow, I led her straight to the bedroom. "How do you feel about a bath? There are bubbles, more candles, and more rose petals."

"I can definitely get behind that," she said as I circled her waist with my arms and drew her to me until we were so close we were sharing air. "Thank you for tonight, Jaxon. I'll never forget it."

"It's not over yet." I lowered my mouth to hers, claiming it in a soft, slow kiss that rattled loose all kinds of things in my brain.

Warning bells went off, but I didn't stop kissing her. Nor did I change up the pace or do anything to dispel the intimacy building between us.

We might have an agreement to live in the moment tonight, but it was still our last night together. Our last *time* together. I wanted to experience all I could with her, even if those blaring alarms told me I might just end up regretting it.

CHAPTER 23

LINDSAY

Everything about tonight felt different. We were both completely relaxed, and yet it still felt like an extended goodbye, and the tension of it was thick in the air.

I couldn't count the amount of times I'd nearly gone back on the "living in the moment" rule and asked about our future. In the end, I hadn't because it was obvious he'd spent a fair amount of time on our last day bringing the evening together, and I wanted to enjoy it for what it was.

A very big part inside me was screaming to just bring it up and get it over with, but that was the part of me that always needed to know what was going to happen next. With Jaxon looking at me with molten heat in his eyes as he slowly unzipped the dress he'd gotten me in the steam-filled bathroom, I knew enough of what was going to happen next that I silenced that part of me.

After a kiss that I'd felt all the way to my soul back in the bedroom, he'd taken my hand wordlessly and led me in here. He moved around the room, lighting the candles before dimming the lights as low as they could go. I hadn't been able to tear my gaze off him.

Now the bath was drawn, the petals were scattered on top of the bubbles in the claw-footed bath, and it was time to get in. His fingers brushed against the bare skin of my spine from where he had pulled the zipper down torturously slow, then pushed the broad straps of the dress from my arms with equally deliberate movements.

A pleasured sigh escaped me when the material pooled around my feet on the floor and he dragged his fingers up my sides to unhook my bra behind my back.

When I was left in nothing but my heels, I turned to face him and gave him the same attentive treatment. He looked so damn handsome in his charcoal suit pants and black button-down shirt with his sleeves rolled up to his elbows.

Why is it always so damn hot when men do that? It was like lady-part Kryptonite. I wondered if they all attended a class at some point in their lives where they were taught that.

My thoughts fled when I got to the last button of his shirt and pushed it off his defined shoulders. I'd had a week of seeing him shirtless, but I'd never felt as free to ogle the ink that decorated his skin as I did now.

All of the work was intricately done, the details precise and beautiful. Over his heart was a black and gray compass with clean lines, and I was pretty sure I knew what that one meant. I glanced up at him to confirm as I tapped a nail softly on it.

"Always follow your heart?"

He nodded, his gaze heavy as he watched me take him in like I hadn't had the guts to do before. On his ribs, there was plain lettering reading "I am the Captain of my Fate and the Master of my Soul," while the word on his inner bicep was simple, "ALIVE."

A gorgeous Celtic cross decorated one of his shoulder blades, while his back and the other shoulder were like a patchwork canvas of stars, flames, and a nautical star symmetrically placed across from the cross.

"Do they all have meanings?" I asked, my breath catching as I thought about all the hours he must've spent under the needle to get it all done, and wondering how many more he'd spent deciding on what to get done.

Again, he nodded, but this time, he brought his hands up to mine, pulling them away from his body but holding them tight. "Let's get in before all the bubbles are gone and the water goes cold."

"I can spend hours just looking at all of those," I admitted just before removing my heels and and lifted one leg into the tub while he held my hands to provide balance.

He smirked, turning me around before I sat down. I heard him lowering his zipper and the slight rustle of clothes as he dropped his pants, then felt him climbing in behind me with his chest to my back.

"You've got two choices at this point. We have hours left, but would you rather spend them looking at me or touching me? I can't promise I won't touch you if you choose looking at me, though."

My throat nearly closed up at the thought that we really did have only hours left. I was about to try maneuvering myself around to face him so I could do both at the same time when his hands came around my waist.

He dragged his fingertips over every part of my torso but avoided my breasts like the plague. Chills—the good kind—raced across my skin and left gooseflesh and raised hairs in the wake of his skilled hands.

Letting my head drop back against his shoulder, I planted my hands on his thick thighs on either side of my legs. I ran my fingers along the corded muscle I found there, feeling him growing even harder against the small of my back.

I moaned when one of his hands traveled lower, delivering the gentlest of brushes against my core while the other traced the underside of my breast. In response, my own fingers went higher on his legs until I felt the very top of them.

We built each other up as if we had all the time in the world. As if this really was our honeymoon and this was only the first night. Our soft moans and gasps mingled in the steamy air, the only sounds except for the occasional mumbling of my name or his.

Once the water was cool but my blood was boiling, we got out of the tub. Jaxon held up a thick bath towel and patted me dry everywhere but at the dripping apex of my thighs. I did the same to him, but I'd admit to copping a feel and maybe giving him a stroke or two as I worked around his raging erection.

The thing looked downright angry, but I wasn't afraid of its wrath. Might even welcome it.

When we finally tumbled into bed though, he didn't slide into me straightaway. Instead, we spent more time exploring each other with our hands and mouths until he gritted his teeth and let out an almost pained groan.

"I need you now," he grunted, tapping my shoulder to get me to release the steel rod his cock had turned into from my mouth. "I can't take anymore."

"Thank fuck. I was there ages ago." I climbed on top of him.

He used one hand to cup my cheek as he brought his lips to mine, the other on my hip as he guided me down. I took his length greedily, faster than the rest of the evening had gone, but I didn't hear any complaints from him. We kissed each other with such passion that it was like we were trying to share our souls with one another.

I didn't know about him, but I certainly felt branded when we fell apart holding each other and swallowing each other's moans without stopping our kisses time and time again. Well, I fell apart many more times than he did, but he always seemed to regain his strength faster than I'd have anticipated and was ready for me.

It had to be the early hours of the morning before we fell to the mattress in a tangled heap. Our skin was damp even though the air-conditioning was on, and my limbs were trembling so much that I let him handle our landing.

Jaxon rolled onto his back with his strong arms still holding me. I landed with my head on his chest, listening to the erratic beats of his heart slowly returning to normal.

His fingers burrowed into my hair, twining around the long strands before he brushed through them. It was a strangely soothing gesture, and after the intensity of what had just happened between us, I'd never been more tempted to ruin a moment.

I wanted to talk to him more than anything about whether he thought we might have a future together, but this moment seemed so fragile, so precious, that as tempted as I was to break my silence, I swallowed the words down and pressed a kiss to his bare skin instead.

"I don't want to say goodbye tomorrow," I whispered, settling for telling him the simplest, most important part of the truth.

In the morning before we went our separate ways, I would tell him the rest. I would let him know how I felt, and then I would go the airport. Hopefully, there would be time to get his take on the matter as well.

If there wasn't, at least I'd know I'd said my piece. I wouldn't have to live with the what-ifs, and I'd be able to plan my immediate future accordingly. None of that had to happen tonight.

It'd been the most perfect, if bittersweet, last night I could've imagined. When Jaxon kissed the top of my head in response to my statement instead of bolting, a strong surge of hope bloomed in my chest.

I held on to that hope as I drifted off to sleep in the arms of the only man I ever wanted to hold again.

CHAPTER 24

JAXON

What the fuck was that?

My heart was thundering even after Lindsay fell asleep. It had nothing to do with the physical effects of sex anymore, and everything to do with having had the most feelings I'd ever had while fucking someone. On the other hand, I knew what *fucking* was, and *that* hadn't been it.

We hadn't known each other nearly long enough for it to have been the other thing, so it had to have been something between the two. I'd accepted it, though.

That wasn't what was keeping me awake. The reason why I couldn't sleep was because of the pain I'd heard—even in her whisper —when she'd told me she didn't want to say goodbye to me tomorrow.

I didn't really want to say goodbye to her either. If we had two more weeks together on this island, I doubted I'd even be ready to say goodbye then.

The alternative, however, didn't bring me any joyous thoughts either. Moving carefully so I wouldn't wake her, I went to get my phone and checked the flights back to Houston again.

Yesterday between all the arrangements I had to make, I'd scrolled through the options and decided to choose one later. If I was being completely honest, I hadn't wanted to book my flight because that would've put a definitive end time to my little adventure in the life of a man married to Lindsay.

I'd promised her time and time again that I wouldn't let her get hurt, though. I told her I would protect her and asked her to trust me. Every time I'd asked, she'd put her faith in me and agreed to whatever it was I had asked of her.

Now it was time to earn that trust. That faith she'd put in me. I owed her that much. Even if it was myself I had to protect her against, or the hurt I would inflict on her if she had to say goodbye.

As quietly as I could manage, I rifled through my bag and pulled on a pair of pants, made a cup of coffee, and carried my phone and the hot drink outside. I figured there was even less of a chance of me disturbing her when I wasn't even in the bungalow.

The beach was deserted at this hour, and it just about ripped a hole into the very fabric of my being when I realized this was the last time I would see it like this. With Lindsay pretending to be my wife in the room behind me anyway.

I already knew that no return trips I might make here would be the same. This was the end of the line for Lindsay and me, and this place, as beautiful as it was, would always be empty to me without her.

Walking to the beach, I sat down on the sand and sipped my coffee while I got the unavoidable done with. I needed to do this—for both of our sakes.

The first flight out was in just a few hours. It was on a different airline, but I knew a few people who worked there, and despite the time, I had my ticket sitting in my email inbox ten minutes later.

I finished my coffee slowly, lost in thoughts and memories and doubts about whether I was doing the right thing. Lindsay being upset tomorrow was the last thing I wanted. I wanted her to have a good memory of me, and it was probably best if my big romantic gesture was it.

While I'd been in town to choose the dress, I'd had a photo of us printed off my phone and bought a handcrafted frame for it to go in.

In the picture, our cheeks were pressed together while we sat on the beach one afternoon, and we were both smiling like we'd never been happier.

Slight stubble dusted my chin on the image, my eyes vibrantly alive and my features relaxed. I knew it was probably one of the best pictures I had of myself, but I also knew it was only because she was in it.

God, those eyes. Even though the picture had been taken days ago, I felt like she was peering straight into my soul. Her mouth was tipped into a smile, and I remembered the joke I'd made just before.

Her nose was slightly wrinkled, but I recalled the exact moment it'd scrunched up when I'd whispered the dirty joke into her ear a millisecond before I'd snapped it. In that moment, neither of us had been thinking about this day. The day when we'd have to face the realities of going back home.

We both had jobs to get back to. Lives that wouldn't wait on us forever. But in that moment, that had been *our* life and it'd been pretty fucking good.

Quietly pulling the framed copy I'd had made for her out of my bag once I got back inside, I padded back into the bedroom and put it down on top of her suitcase. With yet another task done before it was time to leave, the weight in my stomach became heavier and heavier.

This is really fucking happening. I'm leaving. It's over.

When I'd approached her and asked her to play along that first day in the lobby, I hadn't thought it would *hurt* when the time came to go home. But it did.

I was no stranger to pain, and I'd endured my fair amount of it, but this was different. It felt like someone was taking a blowtorch to my insides and wouldn't fucking let up when I said mercy.

I gathered my things without making a sound, efficiently wiping every trace that I'd ever been here from existence. The sofa-bed wasn't even rolled out anymore, considering that I'd only used it the first couple of nights.

Once my duffle and my backpack were packed, I gave the bungalow a last onceover and noticed my dirty mug standing there.

With a heavy heart, I walked over to the sink and rinsed it out, removing even that.

When Lindsay woke up, it'd be like I'd never even been here. That was the best I could do for her. If she didn't want to say goodbye, I wouldn't leave anything behind for her to say goodbye to.

Except the picture.

Because I couldn't simply erase the whole week. I just couldn't. I wanted her to have something tangible to remember me and the memories we'd made. That picture was the best representation of those memories I'd been able to find.

Softly letting the door click shut behind me, I walked away from her feeling like I was being flayed from the inside out by that fucking blowtorch. I breathed through the pain, but it was difficult. Much more so than it should've been.

I'd been shot, for God's sake, and that hadn't hurt as much as leaving her did. It wasn't just the pain I had to deal with either. There was also the intense urge to chuck this fucking plan out the window, run back to the bungalow, crawl into bed with her, and then try to come up with a different plan that didn't involve us leaving at all.

But I couldn't.

Because I'd promised, more than once, that I'd always protect her and that I'd never let her get hurt. She hadn't asked for anything in return when she'd put her faith in me to keep those promises, but she had told me she didn't want to say goodbye to me today.

So this was what I had to do.

Big Mac was in the lobby when I passed through about an hour before the sun rose, lugging a crate of fresh bread across the floor. His brows lifted when he saw me. Then he broke out in a wide grin.

"Jaxon! What are you doing up so early?" He noticed my bag and studied my face, dropped the crate on a side table, and came over to grip my upper arms with the most serious expression I'd ever seen in his eyes. "Where are you going?"

"I'm leaving," I said, my voice raspy thanks to the pain I was doing my best to keep bottled up inside. "I have to leave, man."

"Why?" He frowned deeply. "Did something go wrong last night?"

"Nope. Just the opposite." I knew Lindsay had told him the truth about us, and I could see the genuine concern he looked at me with. "She said she didn't want to say goodbye. If I don't leave now, I'll still be there when she wakes up. Girl never sleeps in."

I barked out a laugh, but there was no humor in it. Big Mac obviously knew I was full of shit because he crossed his arms over his wide chest and stared me down.

"Did you speak to her at all last night?"

"Yeah. We talked for hours." I gave my head a light shake, trying to force those memories from my mind for right now. If I thought too much about them, I was abandoning my attempt at giving her what she wanted and going straight back to bed. *With my fucking wife.* "Look, man, it doesn't matter. Nothing has changed since we talked yesterday morning. We've both got to go back to our lives."

"Why can't you go back together?" He narrowed his eyes. "You seemed to do everything well together while you were here."

I ran my hand up and down the back of my head, trying to come up with a good enough answer. "It's complicated. We're both really busy back home and she's been through a ton recently. I'm not adding to that."

"You don't look so hot yourself," he commented.

I shrugged. "I'll live. It's not about me anyway. It's about doing what's right for her. All I need is to figure out how the fuck I'm going to forget about her."

"Don't. It's as easy as that." His gaze bored into mine. "You're sure you're doing the right thing by leaving, Jaxon? You don't want to give talking to her one more go?"

"I can't." I closed my eyes, breathing in deeply. "I've made my promises to her, big man. I need to keep 'em now. It's better that I'm just a memory for her at the moment anyway, and I really don't want to hurt her."

"You're not making a lot of sense." He slapped me on the shoulder. "You sure I can't cook you up a plate of bacon and we can hash it out over breakfast and coffee?"

"No, I have to go."

He regarded me with what seemed like pain in his own eyes before he wiped his face blank. Sticking his meaty paw into his pocket, he came back with a plain white rectangle of cardboard paper with a number scrawled on it in ink.

"Call me if you ever need me. I'm always available on that number."

"Thanks for everything, man."

He enveloped me in a bear hug, thudding me hard on the back before letting me go. "You're welcome, brother." He pointed at my aching chest after he took a step back. "Come back here sometime, you hear?"

I forced a grin, not wanting to tell him that while leaving was one of the most difficult things I'd ever done, at this very moment, I couldn't imagine ever stepping foot inside this lobby again. "Yeah. Maybe. We'll have to see."

CHAPTER 25

LINDSAY

When I woke up, I knew in my heart of hearts that Jaxon was gone before I'd even opened my eyes. I felt around on his side of the bed, but the sheets were ice cold.

Not only that, but his presence was gone too. I didn't know how to explain it other than I'd always felt this awareness of him in this room, and I couldn't feel it anymore.

My suspicions were confirmed when I sat up slowly and took a good look around. It took me no time at all to notice what wasn't there anymore.

I could see the bathroom from this side of the bed, and the basin that'd had his toiletries next to it was empty. Last night when I'd fallen asleep, clothes had been strewn all over the floor in there, but it was all cleaned up now.

My dress hung neatly from a hanger hooked over the bathroom door. Even the rose petals were gone. How he'd managed that without waking me, I didn't know.

Then again, he'd worn me out pretty thoroughly last night. My heart started pounding when the thought hit. *Was he planning this all the time? Did he give me all that pleasure just so that he wouldn't have to deal with my pain in the morning?*

Jumping out of bed with a pathetic little string of hope still tied to my heart, I searched the entire bungalow but it was like he'd never even been there at all. There was nothing left of him. It was like I'd imagined him and he'd never been real.

If not for the aches in my body after our nocturnal activities, I really would've started questioning my sanity.

How could he do this to me? A sob rose in my chest. I couldn't believe he would just leave. He knew what'd happened to me just weeks ago. *What a way to end this trip, by getting left again.*

Had I been fooling myself all week? Last night, I could've sworn I saw real feelings when he looked at me, felt them in the sweet way he'd made love to me, and now this? I really couldn't believe it.

My hands started shaking and tears welled up in my eyes, their onslaught never ceasing once they started spilling out. Hurt, pain, and rage like I should've felt when Will walked out on me raced through me now—like a lightning strike that'd somehow been delayed.

Although dealing with being abandoned once was bad enough. Having to deal with it twice in as many weeks? That was unthinkable. Unimaginable.

Loathsome thoughts churned in my brain, and I couldn't get them to stop while I packed. *Am I really just that unbearable? Am I unlovable? Would I ever find anyone who would really stand by me and have my back?*

Sobs kept wracking through me. I couldn't stop crying. This was the kind of pain people had been expecting me to feel after my wedding had fallen apart. Yet I hadn't felt a damn thing.

But throw me into paradise and toss a hot guy into my room, and I get my heart broken. *Pathetic. I'm utterly pathetic.*

I'd never felt quite so downtrodden, quite so defeated, or quite so used. *Where do I even go from here?*

None of these were thoughts I'd ever had about myself, yet I felt every stinging word of the truth now. *Gah. Had I really just been such an easy, vulnerable fucking target for Jaxon? Why yes, darling. You even threw yourself at him.*

After a few minutes, I slammed my back into the door and sank down until I was sitting on the floor, hugging myself as I tried to weather the storm of emotion I'd known was coming but had been counting on Jaxon being here to see through with me.

Every nickname he'd called me, every smile and heated look.

Lies.

All of it had been nothing but lies. It couldn't have been anything else. If he cared about me at all, he wouldn't have left me without so much as a goodbye.

My whispered words in the early hours of this morning came back to me. *I don't want to say goodbye to you tomorrow morning.*

Humiliation laced with mortification spread through my veins. It was too early for it to have gone down any other way. He'd already known when I said that, when he pressed that kiss that'd made me so foolishly hopeful to my head, that he wouldn't be here when I woke up.

That he wasn't planning on saying goodbye.

I fell apart on that bedroom floor, finally crying for everything I'd lost in the space of less than two short weeks and everything that had been taken from me. A million miles away from home and without a soul knowing what was happening, I let myself mourn for my future with Will that'd never materialized, but also let myself mourn the end of the best relationship I'd ever had. Even if it'd only been a week long.

The worst thing of all was I was pretty confident Jaxon had ruined me. At least for a while, I wouldn't even be able to look at any other man.

My heart was shattered.

Broken, bruised, and bleeding, and he'd given it a final stomp before tossing it right back at me. And I hadn't even been awake to catch the useless damn thing.

Not only that, but he'd also taken that part of me that being with him had unearthed, because there was no way I'd be able to trust that woman's judgment again.

And so I cried for me, for Jaxon, and for Will. For unrealized dreams and unrealistic plans. For the relationships I'd had and the relationships I'd hoped they would turn into. For the anguish that felt like it'd crawled into my heart for good and for the humiliation that would never leave me.

I reminded myself over and over again that I was a strong, independent woman and that I didn't need a man. A voice in my head whispered that this one breakdown was okay. That no one could be expected to go through the emotional wringer the way I had and begrudge themselves that one ugly cry session.

When I got up from here, I would be that queen again that I'd told Jaxon I was. But for now, I was going to cry because I already missed his hand in mine and the weight of his arm over my shoulder. I already missed being able to count on him—always there, always ready, always right beside me.

I already missed that stupid smirk and the way he made me feel when he looked at me. I was going to cry because the first thing in my life that'd really felt real had been fake all along. I was going to cry because I knew, and I wasn't just being dramatic, that there would never be another Jaxon for me again.

The kind of chemistry I'd had with him had been once in a lifetime, and so had the safety and comfort offered by my marriage to Will.

And it was all gone.

Just gone.

As intangible and irreplaceable as a single puff of smoke in the wind.

Both times without even having had the opportunity to say goodbye.

I must've done something really terrible in a previous life or something to have deserved this.

Just yesterday, I'd believed it when Big Mac had said the universe had pushed us together. I'd believed that maybe it really had been fate that wanted us to be together, and that maybe that meant it would all work out.

What a crock of shit. I knew better than that. *Honestly.*

I let myself fall to pieces before reminding myself that I couldn't sit here like this for days. I had a plane to catch, and it was probably about time for me to start getting ready to catch it. Little by little, I focused on putting the salvageable parts of myself back together and eventually found the strength to get up off the damn floor.

I showered but felt like every one of the warm drops was slicing straight through my being. Not only was every one of those aches in my body now nothing of a painful reminder of what I'd lost and would never have again, but I could still feel him deep inside me with every move I made. Even though he'd known—he had to have already fucking known—that he'd be gone without the courtesy of even a goodbye by the time I felt it.

God. He must be having such a good fucking laugh at my expense right now. I fell for everything he'd laid out for me. Hook. Line. And fucking sinker.

Feeling sick to my stomach after I got out of the shower, I was hunched over while I packed my things in here. If I could avoid it, I didn't want to revisit any part of this bungalow once I was done in it for the last time.

The shower was the last time I wanted to see this fucking bathroom, where just last night he'd confirmed that he had the symbol for following his heart tattooed right over it.

Yeah. Right. What fucking heart?

Where had he followed it to anyway? The next hotel, an attendant on one of his flights, a fucking member of the staff of this very resort? With looks and a personality like his, he could get any woman he wanted and he knew it. *Probably just another reason why he decided to dump poor Lindsay without a goddamn word when he was done with me.*

Was I that worthless I didn't even deserve a conversation from either of these men? I didn't want to believe it, but the evidence was seriously stacking up against the accuracy of my beliefs.

As I moved back into the bedroom and dropped my vanity bag on the bed, I swiped my clothes from the shelves with complete disregard for the state they would be packed in, then stopped dead in my tracks when I saw something lying on top of my suitcase.

It was a wooden, carved-out frame that looked like something one could buy in the market here. In it was a photograph of the two of us looking so damn happy I could puke now when I looked at it.

Why? Why would you do this to me? I mentally yelled at him, feeling like a thousand red-hot needles stabbed into my heart as I stared. *You sadistic fucking son of a bitch!*

Both of us looked so genuinely happy in that picture that I had to just blink at it for a minute. The man was a damn good actor. I had to give him that. To be able to fake *that* look *that* well, he deserved a fucking award.

I, of course, wouldn't be giving him jack shit ever again. On the other hand, he didn't really deserve anything from me either.

I had half a mind to smash the frame and text him a picture of me hurling the thing into the ocean, but I knew I had to hang onto this. It would serve as an excellent reminder of why I didn't throw the goddamn planner out the window. It would also help keep me grounded if another good-looking asshole with tanned skin and abs for days came knocking at my door.

People said not to hate the player and to hate the game, but right in this moment? I hated the fucking player with a burning rage so all consuming that I wanted to follow through on Ember's threat of ripping his precious cock off with my bare hands.

But I turned all that inward once I'd searched the room to make sure none of my possessions had stayed behind. I refused to be labeled as that mess of a bride who got dumped on her honeymoon and her husband hadn't even said goodbye.

Not that I planned on making any stops, but I wanted to leave here at least feeling like my dignity was intact. No one would ever have to know the horrible thoughts that had gone through my mind back in that bedroom, and no one would ever witness a scene like that from me again.

Well, except for the potted plants in my house, because I was ninety-nine percent sure I wasn't even *nearly* cried out over all this yet.

Unfortunately, I ran into Big Mac on my way out.

The kind-hearted, kind-eyed man who'd had such a soft spot for me and the asshole was honestly the last person I wanted to see. But he seemed to be waiting for me, hanging around near the elevators going up in the lobby.

He pushed away from the wall when he saw me, coming over to envelop me in a hug that told me that once again, he knew more than I thought he did. "Jaxon left a few hours ago. He was afraid of saying goodbye. I'm sorry, honey. I tried to stop him, but he seemed to think it was for the best."

I stifled a sob at his tenderly murmured words. "It *was* for the best."

"It's not. I spoke to Jaxon, saw him, and looked into his eyes, and now I'm doing the same with you. He was just as upset as you are over having to leave you."

That can't be true. He's just a fucking good actor. "I have to go, Big Mac. Thank you so much for everything."

The big guy insisted on walking me out, carrying my suitcase, and even reminded me to pick up my packages from shopping the day before. Then he helped me fit my purchases in before personally calling a private hotel transfer to the airport for me.

Once again, the ride between the hotel and the airport passed in a complete blur, and before I knew it, I'd somehow managed to get my suitcase checked in, go through customs, and I was about to board.

My phone rang with an incoming call from Ember, and I moved off to the side of the crowd of passengers to take it. I relayed the highlights of my morning to her almost robotically, shutting down any emotion for fear that even a single crack would lead to another—much more public—breakdown.

"If you think about it," she said once I'd finished talking. "It really was the perfect way to end it. No feelings of 'there should have been more' or empty promises to stay in touch. It was what it was, and now it's over."

"Yeah. Sure. We're boarding soon. I'll see you later." I hung up on her without another word, staring at the boarding pass in my hand and wondering why the hell I was going back.

What do I even have left there?

CHAPTER 26

JAXON

Being back at the hangar with my tools in hand and grease covering my clothes, it felt like my time in Fiji had been nothing but a dream. Almost like I'd spaced out during my last conversation with Kavan and was coming to with all these made up memories of things that hadn't really happened.

The heaviness in my chest and a deeper tan on my forearms as I worked were the only evidence that it had really happened and that I wasn't likely to forget about it anytime soon. Big Mac's advice not to forget about it at all turned in my head, but it was better if I did. The sooner I let it all go, the sooner I'd start feeling like myself again.

Kavan walked in about an hour later, his face breaking out into a grin and his arms widening to his sides when he saw me. "Welcome home, brother. When did you get in?"

"Yesterday." I tightened the bolt I was busy with, feeling his gaze heavy on my back. "I don't want to talk about it. How're Shira and the baby?"

"Doing well. We're counting down the days until the little princess arrives." He walked around me and leaned against the engine I was working on, concern furrowing his brow as he folded his arms loosely over his chest. "What exactly don't you want to talk about? Fiji, or your fake marriage while you were there?"

"Both." They were so rolled up in each other that there was no telling how to speak about one without the other. "All that I'm willing to say is that I wished it had ended differently."

"How did it end?"

I scowled at the metal under my hands, even though it was completely innocent in all this. "With me leaving in the pre-dawn hours without saying goodbye."

Kavan made a strangled noise at the back of his throat, his brows shooting up. "Seriously? You of all people sneaked away under the cover of darkness? What the fuck?"

"I didn't sneak away." I scoffed, giving him a narrow-eyed glare. "She said she didn't want to say goodbye to me in the morning, so I didn't make her say goodbye. I caught the first flight out and here I am."

He covered his face with his hands, groaning and shaking his head. "Dude, I don't know this woman, but I doubt she meant that as literally as you took it."

"What?" I snapped. None of this was Kavan's fault either, but I was in a shitty mood, and he was pushing for information I'd already told him I didn't want to give.

"If she said she didn't want to say goodbye to you, it meant she didn't want your time together to end. Not that she literally didn't want to do the goodbye part."

"You know what? You're right." I turned my glare on the engine again. "You don't know her."

My friend, who was obviously in the mood to get a fist to his jaw because he kept pushing, let out an exasperated sigh. "Maybe not, but I know women and I know relationships. I've only been with Shira for over a decade. What was your longest relationship again?"

"You and Shira were meant to fucking be. You never went through anything like this."

Blue eyes turning to ice, his jaw tightened and his fingers curled into a fist on the engine. "Your memory seems to be failing you in your old age.

171

Maybe we didn't meet in a tropical fucking paradise and our biggest obstacle wasn't how to tell each other that we wanted to keep seeing each other. You know what our obstacles were? Continuous deployments for the first few years we were together, my injury, her not knowing whether I was alive, my rehab, depression when I got discharged, trying to build a new life for ourselves, fertility issues and treatments. The list goes on and fucking on, but why don't you tell me again that I don't know what I'm talking about because we never went through anything like that?"

My anger and frustration deflated like he'd popped the ever-growing balloon with a pin. I shoved my hands into my hair and looked up at him properly, letting out a sigh as I tilted my head toward the ceiling.

"Fuck. I'm sorry. Sometimes I forget all that shit, but when you summarize it all like that, you two really have been through a lot."

He nodded, clenching and unclenching his fingers and rolling his neck. Then he let out a deep breath of his own. "Let's go get some coffee and you can actually talk to me without pretending like you're the only person in the world to ever have had problems with a woman."

"Still don't want to talk about it." But I was already placing my tools back in their container and following him to the break room.

He turned his head to the side to look at me over his shoulder, making sure I could see his exaggerated eye roll. "Do you know how many times I've said those exact same words to you? You kept coming at me anyway, and it helped. I'm returning the favor."

"Would you like to braid my hair while we're at it?" I smirked, knowing I was being an asshole but really wishing he'd leave me the fuck alone about this.

He flipped me off and sent me a warning look. "Cut that shit right the fuck out. I'm about to have a little girl. Those condescending types of comments about what they do aren't going to fly with me anymore."

"You really think it's condescending?" I scratched my chin, thinking about his statement as a distraction from my own bullshit.

"Of course, it's fucking condescending," he growled and slammed the empty pot into the coffeemaker. "Now pull your head out of your ass and start talking."

"I think I'd rather have you braiding my hair." I got out our mugs, as was the routine, but walked back and dropped into one of the threadbare couches. "This might come as a surprise to you, but that tone doesn't exactly invite candor."

"Quit stalling." He turned with his back toward the counter housing the coffeemaker and gripped the edge of it as he stared me down. "You're not getting out of this, so you might as well get it over with."

"Such an asshole," I muttered under my breath.

"Takes one to know one." He pretended to blow me a kiss, but his eyes were firm and impatient on mine. "Can you *please* quit stalling now? I have work to do and I'd really like to get back to my wife at some point this week."

"I don't even know where to start," I admitted. "My sides just feel so empty."

"Your sides?" He looked thoroughly confused. "Pro tip, don't start there. That makes no fucking sense."

"It makes sense to me." Starting from the beginning, even if I knew he'd already heard some parts of it, I told him everything that had happened between Lindsay and me, ending with how I'd gotten so used to having her curled up into one of my sides that it now felt weird having only my arms next to my body.

Understanding washed over his features when I explained that part. "Okay, I get it now. You said earlier that you wished it had ended differently, so why didn't it? You've never been one to just let the chips fall where they may."

"Honestly? It would've killed me to know she was in the same city but that she wasn't mine anymore. Even if she never really was."

"What would you have done if she could've been yours? If she is in Houston, why not go after her?"

"She's not the kind of girl who's going to jump into the next relationship when she's still reeling from the last. She deserves time and space to work through it."

"No offense man, but that's not your call to make."

"Isn't it?" I tipped my head to the side. "I promised her I'd protect her. Her relationship and her wedding fell apart a little over a week ago. Jumping into something with her that she isn't ready for, or forcing her to make a decision about it right now, isn't fair."

"Making the decision for her isn't fair either," he countered. "Yet you had no problem doing that."

"I didn't make the decision for her. She didn't want to say goodbye, so I fixed things so she wouldn't have to. Done. End of our story. Now she can move on with her life without any complications while she figures out how to do that."

His reply was interrupted by my phone ringing. The name on my screen when I fished it out of my pocket belonged to my supervisor at the airline. "Shitty fucking timing, but I have to take this."

The timing could've been way shittier, to be fair, but that didn't mean I wanted to speak to him right now. I answered anyway. It was my job, after all.

"Where have you been?" he asked after exchanging terse pleasantries. "I checked with the HR department, but there was no vacation time authorized for you this week."

"Funny. I did put in for it." I'd sent an email to the general account for the department while waiting for my flight. "I had a ton of time off saved up. I'm sure they'll just take it off."

"I'm afraid it doesn't work like that." His tone was filled with regret, and my gut clenched. "I have to send your file up for termination, Jaxon. You can't just take off without any notice. It's against our policies and procedures."

"But—"

My protest fell on deaf ears. "It's out of my hands. There are disciplinary procedures that must decide your fate now."

He ended our call abruptly shortly after, not budging an inch despite anything I said. Kavan had a worried crease between his brows and he lifted them at me when I tossed my phone down on the rickety coffee table.

"Trouble at work?"

I nodded, staring at my friend in complete disbelief. I really hadn't thought it would be an issue. I had the time saved up and I'd sent them an email. Fine, I hadn't waited for a reply and I hadn't really asked so much as tell, but it was only a few days longer than I would've been home anyway, so it wasn't like I'd missed any scheduled flights or they had to replace me at short notice.

"I'm going to have to call the HR department myself. This is fucked up. They're trying to fire me for going to Fiji."

CHAPTER 27

LINDSAY

Ember had dropped me off after I got in late in the night. As soon as she'd greeted me at the airport, she'd known I was in trouble.

It had taken some arguing, but at least I'd eventually convinced her that I just needed to get some sleep. The compromise we'd reached was that today would be a girls' day and that I wasn't allowed to try to get out of it at all.

I'd given in because I really had been weighed down with bone-deep exhaustion and was desperate to tumble into my own bed. It'd seemed like the fastest and easiest way to get her to stop looking at me like she was afraid she needed to take me for mental observation instead of my house.

Now that it was morning and I'd had a shower, I regretted agreeing to her terms. Not that I hadn't missed her or didn't want to spend time with her. I wanted both of those things desperately. I just didn't want to hear her take on how Jaxon leaving the way he had was for the best.

I felt like I'd gone several rounds with an Amazonian warrior princess as it was. I didn't have it in me to have to be realistic about it right now.

Jaxon didn't have the power to break me, but he'd definitely left me feeling tender. Having to endure more emotional blows when I was in rough shape already wasn't something I was looking forward to.

I'd texted her earlier to be gentle with me, which was a request I hadn't made of anyone before and she knew it. My best friend wasn't one to pull her punches, though. My fragile state and her idea of gentle might not be well matched.

Which was why I held an extra-strength cup of coffee in my hands, facing the window in my living room and bracing myself for making it through another world of pain today when she unlocked my front door.

"I brought vanilla, peanut brittle, strawberry swirl, and blueberry," she said, calling out all my favorite ice-cream flavors, and slammed the door behind her. "Where are you? What was with that text this morning? It didn't sound like you at all."

She came to an abrupt halt when she spotted me, dropping her shopping bags at her sides, and gave me a long onceover before she came rushing at me. She just about tackled me into her hug, stroking my hair and holding me tight when my tears rose again purely from being in her arms.

Tepid brown liquid sloshed over the side of the mug between us, but neither of us seemed to care.

What is it about seeing moms or best friends that just makes it feel okay to cry?

Ember led me over to the couch, took the coffee from me, and set it down before patting her shoulder. "Okay, girl. Lay it on me. What in the hell happened to you? You look like shit."

"Thanks." I managed a small smile. "You mean you don't like my new look?"

"I don't know." The corners of her lips pressed in as she swept her gaze across my face before I laid my head down on her offered shoulder. "Pale skin, glazed-over, puffy eyes, and a pinched expression like you're a walking ball of anguish might not be the best look for anyone. It's definitely not a good look on you."

"I didn't think so either." I exhaled heavily, screwing my eyes shut to keep the tears at bay. "What have I done to my life, Em? I feel like I've fucked it all up and I have no idea how to get back to it."

She twined her fingers into my hair, and the shaking of her head moved my hair. "You haven't fucked anything up. Will left you, which obviously changes your life a little bit from what it was before, but you don't want to get back to that anyway."

"No, I don't, but I just don't feel like I have control over anything right now." My gaze zeroed in on her dropped packages. "Hang on. We're going to need a solid breakfast for this conversation."

Chuckling lightly as she got up, she retrieved the ice cream, stashed the tubs we weren't going to have right now in my freezer, and took the spoon I held out to her. "It's the breakfast of champions, but only if we have some fresh coffee with it."

We spent a few minutes getting ourselves organized before heading back to the couch and settling in for the heavy part of the day. Hopefully once it was done, we'd get to watch horror movies and stuff our faces with pizza.

"I can see I've been going about this all wrong," Ember said once we were seated. "This Jaxon didn't just feel like a holiday fling to you, did he?"

"Nope." I ground my teeth at the mention of his name out loud. "I know it sounds really stupid, and I know thousands of people make out with other tourists in tropical destinations all the time, but it just didn't feel like that to me."

"That's why you asked me to be gentle?" she said quietly. "You don't want to hear me talking about it like I have been."

I made a noncommittal sound. "I know what you've been saying is true. Don't get me wrong. It just hurts to hear it."

"I'm sorry." She gave me another quick hug. "I really didn't understand until I saw you last night."

"It's not your fault." I squeezed her back. "I'm the one who ran headfirst into a brick wall of muscles, tattoos, and guaranteed heartbreak and still went for it."

"If it makes any difference at all, I'm proud of you for going for it. I know it might not feel like it right now, but you're going to look back at this experience one day and be happy about it. You've learned from this, and that's why you're going to look back at it fondly."

I laughed as we separated, but the sound was humorless and sad. "It's going to take some time for me to get there."

"It will, but you'll get there eventually."

"What if I don't want to?" I asked, revealing the actual crux of my innermost problem. "Jaxon made me feel things I've never felt before. Tingles, butterflies, that crazy need for someone that makes you feel like you're going to explode if they don't just take you right now. What if I don't want to look back at it fondly because I don't want to let it go at all?"

"If you want tingles and butterflies, then that's what you'll have. Just maybe not with him."

"That's the problem, though. I've only ever felt it with him. I know you don't believe in love at first sight, and frankly, neither do I. But the chemistry between us was insane. It felt like a once-in-a-lifetime, forged-by-the-universe kind of connection."

"Forged by the universe?" she repeatedly slowly. "Girl, who have you been speaking to? Because none of that sounds like you."

I told her about Big Mac and his observations about our relationship. "I couldn't disagree with him. Everything he said felt spot on."

Her gaze held mine, and once she'd worked through the confusion of hearing me spouting off about the universe, she smiled. "Then you're lucky to have had it at all."

I nearly fell off the couch. "Now who's the one sounding like she's been body snatched?"

"No, it's not like that. It just kind of proves my point that your trip, and even the way it ended, is nothing to be sad about." Her hand shot out to grip my shoulder. "You got to parasail, Linds. You swam with sharks and had sex with an amazing guy. You got to experience the kind of connection other people can only dream about. That's one hell of a fucking trip. You can't possibly be sad about that."

"Maybe not, but I can still miss the guy who made it possible." My voice was too small for my liking, and Ember sniffed in response.

"Jaxon didn't make it possible. He was simply along for the ride.

You, my friend, are the one who made it possible. You're the one who went to Fiji instead of hiding away at home, you're the one who grabbed all those opportunities with both hands, and you're the one who put on your damn lingerie and walked out of that room."

While she spoke, my spine straightened out and some of those doubts I'd been having about myself melted away. "You're right."

"Of course, I am." She broke out into a wide grin. "It's okay to miss him, Linds. As much as I really believe it made it easier for you that he left without a long drawn-out goodbye and promises being made that neither of you would know if you could keep, it's also normal to feel like there's some unfinished business there."

"So how do I get over him?" It didn't escape my notice that Will was no longer coming up in the conversation at all.

While I was still not happy about the fact that he walked out without even telling me he was calling off the wedding, I couldn't help but be grateful that he *had* called it off. If there was one thing this week had shown me, it was that marrying him would've been an even bigger mistake than trusting Jaxon had been.

In fact, if I ever saw my ex again, I might even buy him a beer to thank him. Then we'd also have to have a conversation about the polite, decent way to go about letting someone know you were leaving them.

Ember, meanwhile, was still pondering my earlier question. "You're going back to work tomorrow, right? Maybe that will be a good distraction while you figure out how to get over him. It's not like I can suggest getting under someone else to get over him, seeing as how he was the someone else you got under."

Her eyes shone with humor over her joke, and I couldn't hold back a tiny burst of laughter even as I smacked her arm. "That wasn't what I was doing and you know it. Be that as it may, I do have to go back to work and I'll probably have to spend the next week going over the shitload of messages I missed. So yeah, it will definitely be a good distraction."

Hopefully.

"You can't even pretend to complain about having to go back

through so many messages. I know how much you love your job. There's no point trying to hide it from me."

"I'm not trying to. I love that I have to go back. I really need it. I just..." I didn't even know anymore.

Ember, as it turned out, did know. "You just need some time to process everything that's happened and to try to put your vacation romance behind you."

"That's exactly it." I needed to get to a point where I didn't automatically reach for his hand when a thought hit me, and when I didn't keep expecting to feel him slinging his arm around my shoulders or tugging me against his warm chest from behind. "I need to figure out how to close my eyes without seeing his."

"How about we replace some of those images of him with people being murdered on screen? Would that make you feel better?"

"Yes." Watching some violent movies might ease the urge I had to look him up only so I could punch him right in his handsome face. It would probably end up hurting me more than it did him, but I'd taken some self-defense classes. I was eighty-percent sure I wouldn't break my thumb if I tried it.

Ember hopped off the couch to grab the remote and more ice cream, and we spent the rest of the day talking and watching movies. Ultimately, I still wished things had ended differently with Jaxon.

If I'd just had the closure of having spoken to him before we left, like I'd been planning on doing, I felt like there wouldn't be this huge, gaping wound in my chest. Even if he'd shot me down when I suggested we try a real relationship, at least I would've known where we'd been standing all along.

Instead, I just felt hurt and confused.

Jaxon was exactly what I'd needed out of that trip, but he'd still left me all cut up inside. It was less than ideal, and if I ever saw him again, he was definitely *not* also getting a thank-you beer from me.

CHAPTER 28

JAXON

"When is the person in charge of that part of the department getting back then?" I barked into the phone while I parked in front of my mother's house. "This is the third time I'm being told they're not available."

The annoying voice at the other end of the line belonged to an assistant at the airline, and she definitely didn't grasp the meaning of the core part of her job description. She wasn't *assisting*. She was fucking pissing me off.

"Yes, sir. I understand that. She's been out of the office, but I'll be sure to pass your messages along."

Fat chance of that happening. It seemed like my messages from before I'd even gone to Fiji hadn't even been passed along yet. "Yeah, you do that."

I ended the call with a frustrated grunt. Obviously, our HR department was a fucking mess. What made it worse was that any time I thought about human resources, I thought about Lindsay. I'd never even found out which company she worked for, but wherever it was, any department she was a senior member of would be much better run than ours was.

My mother walked out of her house smiling until she caught sight of my expression when I got out of the car. She rushed over to me, cupping my face in her hands and fixing me with her worried stare.

"What happened? No one should come back from a week on an island looking like that. Are you okay?"

"I wish people would stop asking me that," I snapped before remembering who I was talking to. Smiling sheepishly, I pulled her into my arms and hugged her. "Sorry. I'm just really annoyed."

"I'd say." She ushered me into her kitchen. "Sit down. Tell me about your trip, and then tell me what's got you so riled up."

Just being in her small but familiar space calmed me down some. The magnets I'd brought back from all the places I'd been were stuck to her fridge, and the scent of roast chicken always seemed to be present.

I sat down on the closest stool, watching as she rummaged around for two tumblers. She came back to me carrying the glasses and a bottle of whiskey.

Fuck, I love my mother.

After I filled our drinks to the brim, I pushed one over to her and picked up my own. We clinked them together, each taking a long drink while she waited patiently for me to spit it out.

"Thanks for this," I said finally. "I was really hoping you weren't going to offer me tea."

She made a disgruntled sound. "Who do you think I am? You're not wearing a face that says you're in the mood for tea."

"Well spotted." My mother read me better than anyone else. She definitely wasn't the typical mom either. She never had been. "We might need another bottle. That one looks pretty empty."

She pursed her lips. "Do I really have to ask you again who you think I am? There's another bottle in the cabinet. Now quit stalling and tell me what's going on."

"You sound just like Kavan did. He even used those exact same words."

Her eyes shone with satisfaction. "I knew I liked that boy. It's good to know I've rubbed off on him."

"You sure did." Between my mom and Shira, the guy was becoming way too... something. I didn't like it. "I've already had to sit down and tell him everything."

"Tell it again," she said firmly. "Everything this time. I know you well enough to know that you'd have left out some details when you spoke to him."

I shrugged. "He wouldn't braid my hair. I might've left out some stuff as his punishment."

She smacked my arm. Hard. "I'm assuming from that statement that what you left out pertained to some of your feelings. Here's a heads-up, honey. Women don't have to braid each other's hair to share those. We drink wine and bitch about you guys because you're too scared to admit you even have any feelings. We feel what we feel, we tell it like it is, and then we can move forward without being burdened. We have the ovaries to admit what we're feeling without turning into broody messes."

She hardly took a breath and yet she didn't seem at all desperate for air.

"Are you calling me a broody mess?" I downed half my glass, feeling the alcohol burn in the best possible way down my throat.

She batted her lashes innocently. "Am I calling my own son a broody mess? Why yes, I am." Her face turned serious as she took another swig. "Do I need to be worried about you? I've never seen you looking quite like this before."

"I met someone," I admitted. "I've never looked like this before because I've never felt like this before. Are you happy with the size of my ovaries yet? Or do you need more feelings?"

"Please." She waved her hand. "Saying that you've never felt something before is only the tip of the iceberg. I still have no idea how you're feeling. Although I'm willing to venture a few guesses."

Mom listened while I told her about my trip, chiming in with questions about how things had made me feel every time I tried to gloss over it. When it happened again right when I got to the part about me leaving, I narrowed my eyes in a mock glare. "Are you going to charge me for this session?"

"Of course. Dinner is on you tonight." She gave me a delighted grin. "There's a magnificent new burger joint that delivers. I'll have the Chicken Supreme."

"Dinner was going to be on me anyway."

She shrugged. "In that case, you're paying for this session by giving me the peace of mind that my son has the balls to face what he's feeling."

"Mothers should *not* be allowed to say the word *balls*," I grumbled.

Arching her eyebrows as an amused smile swept across her face, she tucked her chin closer to her chest. "Why not? You're forgetting the fact that mothers knew what balls were before you kids were even conceived, and also that we were the ones to wipe them for you when you were still in diapers. All things considered, I'm quite confident I know more about balls than you do."

I choked on my own laughter. "Have I told you lately how much I love you?"

"Yep. You texted me yesterday. Did you tell this girl how much you love *her*? I think that's the more pertinent question here."

"What? I don't love her. I've known her for a week."

She gave me a headshake and looked at me like I was stupid. "You say that like it means something. Do you want to know what I think?"

"Sure." I was curious to get her take on it. "Bring it on."

"Something is different when you talk about her. I suspect you already know that, considering that you've already admitted that you've never felt like this before."

I nodded. "She's something special all right. It's really too bad she deserves someone better than me. Hell, I might not even have a job right now."

"You're such a man." She pinned me with knowing eyes. "You should've given her the goodbye she deserved, even if it hurt. You also should have told her that she was someone special to you. In which case, you might not even have had to say goodbye."

"I was trying to do right by her."

"Maybe that's what you've been telling yourself, but it's a lie. Since when do you lie to your mother, and since when do you have such self-esteem issues that you think she deserves better than you? You, my darling, are the absolute best. If this woman is as smart as you think she is, she already knows that."

"Her fiancé left her at the altar less than two weeks ago. Let that sink in, Mom. The guy she thought she was going to spend the rest of her life with left her—on their wedding day—less than two weeks ago. She deserves better than being hounded by some guy she met when she was supposed to be on her honeymoon that now can't leave her alone."

"Does she?" She cocked her head in a way that made me think Kavan had rubbed off on her just as much as she had on him. "Let's put that a little differently, shall we? Does she deserve a guy who knows her worth and is so crazy about her after only a few days with her that he's willing to stand by her side no matter what? How about a man who recognizes and respects that she's been through a tough time and doesn't abandon her just because of it?"

"Fuck." I hadn't thought about it like that. "I could've been that guy."

"Yes, you could have." Mom drained her glass and set it down with a thud on the counter. "What are you going to do about it?"

"It's too late now, Mom. It's already over. I've already left."

The long look she gave me told me she disagreed. "One day, you'll learn, darling, that while you still have breath in your lungs and fight in your heart, it's never too late. Now, refill my drink and let's deal with this one step at a time."

CHAPTER 29

LINDSAY

I'd always liked our office building. It was near the airport, so there were constantly planes coming over, but I'd gotten so used to it that I hardly heard the noise anymore.

Since my employer was an airline and the employees I wrangled worked for it too, it made sense for us to be within spitting distance from the actual airport. Our offices were light and airy, and we looked out over a collection of runways with wide expanses of green grass between them.

My first day back at the office had been chaotic, and my second day wasn't shaping up to be much better. It wasn't even nine yet, but I was already putting out fires every time I turned around.

On the upside, it didn't leave me much time to think about Jaxon. While I usually prided myself on having everything in hand and neatly organized, the chaos I walked in on offered a welcome reprieve.

Anna, my newish assistant, stood in front of my desk with a tablet in one hand and a takeout coffee for me in the other. "Yesterday was all about sorting out the most urgent things that happened while you were gone. Today we'll have to work on returning a ton of calls and messages."

"Let's do it." I waved her into the wingback chair across from me and held out my hand. "Thanks for the coffee—and for holding the fort down while I was gone."

"Just don't go away again anytime soon." She smiled as she slid the coffee across the desk. "I swear it was like people could smell you were gone. The entire workforce seemed to have a collective meltdown."

My nose wrinkled. "Was it really that bad?"

"Yep." She turned the screen of her tablet to me so I could see how many unread emails there were in her complaints folder as she scrolled. "A bunch of the ground staff got drunk on the premises again, the luggage handlers might be planning a strike for the end of the month, and there have been a string of infractions by individual employees."

I rolled my head back and said a quick prayer for patience before jumping in. Picking up my coffee, I opened the corresponding folder in my emails that she had open on her tablet. "Is there anything that needs our attention more desperately than any other matters? Or can we work through it systematically from oldest to newest?"

"Systematically should be fine." She glanced down when her device started vibrating in her hands, an annoyed scowl flickering across her features. "Actually, maybe we should start with that one first. He's been calling all day and he's put in a few calls over the last couple of weeks. He's getting terminated."

A loud huff came out of her when the vibrating started up again seconds after it ended. "I don't think he actually understands English. I've told him so many times that you'd get back to him as soon as you're able to."

"People tend to get worked up when they're threatened with termination," I said calmly. "Let's get his papers in order and we'll call his managers before we speak to him. Have you got his file on there?"

"Yeah. Name's Jackson." My heart skipped a beat, but then I realized that the spelling was probably different, even though the pronunciation was the same. "They've sent him to us because apparently he didn't show up to work for a week or something."

My stomach twisted, but it had to be a coincidence. Taking in a reassuring breath, I exhaled it slowly and focused on my job. I could *not* allow not-my-Jaxon to distract me here.

"What's his direct manager's number? Have you got it?" Mentally running over our termination checklist, I identified the next steps we had to take. "We should double-check our own system, speak to management, and get all our ducks in a row before entering into official communication with the employee."

Terminations could get rough. Coming across unprepared or not having all our evidence on hand only made it so much worse. Anna nodded and tapped on her screen a few times, and a contact email from her popped up on my laptop a few seconds later.

"The manager is Steve Robertson," she said. "He's also the one who sent the file over here. They've already been in contact with the employee to alert him to the fact that steps are being taken against him. There's a note on the file about the call."

"It's a good thing they've gotten the ball rolling." I took a few sips of my rapidly cooling coffee, but I'd rather have cold coffee than a hot office. The air-conditioning in there was even more effective than the one—

No. Stop it. Not here. Not now. Not him.

"Can you check our logs to see whether we've had any communication from him prior to the incident in question or his incessant phone calls now?" I asked Anna. "I'll get Steve on the line, but we need to update him about what we've got as well."

"Checking now," she said. "Our office didn't receive anything directly, but I'll include a search to our general administration emails as well. I suppose most communications with the entire department go there, whereas we only get the stuff specifically addressed to our own email addresses."

"True." I'd have thought she would know that I needed a wider search, but she was probably just a little overwhelmed. She'd only been with us for a few months, and I loved her, but leaving her alone for so long would've been intimidating.

Most larger companies, like ours, had hundreds of people working in their HR departments. Employees working in other divisions of the company hardly ever knew our names or exactly which person to send things to.

We were the backbone, the people who kept the order among the most important assets of any business—its workers—and made sure the employee lifecycle was properly managed. Most of the people we actually worked for, the employees, avoided us like the plague because our role was often misunderstood.

Even those who understood what we did rarely knew anyone within the department's responsibilities so well that they knew who to contact. It was slightly worrying that Anna hadn't performed the proper search when the phone was already ringing for Steve's office line, but I'd deal with her in a few minutes.

Perhaps I should've gotten someone a little more experienced to stand in for me. We would have to tread carefully with this particular termination. If the employee whose name I'd rather not think about, even though it was spelled differently, was already blowing up Anna's phone, he wouldn't take getting fired lying down.

We had to follow our procedures to the letter. If the ball had been dropped already, we'd simply have to pick it back up.

"Hello?" Steve said when the call connected.

"This is Lindsay Flinn calling from Human Resources. I understand you've referred an employee to us for disciplinary steps to be taken."

"Yeah. Guy took off without notifying anyone here. He claims to have had some vacation days saved up and says he did contact you, but I obviously wouldn't know anything about that. It's your domain, so I referred his file."

"Sure." I didn't like the manager's tone, but managers were employees too. They were as loathe to speak to us as anyone else most of the time.

Anna caught my eye, so I asked Steve to hold. He didn't sound too happy about it, but he'd just have to wait. I was back, and I was making sure everything was getting done properly.

If he'd thought his referral was where his role ended, he was sorely mistaken.

"It looks like he did reach out to us before he disappeared." She frowned. "I didn't see this before."

I let out an internal sigh. *This is why I don't like going away. First, I get my heart broken and now, my portfolio is broken.*

"That's okay. We'll go over some of the departmental guidelines when I'm done with Steve. It'll be good for both of us to brush up."

She smiled as she nodded, and I went back to the phone. "It would appear that he did reach out to us before he absconded from the job. We'll go over what we have and contact him. I'll keep you apprised of the situation."

"Yeah. Thanks." He hung up without saying goodbye.

Story of my fucking life.

I'd been meaning to ask him some questions about the employee and his service record, but I'd have to do that in a follow-up call.

I also needed some more details about the guy, and then I needed to compile a separate file for the disciplinary proceedings. Ember had no idea why I loved my job so much, but I really, really did.

"Will you get Jackson on the phone for me please?" I asked Anna. "We need to ask him to come in. I'll get started on the forms we need to fill out."

"Sure thing." She smiled as she returned his earlier calls. "Thank God I finally have something legit to say to him. That man does not like hearing no for an answer."

No one does when it involves losing their jobs. I definitely needed to spend some more time on Anna's training. She was clever, though. She'd pick up on the finer details soon enough.

Her smile slipped when he didn't answer. "What do I do now?"

"Send him an email to the same address he contacted us from, as well as any other addresses listed in his personnel file. Ask him to come into the office and tell him that we'll talk about the issue."

A few minutes later, before I'd even gotten around to printing all the paperwork from his file and was only about halfway through the official disciplinary forms, her tablet chimed with a response. "He says he'll come in immediately."

Well, at least now I know it's not my Jaxon. He would never be so prompt.

CHAPTER 30

JAXON

S lightly hungover from my afternoon with my mother yesterday, I walked into the office fully geared for a fight. Over the years, I'd had a couple of offers from other airlines, but I liked where I was.

If they made me start over at a different company, I would, but I wasn't just taking this bullshit termination crap lying down. I was finally at the point here where I pretty much got to choose my routes, had more downtime between flights, and could theoretically be home more often if I chose to do it.

The airline was affiliated with one of the charities I volunteered at, and they were even counting my hours there now as actual work. It had taken me a long time to get to this stage of my career, and I wasn't just leaving.

A young brunette girl greeted me in the waiting area of the office number she'd told me to report to. She sat with her back toward the runways, and her eyes widened as if she was in shock to see me there.

"Are you Mr. Scott?" she asked when I walked in. I was wearing my full uniform and had my hat tucked under my arm for good measure. It was time to remind them of who I was and that they'd be firing a pilot they'd courted for years if they went through with this.

I nodded once. "Yes. Ms. Bowman, correct? You summoned me?"

Her head bounced up and down, but there was definite tension in her movements. "We just need to discuss with you what has happened. Then you'll be on your way. Today's meeting shouldn't take too long. If disciplinary steps follow, I'll be in touch about the procedure from here on."

Delightful. "Sure. Can I go in?"

"In a minute. They're just finishing up a conference call about the strike." She flushed like she knew she wasn't supposed to have mentioned it and then cleared her throat. "It'll just be a minute. Please have a seat. I'll let you know as soon as she's ready for you."

"Guess I'll wait some more." I planted my ass on the seat closest to the door marked only with the airline logo, and I tapped out a text to Kavan, canceling the plans we'd had later this morning. Shira wanted me to help with painting a rainbow on the baby's wall. Instead of being there helping them prepare for their new arrival, I was here trying to reason with a department that was clearly in disarray.

My knee bounced while I sat there, my mind half still stuck in Fiji as it had been since I'd gotten back, and half going over the job offers I'd had before. One would require moving to New York, but at this stage, that didn't seem as bad as it used to. Except for the fact that Mom would never move and she'd have my diaper-cleaned balls as payment if I tried going without her. But there was one in Dallas as well. She might go for that one if push came to shove.

A few minutes later, the receptionist cleared her throat again.

"Please follow me, Mr. Scott." She smoothed out her skirt after she stood, giving a terse nod in the direction of a short hallway behind her desk.

I followed her to an opaque glass door at the end, my heart slamming into overdrive when I read the name on the door. There was no mistaking it, though.

In big, bold, capital letters, there was Lindsay's name.

Ms. Lindsay M. Flinn.

Oh shit. Also, I wonder what the M stands for?

I had literally no time to think about how to handle facing her again. Her assistant rapped her knuckles against the glass and pushed the door open without even waiting for a reply.

"You can go in," she said without making any move herself. "I'll be at my desk if you need anything. Ms. Flinn will take it from here."

I'll just bet she will.

Lindsay rose behind her desk when I walked in, her hand stretching out ahead of her like she was about to shake mine, but then she lifted her eyes away from her computer and saw it was me. Her hand froze in midair before dropping back to her side.

I gave her a smile, but her eyes turned to steel as she glared at me like I'd never been glared at before. "Oh, joy. It's you."

Clearly, she was just as surprised to see me as I was to see her. "Hey, Linds. You never told me we worked for the same company."

"I didn't know."

I cocked my head, still clutching my hat underneath my arm. "You didn't think to ask who I flew for when I told you I was a pilot?"

"We only ever talked about our current positions our first day there." Her eyes spat fire at me while her voice was as cold as a fucking glacier. "Forgive me for not taking more of an interest in the employer of the man who, shortly after asking me what I did for a living, told me I hadn't cared about my fiancé."

"Come on, Linds. It wasn't—"

Her expression turned thunderous. Eyes narrowing into slits, her nostrils flared and she held up a hand to interrupt me. "Don't call me that. Don't you even begin to think about speaking to me like we're still on that island."

She marched out from behind her desk, but instead of coming to me, she walked around—giving me a wide berth—and slammed her door. I didn't want to make her madder than she already was, but I was genuinely confused.

"Why are you yelling at me?"

She spun to face me from the door, eyes still blazing as she planted her hands on her hips. "Who the fuck do you think you are, leaving me alone in that hotel room? I'm not some worthless slut you fucked on your way into or out of some country, and even those women aren't worthless."

Her chest heaved, but she wasn't done yet. This was a side of her I hadn't seen before, but I couldn't deny that I liked it. Even when her fury was aimed directly at me, she was fucking hot.

Angry sex hadn't really been my thing before, but looking at her now, I would definitely be okay with it. Not that I thought it was about to happen.

"Did you even think for one fucking minute what it would do to me to wake up alone after a night like that?" she asked. "Not even just a night. A whole fucking week. A week where you pretended to be this good, supportive guy when you were really nothing but a bottom-feeding scum leaching off a vulnerable woman's emotions?"

Her words hit me like an arrow to the heart. "You know that's not what it was. I thought it would be best for both of us not to say good-bye. We had a pretty fucking awesome night, and it felt right to leave it with that as our final moment."

She'd walked back behind her desk and slammed her palms down on the glass top. "Right for who? Best for who? Not for me. That's for fucking sure."

With the amount of F-bombs we were both dropping, it was no surprise that the tension between us was thick enough to cut with a blunt knife. That same electricity from before zapped between us, but this Lindsay, the one with the hair tied up into a firm, sleek bun and wearing a navy dress like it was body armor, showed none of the signs that had become familiar to me that she felt it too.

I showed her my palms after tossing my hat down on the chair I was supposed to have taken. "We need to talk. I'm starting to get that maybe I made a mistake, but this really isn't going to get us anywhere."

The only place it would get us was with her bent over her desk and her skirt bunched around her waist. If that was what it took, I wasn't opposed to using our emotions against both of us.

She stared at me with her blue eyes wide. "It wasn't going to get us anywhere for you to leave either, asshole. But I get it. You got what you wanted, so you left."

Disbelief clouded my vision and scrambled my thoughts. "*You* were the one who said you didn't want to say goodbye, *Ms. Flinn.*" I emphasized her name because she'd told me not to treat her like we were back in Fiji. "I gave you what *you* wanted. Let's just be clear about that."

"What *I* wanted?" She was practically shouting now, her body wound tight as the knot my earphones got into in my pocket. "*None* of this was what I wanted, Jaxon. It was never about what I *wanted.*"

I stiffened from head to toe, my own lids lowering until I was staring out of slits. "Can I just say, for the record, that you were complicit in everything? Consulted in everything. Don't make it sound like I forced any of it on you, Lindsay. That's beneath you."

"Beneath me?" Wildness crept into her eyes as she jerked upright. "You know what was beneath me four fucking nights ago, Jaxon? You. Do you know what was there when I woke up? No one. Nothing. Not even a single fucking rose petal."

"I took care of it before I left." Admittedly, there were better things I could have said.

She let out an incredulous laugh. "That was so kind of you. I'm sure the staff thanked you immensely for your dedication to helping them when you had to have picked up each petal by hand and they could've vacuumed it all up after we left."

"It felt important to do it by myself." I stalked up to her, my eyes never leaving hers as I planted my face right in front of her. "I did it for you, Lindsay. Do you hear me? I stayed up, I cleaned up, and it was all for you."

"None of it was for me." She shoved me away from her and dropped into her chair, flicking a finger at the one with my hat on it. "Do you want to have this meeting? Or are you going to sign my forms, agreeing to mutual separation of employment, and get the fuck out of my life?"

I grinned but even I knew it didn't reach my eyes. "I'm not signing shit, baby. I made it easy for you to get rid of me once, and look where that's gotten me. Apparently, it was the wrong thing to have done then, and it sure as hell is the wrong thing for me to do now, so I suppose you're stuck with me."

"Stuck with you?" she hissed out between clenched teeth. "No. I'm not *stuck* with you. I'm *done* with you."

"What happened to our meeting?" I challenged her, not willing to walk away again until she asked me to in so many words. "I thought this was about my termination, not my actions taken in my personal capacity on my time off."

"Your time off? You didn't have any time off, Jaxon. If you think I'm going to do fucking shit for you to try to save your job, you're sorely mistaken."

"I suppose that's fair." I picked up my hat and leveled a stare at her. "But this is far from over, Lindsay."

"Get out," she ordered between shallow, panting breaths, her eyes still shooting daggers at me. The dark blue depths I'd admired so many times were black. "Get the fuck out of my office and don't bother saying goodbye. You had your chance to do that, and you missed it."

CHAPTER 31

LINDSAY

J axon's golden gaze locked on mine, and a muscle ticked in his jaw. I could practically hear the thoughts screaming in his head, but he didn't voice them. He thought I was overreacting. Perhaps that I was being unfair.

Maybe I was.

If any other person had walked through my doors, I wouldn't have been treating them like this. I definitely wouldn't be throwing them out of my office before we'd even gotten to the purpose of the actual meeting.

Unfortunately for him, he wasn't any other person. He was the guy who had walked out on me just days ago. The guy who had been instrumental in showing me new heights—and I wasn't just talking about parasailing—and then left me lower than I'd ever been.

I *couldn't* treat him like I would anyone else. Not right now. Maybe not ever.

The proper thing to do would've been to kick his case to a colleague and let them deal with him. If I was capable of rational thought while being pinned by those eyes, I'd have handed over his file and been done with it.

As it always did when I was anywhere near Jaxon though, my brain was malfunctioning. No matter what he'd done to me, that humming electricity was still present between us. Especially when neither one of us was willing to look away.

A long minute, or maybe more, passed before he thrust his chin up, shook his head, and turned on his heels. There was a distinct frustration in the sharp, almost robotic movements of his body, but that wasn't my problem.

I knew he'd seen how hurt I was while he looked at me. There was no way I'd have been able to hide it from him when he stared at me like he was peering right into my heart, and he still hadn't said anything. Still hadn't acknowledged it in any way.

Gripping the door handle so hard his fingers turned white, he paused for a second without turning back to me. His shoulders rose like he'd sucked in a deep breath, and when they fell, he twisted the handle and strode out of my office with his spine rigid.

I brought my fist to my mouth, and my eyes narrowed as I let out a silent scream. The door slammed shut behind him, and just like that, Jaxon was gone again.

The fresh, masculine scent of him permeated the air like he'd left it behind on purpose to be a painful reminder of all the times I'd breathed him in. The very oxygen I was breathing was now tainted by him.

Asshole.

My heart was going crazy, my blood pounding in my ears. I felt like I'd been hit with a battering ram in the stomach, and my arms shook when I wrapped them around my torso. I knew I wasn't literally about to fall apart, but I still felt the need to hold myself together.

I have to calm down.

I'd never gotten this upset in the office, and I wasn't about to start now.

A soft click when my door opened sent my pulse into a frenzy again, only to hit rock bottom when Anna walked in.

Stop it, body. We didn't want it to be Jaxon anyway. Stop reacting like we're disappointed it's not.

I turned to face the window to hide the expression I was undoubtedly wearing, but it was too late. The sound of Anna's heels clicking against the tiles stopped abruptly, and there was a brief awkward pause.

"Lindsay? Are you okay? Did he hurt you?" Alarm rang out in her tone. "Let me alert security. Hang on a second."

Before she could leave, I swiped my fingers under my eyes and shook my head. "No. That won't be necessary. It's not what you think. There's no need to get security involved."

My voice was strained, but at least I'd stopped her from calling in even more people to witness my emotional wobble. I cleared my throat and walked back to my desk slowly, moving like I was in physical pain.

"Did you need something?"

Confusion and uncertainty flashed in her eyes before she shook her head. "No, uh, I just wanted to find out if you wanted to do the progress report for his manager. We can do it later."

Fuck.

I'd forgotten all about that. "There's nothing to report at this time. I'll have to investigate further and update them when I'm done."

Her brow creased. "I've been looking at the manual, and it says that after every meeting, we have to—"

"I know what the manual says," I snapped at her. "I wrote it. I just need some time."

Once again, a tsunami of guilt slammed into me and I softened my features. "I'm sorry, Anna. I shouldn't have spoken to you like that. I'm just... it's a personal matter. I'm going out for lunch early. When I come back, we'll get into the rest of the day."

I hadn't been planning on going out, but now I couldn't stay in here for another minute. I needed fresh air—air that didn't still have his presence lingering in it. Gathering up my things, I stood up and slung my purse over my shoulder.

"I'll see you in an hour or so." I managed a small smile before giving her a curt nod of my head, leaving her standing in the middle of my office.

On my way out of the building, I fished my phone out of my purse and texted Ember. My friend lived for early, long lunches and she somehow always made it work.

Before I even reached the parking lot, she replied with a string of grinning emojis and sent me the name of a restaurant I hadn't been to before. I didn't really care where I met her, though. I just needed to get out and she was the only person I wanted to see.

Thirty minutes later, I walked into a modern bistro with a few rustic elements blended in here and there. The atmosphere was lively and friendly, and when I saw Ember waving at me from the patio, I already felt the tension bleeding out of me.

I was here. I was fine. I'd come face to face with Jaxon after he'd left me there naked and vulnerable, and I'd come out the other side with my dignity mostly intact.

My friend's smile disappeared when I got closer to the table, her eyes narrowing to slits as her gaze flitted over me. Already on her feet when I stopped in front of her, she pulled me into a bone-crushing hug.

"Work or Jaxon?" she asked once we were both seated.

"Both." I took the carafe of wine she'd ordered, filled a glass with the tangy white, and took a giant gulp. I'd need a mint and some perfume before I went back to the office, but as long as I didn't turn up wasted, I wasn't breaking any rules.

Ember's nose twitched. "What do you mean 'both'?"

"I mean Jaxon came into work today. *My* work, which also happens to be *his* place of work." I took another mouthful of wine while her eyes went wide, nodding as her rapid blinking told me she was getting it. "Yep. In a cruel twist of fate, it turns out that he's a pilot for my airline."

For once, my friend was so shocked that she was speechless but it didn't last long. "How did you not know that?"

"We didn't really talk about work, much more than asking what the other did for a living on our first day. When he said he was a pilot, I guess I just assumed he didn't fly commercially. He sure as hell doesn't *look* like the rest of our pilots."

"He never asked where you worked?"

I shook my head. "I told him I was a senior consultant in human resources and the conversation went in a totally different direction after that. In fact, he made a comment about my relationship with Will a few minutes later and I blew up at him."

"It never came up again?" she asked, eyes still wide. "How?"

"I don't know." I shrugged, even though she was right. I felt like a total idiot for not having asked him about it again. "I think maybe because the conversation about our careers ended the way it did? Jaxon promised he wouldn't ask about Will or say anything about my relationship with him again. That promise was the only reason I agreed to spend more time with him. We steered so far clear of that subject that I think, even if it was subconsciously, the job thing just ended up in the same category."

"Did he keep his promise?"

"Mostly." A waitress came to take our order, and I asked for the first thing I saw when my eyes landed on the menu in front of me.

Ember ordered the smoked salmon salad too, then motioned for me to continue when the waitress left.

"I don't know," I said. "We talked about it eventually, but we never went back to the job thing. There were so many other things to talk about and it didn't seem important. Our last day, he mentioned something about how his work would be calling him back soon. It reminded me that I still didn't know, and I was about to ask, but he beat me to it. Instead of asking about work though, he asked about my brother."

"Wait." She frowned, her pursed lips moving from side to side. "Your last day? That was when you phoned me and said you were in town alone."

"Yep." I tapped the side of my nose. "When I got back, he suggested we live in the moment for the night and not talk about leaving or anything else that was painful. And again, the job thing was linked to the conversation about my brother."

"So you just never got around to talking about it," she finished for me. "It makes sense, I guess. If you clicked with him the way you did, I suppose there were never any awkward silences to fill with small talk about the real life you were taking a break from."

"Exactly." I released a breath through my nose. "In hindsight, it was stupid. As soon as he told me he was pilot, I should have asked him."

She gave me a look. "You said he told you that on your first day, which means you'd have been jetlagged, traumatized after having been stood up, and then claimed as the wife of a total stranger who'd just told you he'd be sharing your room. I think you can forgive yourself for not making the immediate assumption that just because he was pilot, he had to work for the same company you do."

"Yeah, but I should have asked him what kind of pilot he was at least. I think knowing that he used to be Air Force just made me automatically assume that he was still in some way affiliated with a company contracted to the military."

"It's not an unreasonable assumption to have made." She tried to defend my stupidity, but when I lowered my chin and lifted my eyebrows at her, she conceded. "Okay, so it does feel like the kind of thing you'd have eventually thought to ask about, especially considering that you work in aviation yourself, but it wasn't exactly the easiest week of your life."

"What, being left on my wedding day and then falling in lust with a hot, alpha asshole on my supposed honeymoon is an excuse for being completely dim?"

She laughed but it wasn't mocking or judgmental. "Well, if anything's going to be an excuse for an oversight or a lapse in logical thought, I think that's a pretty decent one."

I snorted softly. "Thanks. Strangely, that doesn't make me feel much better."

"What brought him to human resources?" she asked, moving her glass out the way when our salads were delivered.

"Oh, that's the best part of all." I grinned, and I knew I looked more than a little unhinged in that moment. "He never got approval for the time he took off to go to Fiji. They sent his file up to us for termination."

"What?" She dropped her silverware with a clatter, a wicked gleam in her eyes as she shot me a wide grin of her own. "What are you going to do? Are you going to get him fired?"

"I don't know. I thought about it all the way over here. I fucking hate the guy with a passion, but he did try to get ahold of us before he left."

Her grin grew even bigger and she lifted her hands to rub her palms together as if she was a real-life villain. "Who cares? You have the power now. The only question that remains is what you're going to do with it."

CHAPTER 32

JAXON

Kavan's blond hair was disheveled instead of in its usual faux-hawk when he opened the door for me. There was paint splattered on his shirt and over his forearms, and several band-aids stuck to his fingers.

I took a step back. "Whoa. What the hell happened to you?"

"Putting together a nursery happened," he grunted before letting me in. "Thanks for coming to help me assemble the crib. I only have so many hands and I don't want Shira lifting anything that heavy right now."

"No problem." I followed him into their kitchen. "Where is she?"

"Having a mommy massage at the spa. Your mom got it for her actually. She said every woman should have one last spa day to relax before the baby is born." His blue eyes cut to mine before he opened the fridge to extract two beers, a baffled sheen in them as he gave his head a quick shake. "I don't get it. What's so great about a spa?"

I chuckled, accepting the ice-cold bottle he handed over. "Dude, you should go try it. You wouldn't have to ask once you have. It's pretty fucking great. I'd never have thought about getting someone a gift like that, but I'm glad Mom did. I'm sure Shira's loving it."

"Like you've ever been to a spa." He scoffed and twisted the cap off his beer.

"Look who's the enlightened one now." I smirked at the way his features contorted in disbelief. "I went while I was in Fiji."

"Ahh. That makes more sense." He drank deeply, draining half of his bottle in one go. After he swallowed, he hopped onto the counter and stared at me with questions in his eyes. "How are you doing with that whole Lindsay and Fiji situation anyway? Feeling any better yet?"

A shout of laughter left me, but I wasn't in any way amused. "Do you remember when I got that call about how they wanted to fire me because I went?"

He nodded. "Of course. It was only a few days ago."

"It turns out that Lindsay is the person in charge of making that decision. *She's* the HR director or consultant or whatever I could never get ahold of because she was out of the office."

His jaw loosened. "Are you serious? How did you not know who she was?"

"Beats me." I shrugged one shoulder, wishing I had a better answer for him. "It never came up, I guess. We were too busy—"

"I don't want to know what you were too busy with." He flashed me a knowing grin. "My wife's pregnant. Trust me. I know all about how that works."

"That wasn't all we did." I glowered at him.

My friend, however, kept right on grinning. "Sure. You went to a spa as well. Point taken. Carry on."

"Anyway, the woman who took me to said spa and knows very well that I wasn't at work is now the one who gets to decide my future."

He whistled between his teeth and pointed the open top of his bottle at me. "You, my friend, are up shit's creek with not a paddle in sight."

"You think I don't know that?" I sighed. "It's not even so much about the job as it is about the idea that she's been this close to me the entire time. Now that I've seen her again..."

"Wait. You saw her?" He chuckled before taking another swig of his beer. "How was it?"

I scraped my palm over my chin while I tried to find the right words to describe the disaster that meeting had been. "Let's just say it could've gone better. I'm going to have to make some calls about the offers I've received in the past. Find out if any of those people are still interested."

"It couldn't have been that bad. You pulled a dick move by leaving without saying goodbye, but surely, she won't fire you because of that."

"Oh, no. I think she will." The memory of the way she looked at me before I left her office would haunt me for the rest of my days. "She fucking hates me, man. Like, can't stand to be in the same room as I am, hates me."

"Told you she hadn't meant it literally when she said she didn't want to say goodbye." He held up his hand to show me to give him a minute when I moved to flip him off. "The upside is that if she hates you, it means she does care about you."

"Not enough to piss on me if I was on fire." I rolled my head on my shoulders, trying to block out the pain and the universe of hurt behind her gaze when she'd stared at me. She hadn't wanted me to see it, but I had. "I think I really fucked up."

"You don't say?" He drained what was left in his bottle, grabbing two more before we made our way up the stairs to the nursery. "You two had this idyllic week together in paradise. Then you spent the night together. Then you took off."

"Because I thought I was doing what she wanted," I burst out much louder than I had intended to.

Kavan turned on the step two above the one I was on, shooting me a look before he carried on walking. "Don't yell at me, man. I didn't tell you to do what you did. In fact, if you'd just have fucking phoned me when you came up with this idiotic plan, I'd have told you to can it and figure something else out."

"So what? I deserve to lose my job because I made a mistake?" I knew that was what I had done now. Between Kavan, my mother, and seeing Lindsay again, there was no doubt that I hadn't done the right thing. "I didn't mean to hurt her. I was specifically trying *not* to."

"You know what they say about the road to hell, right?"

"That it's paved with good intentions?" I squeezed the back of my neck with one hand and finished my beer with the other. "Yeah, I know. I'm starting to see why they say it too. I didn't want to hurt her, but I didn't even know I was capable of hurting her that much."

I'd thought I was the only one who'd have to live with the weight and the searing pain caused by my decision to leave. It was why I'd made the decision in the first place—to try saving her from having to carry any extra weight.

What a fucking fiasco.

Kavan frowned at me when we walked into the nursery. "Capable of hurting her how much?"

"So much that she literally winced when she realized I was standing in front of her." A stab of pain hit me in my chest. "So much that she told me she wasn't going to save my job and then tossed me out of her office."

"To be fair, it would have come as a shock to her as well." He pointed at an open box lying on the floor. "Let's get started on that while we dissect the terrible state of your love life."

"I don't have a love life," I retorted and dropped to my haunches in front of the box.

"Well, yeah." He rolled his eyes. "Because you turned your back on it and walked out without saying goodbye. Doing shit like that will always throw the world's biggest wrench into the works."

My jaw clenched, but I couldn't argue with his logic. "You're not planning on trying to make me feel any better about this, are you?"

"Nope," he said cheerfully. "I've been waiting to give it back as good as I got it for years. Welcome to payback."

"At least my ideas helped you get Shira and then keep her. All you're doing is pointing out how stupid I was."

"What better place to start?" Amusement lit his eyes as he shrugged. "The first time we talked about this, you still thought you'd done the right thing. Even now that you seem to be coming around to how colossally stupid you were, I'm not hearing how much you regret what you did or even that you're planning on trying to fix it. If you're not there yet, you don't understand."

"You were way less annoying before you knocked your wife up."

He laughed. "You've always been as annoying as you are now, so I have some catching up to do."

I pulled the side panels of the crib out of the box, and we worked in silence while checking the printed sheet of instructions every so often. It took longer than I would've thought, considering that I'd always thought of a crib as a pretty basic thing, but eventually, we had it standing.

Kavan dusted off his hands as he leaned in the doorway, a strange, almost serene look on his face as we he surveyed his handiwork of the last few days. "It's kind of difficult to believe my baby is going to be sleeping in here soon."

I nodded, flashing back to the first time we'd had a conversation about marriage and families. I remembered his arrogant smirk and the confident way in which he'd told a newlywed newbie that he'd willingly walked into a life of captivity.

A lot had changed over the years, but nothing more so than his stance on those particular issues. Although I'd never told anyone, I'd always thought I'd end up meeting my soulmate and having a bunch of babies with her.

I hadn't thought about it much because I always thought it would happen to future-me, but I was starting to realize that none of that stuff could happen to future-me if present-me didn't get his shit together. Running out on the first girl I'd ever really been able to imagine myself with probably wasn't the best way to go about paving the way to having the same look on my face that Kavan did now.

"What're you going to do?" he asked, all the joking and banter gone from his voice. "There has to be a way to fix it if that's what you want to do."

"I don't know if there is." I'd never been looked at by anyone with so much vehemence in their eyes. "I don't know if there's a way back."

"Did you try explaining why you did it?"

"Maybe I could've tried harder."

He slapped a hand on my shoulder, squeezing it as he gave me his version of an encouraging smile. "We flew fighter planes, Jax. We've been in tougher situations and you've always figured it out."

The dark hole inside pulsed and clenched painfully. I shut my eyes against it, shaking my head before letting out a shuddering breath. "I'm not so sure about that. I sure as fuck don't feel like I've been in any tougher situations, and I don't know how to figure it out. This is one clusterfuck I have no idea how to get out of."

CHAPTER 33

LINDSAY

Lunch with Ember had done wonders for my mood, but the feeling of empowerment that had flowed through my veins pretty much shriveled up and died as soon as I'd left her. I might as well not have gone back to the office for the good it did me to be there.

I'd never had a more unproductive day at work, and I only had Jaxon to blame for it. I knew he'd worked there for longer than I had since I'd taken the time to take a very detailed look at his file, but I couldn't help feeling like he'd invaded the sanctity of my workplace. A place that had always been somewhere I'd felt like I was at the top of the world.

In that office, I reigned supreme. There were very few people above me in the department itself, and outside of it, even the highest-ups often deferred to me for decisions relating to our workforce. I was the expert, and they knew it.

I used to take pride in that fact. I used to feel like I was invincible while I was there. Not in the silly, thought-I-could-get-away-with-anything kind of way. It was just that I was comfortable in my knowledge and in my job, and I didn't feel the need to justify or explain that to anyone.

Seeing Jaxon had ripped my confidence to shreds. Maybe not seeing him but not knowing what to do with his case. I'd never been as uncertain, and yet this was *my domain*. My forte.

My brain said one thing, my injured heart another, and sometimes, the two would even switch. I hated the way I was feeling about it. I hated that I felt so much about it even more.

Lying on my couch with my knees hooked over the armrest, French music blasting over my speakers, and running my fingers through my hair, I wished I could teleport back to a time when I wasn't the sad sack feeling sorry for herself over something as temporary as a vacation hookup.

Between my thoughts and the music, I almost missed the banging at my front door. Frowning as I sat up and hit pause on my remote, I nearly jerked when I realized there really was someone desperately trying to get my attention outside.

My heart jumped in my throat. *Jaxon?*

While I was telling myself that I really hoped it wasn't him, I also knew how much I wanted it to be him. I wanted him on his knees groveling for my forgiveness, even if it was only to shut the door in his pretty face.

Yeah. That would amazing. Smiling until I realized I'd never be able to look into those eyes and slam the door on them, I scowled as I flung it open.

Shock radiated through me at who was waiting on the other side, his fist poised to keep banging and his blue eyes flashing with relief when he noticed I'd opened up. "I was starting to think I was going to have to break your door down. Why are you listening to French classics? You only listen to French classics when something's wrong."

My brother grinned and opened his arms, enveloping me in the biggest, most comforting hug I could've gotten after the last few weeks. He rubbed my back when I started shaking in his arms, overcome with joy that he was okay and happy and *here*.

"What are you doing here?" I asked when I could finally form words again. "How did you even know where I lived?"

"I got your letters," he said when he released me, the corners of his mouth turning down. "I kept all of them. I've reread them about a thousand times. I've had your address memorized since you sent it to me after you moved."

Tears pricked at my eyes and I didn't bother trying to hold them back, letting them flow over my cheeks as I put my hands on Ethan's shoulders. "I just can't believe you're here."

I looked him over head to toe three times, checking to make sure that he was real, uninjured, and in one piece before tugging him back into my arms. While I hadn't heard it for years, his chuckle was still as familiar to me as my own when it rumbled in his chest.

"I'm sorry I made you wait so long," he whispered into my hair. "I just wasn't ready to see you before, but I'm on leave, and I really wanted to come see you."

Questions slammed into my mind one after the other, each as burning and urgent as the one before. Asking him about it while he was still standing out in the hall probably wasn't the best move, though.

Ethan and I had a lot of ground to cover, and I didn't want him feeling like he'd come to see me only so I could interrogate him. My brother was almost a foot taller than I was, coming in at six-two, and he might be a badass in the Air Force now, but he was still my little brother. I didn't want to make him regret coming to see me.

God forbid he takes off and doesn't come back for another half decade.

Pulling out of our hug, I waved him into my house. "Come on in. I'm sure you could use a drink. Can I make you something to eat?"

"Nah. I'm all good." His eyes were several shades lighter than mine, making it much easier to pick up the sparkle in them even when he only glanced at me. "I didn't come here just so you could feed me."

"Really?" I slapped a hand over my heart. "Is that your way of saying you don't like my cooking?"

"It's my way of saying I ate before I came so you wouldn't have to cook for me, but you've always been a bit heavy handed on the salt." He winked before his eyes lost some of their shine when he looked around the house. "Husband not home? I thought I'd finally get to meet him. On the other hand, is he the cause of the French music? Are you two lovebirds fighting already?"

A shadow crossed his face, and he wound his fingers around mine, giving them a gentle squeeze before releasing them. "I'm sorry I couldn't make it to the wedding. I tried to fix it so I got home in time, but I only got in yesterday."

"You didn't miss much," I said. "Will didn't show up either. It's difficult to have a wedding when the bride is the only one who makes the effort to stick around."

"He stood you up?" he said after opening and closing his mouth a few times. Then he shoved his hands repeatedly into his auburn hair.

Ethan and I had similarly shaped faces, and we both had blue eyes, but I'd gotten Mom's pitch-black hair while he had Dad's rich, reddish-brown color. He'd also gotten the height, the muscles, and the willingness to exercise them.

We didn't look much alike, but he was my soul's twin. I could see the guilt he looked at me with now and the torment twisting him up inside. "Fuck, Linds. You should've called me! Are you okay?"

"I'm fine about Will and the wedding." I averted my gaze, keeping it glued to the orange ball of the sun dipping beyond the treetops outside. "I've realized I should never have said yes. It felt like the right thing to do at the time, but honestly? He did me a favor by leaving."

"Why the French music? If you're really okay, you'd have been listening to rock. I know you, big sis. Don't try to bullshit me."

"I'm not." I planted my hands on my hips and stuck my finger out so close to his chest I almost jabbed it. "What about you, Mr. I Enlisted Never To Be Heard From Again? If you got my letters, why haven't I gotten any from you? I thought I was sending them to the wrong address or something."

"You weren't." He took a step back from me, holding up his hands to show me his palms. "How about we get something to drink and sit down? It seems we have a lot more to talk about than I thought we did."

I studied his face, my eyes roaming over every inch of the familiar features but also the unfamiliar ones. A healed cut above his eyebrow, the dark stubble he hadn't had before, and the beginnings of creases in his skin.

He still looked like my brother, but he was also right. We did have a lot to talk about, starting with why I hadn't seen him in so long that I hadn't even known about his scar even though it looked like it'd been there for years.

Ethan opted for a beer, so I took out the entire six pack I'd stored in the fridge for Will for after we got back from our honeymoon. Grabbing an ice bucket from the cabinet under the sink, I filled it with the cubes I had in the freezer, stuck the beers in it, and led my brother out onto the patio.

My backyard wasn't big, but the lawn was green. My herb and vegetable garden was coming along nicely thanks to Ember watering it while I was away, and the two deck chairs on the grass had a small plastic table between them.

Light emanated from inside the house, so I left the outside lights off. I had a feeling we'd both want a little privacy during the conversation we were about to have.

"Take turns?" my brother suggested after we sat down.

I nodded. "Me first."

"I can agree to that," he grumbled. "As long as you promise to let me say what I need to without interrupting."

"I'll do my best," I promised. "You know my first question already, so out with it. Why haven't I heard from you?"

He blew out a breath, his eyes on the horizon as he answered. "You've always had everything so together. I'm not blaming you at all. I admire you for it actually. It just wasn't always easy to measure up."

"I never meant to make you feel that way," I said, my voice soft. I didn't argue with him, though. He was finally telling me how he felt and giving me a reason for the distance between us. Nothing I could say could change the way I'd made him feel—whether it'd been my intention or not.

"I know." His hand reached across the chasm between us to squeeze my arm. "It was never about you. You didn't do anything wrong. You ate up a lot more shit from me than I ever should've given you."

I didn't say anything, silently willing him to continue. When he did, I let out a small sound of relief. "I needed time to figure out who I was without you always defending me, or fixing it for me, or trying to help. Like I said. I needed to get my shit together so I could stop being a burden."

"You were never a burden," I said fiercely. "Never. If I made you feel like you were—"

"No. You never made me feel like I was. I just knew that I was. Deep down, every time I fucked up, I felt like I'd let you down. I believe our deal was taking turns, though. It's your turn."

The words reminded me of Jaxon saying the exact same thing not too long ago, and the whole sad story came spilling out of me in one long rush of words. Ethan didn't interrupt, chuckling when I came to what had happened with him in my office.

"That's quite the fucking story. I assume this fake husband of yours is the reason for the music?"

"Yep." If nothing else, I was a creature of habit. I'd discovered the classics like Edith Piaf years ago, and I'd never stopped listening to the woman who was my personal goddess. "I'm so screwed. If I fire him, I'll be carrying out a personal vendetta, but if I don't, I'll have to live with the knowledge that we work for the same company. I don't know if I'll ever be able to concentrate again."

"You've always had a bleeding heart, Linds. Even when people have upset you. It's what makes you *you*. It's one of the qualities I love most about you. If it wasn't for that, you'd have shut the door in my face when I showed up out of the blue after so many years."

"It makes me weak." I ground my teeth. "Not with you, obviously. You're my blood and my best friend, but with him? It's a weakness."

He sat up and swung his legs to my side of my chair, his face serious when he lifted his gaze to mine. "Weak? No, Linds. You've got it all wrong. It's what makes you strong. The capacity for forgiveness over petty vengeance? The ability to do the right thing even if it's the most difficult thing to do? Resilience so remarkable you can overcome anything? There aren't many people who can truly say they've got any of that, and you, my dear sister, have it in spades."

If he kept it up, I was going to start crying again. Not because he was complimenting me, but because after all these years, my little brother still believed in me. And if he could do it, so could I.

CHAPTER 34

JAXON

Mom sat in stunned silence for at least five whole minutes after I told her about my meeting with Lindsay. Eventually, a wide smile broke out across her face and she leaned back in the armchair she'd favored since I was born.

"You, my dear, are up shit's creek without a paddle in sight." Mirth laced her tone, and I stared her down.

"Have you been talking to Kavan?" I narrowed my eyes at her. "Because I've already heard that, and you said it in almost the exact same way."

"Maybe I had another son I never knew about," she mused, her eyes still turned up at the corners. "That boy certainly seems to share a brain with me. His wife too. They're lovely people. Dinner once a week isn't nearly enough time with them."

"You see them once a week?" It was my turn to swallow my surprise. "Since when?"

"Since three years ago when I ran into Shira at the post office. We got to talking, and things happened."

"Three years?" I asked slowly, my jaw nearly coming off. "Why haven't I been invited?"

"You're away so much." She flicked her wrist. "Why? Are you jealous? If you are, you should start being home more often."

"Not jealous. Just surprised." But there was a little flicker of jealousy. Not because they'd all been spending time together or even that I hadn't known about it but because I'd always longed for big family dinners.

Being an only child, that was the one thing I'd never had. I would never complain about not having any siblings, but every only child got that occasional pang to know what it was like. Kavan was the closest thing I'd ever had to a brother, and his wife had wormed her way into my idea of family just as fast.

If I stayed in my current job, I might get to experience it. Chances of staying in my current job, however, were slim to none.

Mom regarded me with sorrow in her eyes. "Surprised but not so much that you'd like to join us next time?"

"I'd love to join you." I braced myself for what I had to say next. One of the main reasons I'd come to see her today was that I had to talk to her frankly about the logistics of what it would mean if I got fired. "I won't be able to if I'm going to be based in Dallas, though."

Her entire body stilled, and for the first time, I really saw the toll the years of my absence had taken on her. "Excuse me? Why on earth would you be based in Dallas?"

"If I get fired." I started when the chiming of an incoming email on my phone interrupted me. "Let me check this. It might be work."

Mom harrumphed but glared at my phone. "Go ahead."

My gaze flitted across the screen. Anna, who I now knew was Lindsay's assistant, asked me to come into the office to discuss what was happening. I sighed, shoving my phone back into my pocket.

"I have to go. I'm being summoned by the powers that be." I got up and kissed her cheek. "I'll let you know what's going on as soon as I do."

"Pick up an application for some other local airlines while you're near the airport, darling. This girl isn't going to help you and I'm not having you move to Dallas."

I gave her a blank stare, but she just shrugged and giggled. "Let me put it to you this way. If she helps you despite what you did, you drop down on one knee and ask her to marry you right then and there."

"She'd say no, Mom." Worse yet, I'd deserve it. "We haven't even known each other a month. Even if she wasn't pissed off as all hell with me, she still wouldn't say yes."

All my mother did was to shrug and let out another giggle. For a woman who had looked so serious not even a minute ago, she sure was cheerful all of a sudden.

I didn't question her, though. Her mind worked in mysterious ways. For all I knew, she was taking this communication from Lindsay as a good sign.

I was a little more pessimistic about it. There was no way she'd have let go of her grudge so fast, and the last I'd heard was an email from Anna addressed to both myself and my manager that they were investigating and would update us in due course.

A day hardly felt like due course, but so be it. Leaving my mother's house, I mentally prepared myself for receiving my marching orders. She was right, though. Just because I was being let go from one airline and had had another opportunity in Dallas didn't mean I had to take it. There were plenty of other local players. I just had to keep my chin up and start over.

Again.

When I got to the office, I struggled to get out of my car. No one looked forward to facing certain termination, but it made it that much worse that I was about to be sent to hell by a woman I genuinely cared about. A woman I could picture myself sitting beside on the porch when we were old and gray, watching our great-grandchildren frolicking in our backyard.

Lowering my head to the steering wheel, I banged my forehead against the leather a few times, my fingers gripping it like the answer would be different if I choked the life out of it. From the corner of my eye, I saw a plain rectangular piece of cardboard in my cupholder.

Big Mac's card.

I'd never believed in signs from the heavens or the universe or the fucking stars, but this sure seemed to be one. Okay, so it'd also been me sticking it in there when I got off my flight, but I hadn't even noticed it again until now.

As if someone outside of myself was making my decisions, I reached into my pocket and extracted my phone. Typing in the numbers on the card, I was halfway to convincing myself he wasn't going to answer when he did.

I hadn't even stopped to calculate the time difference, but he sounded as awake and jovial as ever when he picked up. "This is Mackleroy. How can I be of service today?"

"Mackleroy?" I echoed, trying to stifle a laugh. Just the sound of his voice made me feel like a ten-ton weight had been lifted off my chest. "This is Jaxon, man. Is your name really Mackleroy?"

He laughed, the sound booming and carefree. "Jaxon! I was wondering how long it was going to take you to get in touch. Mackleroy is better than Mackerel, which was my mother's other option, but why do you think I call myself Big Mac?"

"Good call." For just a second, I was transported back to the island and how easy it'd been to strike up a friendship with this man. He was the only one who knew both of us. The only one who had seen us together and, therefore, had any real idea of what we'd had together. "You got a second?"

"For you? Always. What's going on?"

"I didn't check the time before calling. Did I wake you up?"

"Nah. I'm getting ready for the breakfast service, but the minions can handle it for now." He chuckled evilly. "It'll be a good test of how well they listen. Hit me. What's happening over there? You and Lindsay work it out?"

"Not yet." I highlighted our current situation to him, but not surprisingly, he didn't sound distraught or even shocked.

"This is it, my friend," he said. "The planets are aligning. This is your moment. It's your chance to kiss and make up, so to speak. Don't let the moment pass you by, Jaxon. Not many people in your shoes get one chance to get the girl back. You might not get another."

Well, that was heartening. He had a point, though. Once again, Lindsay and I had been pushed into each other's paths. Who knew how many bites we had at the cherry before it was all a distant memory?

Before I become the old guy in the nursing home harping on about how I'd missed my one shot. Obviously, I'd respect her wishes. I wouldn't push too hard and I definitely wouldn't try to insert myself—unwanted—into her life again.

But I sure as hell was going to at least give redemption a try. *Who knows? Maybe the planets and the stars and whatever the fuck else really are rooting for us.*

CHAPTER 35

LINDSAY

My palms had been sweating since I'd told Anna to contact Jaxon. I never thought he'd reply saying he'd be right over.

Maybe I really hadn't known him at all. If I was being completely honest with myself, I'd admit that this prompt side of him made him even hotter. He'd told me he was punctual and structured professionally, but I hadn't really believed him.

The happy-go-lucky side I'd seen on the island hadn't correlated with a man who took his job seriously, showed up when he was supposed to, and replied within minutes of receiving a request from the company that employed him.

Of course, I wasn't currently being completely honest with myself, so I refused to admit it. He had more than enough qualities that made him endearing to me as it was. I didn't need to be adding any more.

Before I'd gotten to grips with seeing him again, Anna's voice came over the speaker in my phone. "Mr. Scott is here for you. Can I send him in?"

"Yes. I'm ready for him." I wasn't. Not by a long shot.

I'd known I was going to be calling him in today, though. So I was as ready as I was ever going to be.

Ethan and I had stayed up so late talking that he'd slept over. Early this morning, he'd even helped me choose my outfit. He didn't know what I was going to do, but I'd been going back and forth about it myself until five minutes ago.

There wasn't really a choice, though. I had to be true to myself. I didn't really know much about what was going on in my life or even who I was anymore, but the parts that I did know, I had to stick to. If I didn't, there was no telling where I'd end up.

That was until Jaxon appeared in my doorway. He paused when he came into view, his golden-brown hair mussed like he hadn't been planning on doing anything today and his matching eyes darker than usual with determination.

A small and yet not insignificant part of me wished he'd looked at me with that gleam on the morning we left Fiji. Wished that he'd stayed and had looked at me that way while telling me that he wasn't ready to say goodbye either.

I stuffed a mental pillow over that part of my brain and smothered the romantic piece of crap. No matter how much I wished things would've been different, they weren't.

Jaxon let out a small sigh. As if he'd seen that secret hopeful part of me being snuffed out and was disappointed about it.

That wasn't my problem, though.

I stood up, just like I would if this was any other meeting, and waved him into a chair. "Have a seat, Jaxon. Thank you for coming in on such short notice again."

His forehead twitched like he'd been about to frown at my tone before he managed to clamp down on his expression. "Of course. I was happy to receive your message."

My heart broke a little at how formal we were both being, but formal, I could handle. It was the familiarity he'd dished my way during our last meeting that'd been unbearable.

"I'm sorry we took so long to get back to you," I said.

His brows moved up a fraction of an inch. "Long? It's only been days, ba—" He mashed his teeth together to shut himself up, and I was glad he had. Folding his hands in his jeans-clad lap, he gave me a tight smile. "It's no problem. I was expecting the investigation to take much longer."

"It might have if it wasn't a cut and dry case."

He cocked his head, his shoulders opening up as his spine straightened. "Cut and dry, huh? Good to know."

I almost smiled. I knew what he was thinking, and I was looking forward to proving him wrong about me. It would be interesting to see his reaction when he heard what I had to say.

"Yes, Jaxon," I said, my voice gentler now. "I've spoken to your manager and everyone else involved in the chain of command. There was no fault on your part. You didn't leave without notifying anyone. We have an email on our server, as well as records of several phone calls. It was an error on our end that your request was never logged."

Deafening silence echoed in my office following my statement. Jaxon looked like he might leave his jaw on my floor, but there was also something new in his eyes.

Hope. Respect. Relief. Maybe even adoration. I couldn't quite pin it down.

"Why are you doing this for me?" he asked eventually. "You hate me. The ball was in your court. Why would you clear all this up for someone you can't stand?"

"It's not about you, Jaxon. It's about me." A cliched line, but that didn't make it any less true. "I am who I am, and I won't change that just because I'm pissed off with someone. Too much has been taken from me. I won't let that go too."

He opened his mouth to say something, but I didn't let him. Exhaling deeply, I rested back in my chair and let my professional demeanor slip.

If I didn't do it now, I was never going to get the truth out. I needed to get it out because if I didn't, I would always be weighed down by it.

That last night in Fiji, I'd been planning on telling him anyway. One of the greatest regrets I had was that he'd left before I had the chance to.

I refused to let the opportunity pass me by again. If I was ever going to be able to move past this nightmare of a month and all the turbulence and emotions it brought with it, I had to start somewhere. I had to purge myself of the words I'd left unsaid.

"Lindsay?" he asked, clearly waiting on me to say what I'd needed to when I interrupted him. "Are you okay?"

"No," I replied truthfully, "but I will be. Look, Jaxon. The trip to Fiji was the best thing that ever happened to me and the worst thing that ever happened to me."

Sensing that I had more to say, he remained silent. His gaze was steadfast on mine. As I looked into those melted-honey eyes I never thought I'd see again, I couldn't stop the wave of emotion from swelling inside me, but I didn't let that stop me either.

I'd made a decision, and just like he had, I was sticking to it. So what if he saw or heard how much I meant every word? So what if I gave away how much it'd all meant to me?

It didn't matter anymore anyway. We were over. If he went to his friends bragging about the poor sap in the lobby who he'd pretended to be married to and who'd fallen for his act, I didn't really care.

I didn't know them, and they didn't know me. For at least this one moment, though, I could know I was still the same woman deep down inside. The woman my brother loved and admired. The woman Ember insisted deserved the best in life.

Most of all, the woman I knew I was when all the noise and bull-shit got stripped away.

"Fiji was the best time of my life," I said again. "I went there expecting the worst. When I left here, I prayed that I wasn't making a mistake, and when I arrived? God. It was like everything was screaming at me that I hadn't just made a mistake, but that I'd screwed the pooch big time."

Jaxon chuckled so softly that I almost didn't hear it. I saw that one half-dimple pop and his chest rising and falling. "You and me both. I thought I'd flown all the way out there only to have a day trip and fly right back."

I couldn't bite back my smile this time, but I also didn't regret him seeing it. At least I wasn't the only one on the honesty train today. It made me feel marginally better, which only confirmed my belief that I was doing the right thing.

The truth will set you free and yada yada.

"Meeting someone like you was the last thing I expected," I said, "but you opened my eyes to a whole new world of possibilities. I'll always be thankful to you for that. I don't know what you saw in me that first day, other than the possibility of a bed for the night, or why you came to join me in the dining area when I'd stormed off on you earlier."

"We needed to look like newlyweds," he answered as if it was the most obvious, simplest thing in the world. "We might not have known each other, but I wasn't going to be that guy who left his wife alone on the first day of our honeymoon."

I wanted to scowl, to cry, or to cuss him out. If he'd just left me alone and been the roommate he had promised to be, the one I didn't even know was there, none of this would've been happening. Or, well, he'd still have been in my office to hear his fate, but none of these bad feelings would've existed between us.

"It might make me sound like a crazy person, but I'm glad you weren't that guy," I admitted eventually. My eyes were growing moist again, but fuck it. As Ethan had said, what I was doing and who I was weren't a weakness. It was a strength, and I was embracing it with both arms open. *As Jaxon had taught me to.*

"Yeah, me too." It was barely more than a whisper, but it rang out loud and clear in my office. He cleared his throat. "So where does this leave us?"

"The same place we were at a month ago," I said. "As nothing. We don't exist to each other. We were never in each other's orbit and we were never meant to be."

The more I'd thought about it, the more I knew it was true. "I got left at the altar, Jaxon. Just when I was forgetting about it and started to believe it'd happened because maybe there was something, some*one*, better out there for me, I got left at the honeymoon."

227

Again, he opened his mouth but I couldn't hear what he had to say until I'd said my piece. "I don't want your apologies. I don't want you to explain or to justify it."

There was so much emotion in his eyes that it almost broke me, but I was so close. How many girls could honestly say that they'd had their alpha-male ex sitting in their offices after having been at their mercy, after they'd run out on them, giving them a chance to say their piece? I didn't know, but I was willing to venture a guess that it wasn't many.

Jaxon's respect as he sat there taking it, not chiming in or arguing, was yet another thing I liked about him. *His mother has to be one hell of a person.*

One of my biggest regrets was that I'd never get to meet the woman behind the formation of this enigma of a man. I was dying to know how she'd raised such a self-assured, confident, caring jerk of a guy who never missed a beat.

"I just want our time there to be left as a good memory and a reminder to keep me from making the same mistakes," I said. "Thank you for the photograph by the way. It's taken up a place of honor in my bathroom. It serves as that necessary reminder that I made a shitty decision."

He laughed out loud at that but inclined his head when he was done. "I expected it to end up as fish food, so I'm glad it made it home. You're one of a kind, Lindsay Flinn."

"Thank you for coming in today, Jaxon. You should be back at work tomorrow. I've made sure this doesn't leave any trace at all on your record."

He nodded and stood up, taking his cue for being dismissed. Once he was on his feet, he stuck his hands in the pockets of those faded jeans and shot me the most hopeful, adorable smile I'd seen in a long time.

"Can I see you again?" He tucked his chin lower, smile turning sheepish. "Outside of work, I mean."

I wanted to say yes. I wanted to throw my arms around his broad shoulders and feel his hard body against mine again. There was nothing I wanted more than to press my lips to his and feel that same rush of exhilaration I would forever associate with being literally and figuratively swept off my feet half a world away.

But it was because of how much I wanted all of it that I injected steel into my voice and said, "No, Jaxon. I think it's best if we don't."

CHAPTER 36

JAXON

I t turned out that Lindsay had been wrong. I had been reinstated after my brief suspension, but I wasn't back to work.

Steve said they'd filled up the dance card while my fate had been uncertain, and therefore, I was still waiting to hear when I'd be taking to the skies again. I was itching to get back, but I was also enjoying my time at home.

I'd even gotten to join my mom, Kavan, and Shira for their dinner the day after my meeting with Lindsay. I was restless but happy to be back for a while.

The evening had been filled with laughter, tears from Mom when she'd felt the little princess kick, and a toast when I'd told them I wouldn't be moving after all. Shira had driven Kavan home after the rest of us had gotten nostalgic over another of Mom's bottles of whiskey, and I'd ended up crashing in my childhood bedroom.

If I didn't start flying again soon, Mom was going to have to start buying her own booze at the rate we were going through it now. Thankfully, I'd been bringing her back a bottle every month or so for quite some time, and since she never drank it unless we were with her, she swore she was okay for the time being.

I'd barely staggered back into my own place when my phone

started ringing. Kavan's name appeared on the screen, and I cursed my friend. "Do you know I've had more alcohol since I've gotten back from Fiji than in the five years before I went?"

"Hey, bro. We're just trying to help you drown your sorrows. No one has been pouring the stuff down your throat."

"Is it supposed to work?" I asked. "Drowning one's sorrows? Because I'm just feeling more sorrowful than I did yesterday."

He laughed, and I had to hold the phone away from my ear. "That's not sorrow. It's a hangover. Consider drinking less next time if you don't like it."

"Yeah," I grumbled. "I'll do that. Just as soon as I can breathe again while knowing that Lindsay is cool with us being a memory she can use to remind her of her mistakes."

"Yeah, that must've been a blow," he said. "Luckily, we've got the convention tonight. That ought to cheer you up. All the old crowd will be there, and we get to make fun of the new recruits. Want me to pick you up?"

"What fucking convention?" My only plans for the day included showering, watching some movies, and sleeping. *Also, thinking about plans hurts.*

My very inconsiderate friend just laughed again. "The Air Force convention, bud. We said we'd go months ago. We can't bail now."

"Ahh, fuck. I forgot about that." Now that he'd mentioned it though, I distinctly remembered my enthusiasm when I'd convinced Kavan to go. "Our one last night out on the town before the baby is born. I talked Shira into it, didn't I?"

"Yep." He whistled happily. "She can't wait for me to leave the house. Apparently, doing hospital drills is getting old. She says there is such a thing as being too prepared."

"Don't pick me up," I said. "I'll get us a cab and come past your place. I still have those bracelets I picked up in Fiji for your girls. Any chance you'll tell me your daughter's name so I can have it engraved?"

His bark of laughter this time grated against my ears. "Nice try. You'll know when everyone else does. You know I've been sworn to secrecy. Shira will have my balls if I tell you before even the grandparents know."

"Yeah," I replied weakly. "We wouldn't want that."

Kavan told me to be at his house no later than six, and then we hung up. I crawled into bed after a quick shower, napped, and binge-watched TV shows under the covers until it was time to shower again.

Unlike any of the other events we got invited to, this wasn't an official thing. The convention was held by one of our former instructors who liked to keep things casual. It was touch-base session. Something he did to remind us that we'd always have each other and that there was always someone to reach out to if you needed it.

It was pretty fucking cool of him actually. He'd inherited well and also headed up a veterans' center, but this was more of a lighthearted affair. It meant no uniforms, name badges, or rank-based dick measuring.

As much as I missed Lindsay with every fiber of my fucking being, I was getting amped up for a night with my brothers and sisters in the service while I got dressed. I couldn't pine for her forever, and she'd made it pretty damn clear she didn't want anything more to do with me.

Big Mac and his planets had been wrong. I'd seen the acceptance in her eyes when she'd told me no, and that was it. Maybe there were some people who couldn't take a firm and sincere no, but there wasn't really a question about it to my mind.

I didn't want to let her go, but what was the alternative?

The taxi I'd ordered was right on time, and the driver didn't make much conversation when he noticed my melancholic mood. Once Kavan was in the car, the two chatted a mile a fucking minute, but at least they left me to my thoughts.

Kavan looked like he wanted to say something once or twice, but eventually, he let it go. I'd heard plenty from him, my mom, and Shira. They knew where I stood on the whole thing, and they'd agreed to give it a rest over dinner at Mom's.

When we arrived, Kavan fist-bumped the driver after I released his payment, together with a healthy tip for having left me alone, and then we were inside. Kavan had done one more tour after I'd gotten injured, and he went to greet some guys he knew from there while I headed to the bar.

I sidled in beside a guy nursing a drink and smiled sympathetically at him. "I see I'm not the only one who's come to this party damaged."

He whirled his head to the side to face me, chuckling as he shrugged. His blue eyes were piercing, but they had that happy shine in them that had nothing to do with booze.

"Yeah. I might've forgotten about this shindig tonight."

I snagged a glass of craft beer from the barman and held it up. "Same here. I guess we'd better just suck it up though, right? No one's going to take kindly to us if we're the wet towels at the party."

He bit out a strangled laugh. "Wet towels, huh? No. I refuse to be known as one of those. Have you smelled those things? They fucking reek."

"Exactly." We clinked our glasses together. "So, who broke you last night? I hope it's a better story than mine."

He groaned, shaking his head slowly. "My sister, if you'd believe it. Of course, I stayed up way after she went to bed, drinking an exotic bottle of rum she had while telling myself I wasn't fucking up all over again. At least she seemed cool about it this morning. She said she'd bought it at the airport but hadn't been planning on drinking it anyway."

"Getting drunk with your sister is better than getting drunk with your mother." I jabbed my thumb at my chest. "My mother and my best friend, who I'm pretty sure she's adopted as her other son without telling me, broke me last night."

He held up his fist and I bumped it. There was something so familiar about him, yet I knew I hadn't served with him. "You get to claim mother *and* best friend, though. I only had my sister. Although she's got enough drama going on at the moment to make up for ten fucking people. Jesus."

My bar mate and I hit it off instantaneously, and a few drinks in, he held out his hand. "I'm Ethan. I'm deploying again in a few days, but I wanted to make the trip out to see my sister. Figured I might as well stay for the party."

"Scott," I said as I shook his hand, reverting to giving him my last name without even thinking about it. "It's nice to meet you, Ethan."

"Yeah. I was worried I would be the only hungover one here."

We talked a little about where we'd been and what we'd seen before he tilted his head to the side, eyeballing me intently. "What's bothering you, Scotty? You're here with me, but you're also not."

I raked a hand through my hair, a little humiliated that I was so obvious. "Honestly? I'm fucked up about a girl."

"Yeah?" He frowned, light blue eyes blazing with confusion as his lips twisted. "No offense, but you don't seem like the type who gets fucked up about a girl."

"That's because I'm not." I tapped my empty glass on the bar for a refill. "This girl though, man, she got under my fucking skin. I can't shake her. No matter what I do."

"Why aren't you with her?" he asked, curious more than anything else. "You're obviously not the shy, reserved type either."

"She shot me down." There was nothing more to it than that. "I wanted to be with her, but she said it would be best if we didn't see each other anymore."

He laughed under his breath. "That sounds exactly like something my sister would say even if she still wanted to see that person. Fucking pride."

"It's not pride," I objected. "It's respect."

"Then respect her enough to fight for her," he roared, slamming his own nearly empty glass down on the counter before shooting me a shamefaced grin. "Sorry. I didn't mean to come across so harshly. I'm just aggravated because my sister's in love with this fucknut who doesn't have any balls."

"Commiserations," I said. "I hope the guy comes to his senses."

Ethan shoved a hand into his auburn hair, clearly frustrated but unwilling to talk about it any longer. "What about you? You coming to your senses?"

"It's not like that with us. I fucked up and I let the only girl that I've loved slip between my fingers. Sad but fucking true."

He gritted his teeth and slammed back against the low backrest of his chair. "Who are you to say she's slipped between your fingers? Has she said it's over in so many words?"

"Pretty much, yeah." I fucking hated to think about the finality in her tone when she'd told me we were better off not seeing each other again, but I'd heard it. Anyone would've heard it.

Ethan let out a bitter laugh. He downed half his refill before he shook his head. "You should fight for her, Scotty. Fight until your fingers are stumps and you can't fight anymore. You know what that's like. You've done it for your country. Now do it for your girl."

"And if she doesn't want me to?"

He snarled. "If she doesn't want you to, she'll tell you. She deserves to know you're willing to. Hell, I wish this dickhead my sister was into would fight for her."

I didn't know who Ethan's sister was, but I knew he was right. Letting go without a fight was not only not in my nature, but it wasn't fair.

Over and over again, I'd been told that I'd made a mistake with Lindsay. I'd come to terms with the fact that I had, but she didn't know that. She didn't know how desperately I wished I could turn back time and find a way to make her mine for real.

She didn't know that I'd hardly slept since I'd last slept beside her. She couldn't know that she was in just about every one of my thoughts or that I'd told my mother about her.

All of these things were my daily reality, but Lindsay didn't know a thing. She thought I didn't care. She thought she was the only one thinking back to Fiji as being the best and the worst time of her life.

I'd listened to her, but Ethan was right. "I should fight. Thanks, man. I owe you one."

Slapping a hand down on his shoulder, I gave him a grateful squeeze before turning to leaving the venue. Ethan clasped his hand around my wrist, stopping me from moving before he held his phone out to me.

"I'll be back in some or other dust bucket before it plays out, but shoot me a text on the other side of it, okay? I need to be able to tell my sister there are happy endings, and I'd like to use yours as an example."

It was a weird request, but I understood where he was coming from. His sister had been hurt and he was leaving again soon. The only way he'd have to comfort her was vicariously through others' stories.

I didn't know if mine would have a happy ending, but updating a guy I liked and got along with wouldn't be a chore. Either his sister would learn something from my story or she wouldn't, but I didn't mind keeping him up to date.

Hell, at least it would mean that there's someone else out there rooting for us. Even if it is just that he's silently rooting for the dickhead dating his sister to pull his head out of his ass.

Hell, if I could come around, couldn't anyone?

CHAPTER 37

LINDSAY

"I'm heading out, Ms. Flinn." Anna popped her head into my office, her eyes red rimmed and glazed from having stared at her screen for so many hours today.

I instantly felt terrible about keeping her so late. Just because I was restless and unable to sleep didn't mean she had to suffer for it. I smiled and waved her away. "Go. I'm sorry we went so late."

She stifled a yawn, blinking the resultant moisture out of her eyes. "That's okay. I know we're still trying to catch up."

"Even so, I should've been keeping an eye on the time." I waved again. "Go, and don't come back until tomorrow afternoon. Take the morning off."

"Are you sure?" She frowned. "Won't that only make us fall further behind?"

"Nope. I've got it. You spent weeks here without me. I'll be fine for just one morning." She gave me a grateful smile, yawned, and nodded. "You shouldn't stay too much longer either. It's getting really late. Tomorrow is another day."

"I'm just finishing up some paperwork. It won't take too long. I promise I'm not too far behind you."

"Good. See you tomorrow." She closed my door with a soft click behind her.

I sagged into my chair and rubbed my eyelids, careful not to smear what little was left of my makeup too much. My lenses stung, but I just had a few last things I needed to get through.

One last push for the day.

I'd been texted a few pictures of an incident that had occurred this morning between some of the support staff, and I needed them to complete the report their superiors would be expecting in the morning. They needed it to conduct their own preliminary investigations before we could officially take control of the management and consequences of the scuffle.

As I scrolled through the gallery on my phone, my heart lurched in my chest when I was suddenly looking at Jaxon's face. It was a picture of the picture he'd left on my suitcase. I'd taken it to keep a reminder on me about why I needed to steel my heart whenever I saw him.

Now that I knew he was close by, I also knew it would be more difficult to stick to my resolve. This picture would always remind me of that moment I'd found it, and of how I'd felt when I woke up that morning without him.

Seeing it now unexpectedly made a ripple of pain pass through me. I didn't know how long it would be until I could look at him without feeling the after effects of him leaving, but I wasn't there yet.

If only I was able to look into his heart, into his mind, to find the answers I knew I shouldn't want but couldn't help thinking about anyway. *So many questions. So few answers.*

He might've given me those answers if I'd just asked, but I wouldn't trust much that came out of his mouth anyway. Forcing my hovering thumb to move, I flicked past that picture and on to the next one before I realized I wasn't even in the right folder of my gallery.

After eventually finding the pictures and compiling my report, my thoughts returned to Fiji. It was like simply seeing a photograph of Jaxon had shocked my heart back to life when I'd been trying to keep it as emotionless as possible recently.

I went through the motions of sending the report to all interested parties but my head wasn't really in the game. It was firmly stuck on the island that had been my own personal paradise for all of one week.

When it felt like I was going to lose my mind if I didn't talk about it, even just for two minutes, I pulled up Big Mac's number from my contacts. We'd texted once or twice since I'd gotten back, but we hadn't actually spoken yet.

I checked the time, did a quick mental calculation, and determined it was early afternoon there. My fingertips drummed on my desk while I waited for him to answer, and my stomach was suddenly riddled with nerves.

Why am I calling this poor man? My issues weren't his responsibility.

Before I could hang up and tap out a text to let him know I'd dialed the wrong number, I heard his voice coming through the line as clearly as if he was standing right next to me.

"Lindsay!" he said in his booming voice. "This is a surprise. How are you?"

"I'm..."I trailed off before deciding that I'd already bothered him. I might as well be honest. "Not so good actually."

I proceeded to tell him everything that had happened between me and Jaxon since he'd last seen us, but as always, I got the feeling he already knew about most of it. I narrowed my eyes in suspicion. "Have you been speaking to Jaxon?"

He chuckled. "The question isn't if *I've* been speaking to Jaxon. It's whether *you've* spoken to him."

"Cryptic." I shook my head at him even though he couldn't see me, but by not answering my question, he'd told me what I needed to know. "What did he say to you?"

"Let's just say I have a feeling it's not over for you two."

So he hasn't spoken to him since the last conversation we had.

I ran my hand through my hair, loosening it from its tie and letting it hang in a sheet over one shoulder. With my eyes pinned to my desk, I let out a soft, shuddering sigh. "It's over between us, Mac. I made sure of it."

"We'll see," he replied cheerfully before I heard his name being called in the background. "I'm sorry, Lindsay. I have to go. We have a wedding on tonight, and I think someone just burned a sauce I've been perfecting for the last seven hours."

He was gone before I could do much more than say goodbye, and a pang of longing speared me in the gut. I hoped those people who were there right now knew how lucky they were and how much they should cherish each moment they had there. Not only because of the place but also because of the people.

Unlike them, however, I wasn't on vacation. I had to work again tomorrow, which meant it was probably about time to get my butt home and to bed. *Maybe tonight I'll finally get some sleep.*

A yawn overtook me. I covered my mouth with one hand while checking that I had everything I needed out of my desk with the other. As I stood up, I thought I heard someone in the waiting area outside of my office.

A frown flickered across my forehead. I knew Anna had gone home, and there weren't usually many other people here this late, but it had happened from time to time.

Relaxing when I remembered the last time I'd gone stiff as a board after hearing something, I smiled at the look of terror that had been on the intern's face when I'd emerged while he was sifting through Anna's stuff looking for spare staples.

Shame. Poor guy.

It was best I didn't scare the living beeswax out of an intern again. Making sure my heels clicked against the floor as I crossed my office, I opened my door with a little more force than was necessary.

Whoever was out there had to have heard me by now, but I still closed the door loudly as well. I was prepared for an intern this time, so hopefully I wouldn't jump a foot into the air again when I saw the intruder.

What I wasn't prepared for was an even more intense physical reaction when I saw who was waiting for me out there. Jaxon stopped at the end of the hall after turning the corner. He looked at me like he couldn't really believe I was there, and yet he had to have come here looking for me.

My heart sped up so much I was afraid it might explode in my chest. My hands got all sweaty and shaky again, which was something they really needed to stop doing. Jaxon just seemed to have that effect on me, though.

I was unable to move when he zeroed in on my eyes with his. There was nothing but single-minded purpose in them. *I just wish I knew what that purpose was.*

He didn't make me wait long to find out. Raising his hands as if in surrender, he stayed rooted to his spot. "I won't come any closer. All I'm asking is for you to hear me out."

"I already told you that I don't want your excuses or justifications, Jaxon. I'm not interested in those, so why are you here?"

Resolve was written all over him. It was there in the set of his shoulders and the tilt of his jaw, the way his nostrils flared and how his muscles were bunched, straining against the confines of his shirt.

"I'm not here to give you excuses or justifications." He lifted his chin, his eyes never leaving mine. "I'm here to fight."

"Fight? About what?" I frowned and drew my hands up slowly to my hips. "Are you drunk or something?"

He shrugged. "I've had a few drinks, but I'm not drunk. I didn't come here to fight *with* you. I came to fight *for* you."

My brows swept up and my fingers gripped my hips tighter. "Oh, yeah? How are you planning on doing that exactly?"

"By telling you everything I should've told you that morning before I left." The world around seemed to blur a little more with every word he said, until there were no conference rooms in the hallways or an office behind me. There was only him. "I've kept quiet so far because I was trying to respect your wishes. If you tell me to leave and never come back after you hear what I have to say, then so be it."

My lids fluttered closed as I sucked in a deep breath. "Fine. You have five minutes, Jaxon. I'll hear you out because you've done the same for me, but I'm not making any promises."

"Five minutes is all I need." He strode across the distance between us, cupped my face between his large hands, and allowed me to see the truth in every word he spoke when he finally gave me my answers.

CHAPTER 38

JAXON

This is it.

Everything was riding on my ability to get through the next five minutes without making an even bigger mess of things. I knew everything I wanted to say, but it was all a big jumble in my head.

"I know I fucked up," I said. "I didn't want to say goodbye to you either, but I still should have. Leaving was the most difficult thing I've ever had to do. At the time, I thought it was because I was doing it for you, even when it wasn't what I wanted."

Arguments flashed in those blue eyes, but she didn't interrupt me even though I saw how much she wanted to. "I've since realized that what I thought was wrong. It's been made very clear to me by my mother and by my friend, Kavan, that I acted like a complete idiot. It just took me some time to sort through it all in my own head."

"You told your mother about me?" she whisper-yelled. "Why would you do that?"

"Because I fell in love with you on that island, and the first time she saw me after, she knew something was different. That *I* was different."

"You..." She stared up at me with disbelief etched into her expression. "You didn't fall in love with me. You wouldn't have left me if you had."

"Oh, but I did." I threaded my fingers into the soft locks at the nape of her neck. "That's why I left, even if I didn't necessarily realize it at the time. I left because I couldn't stand to come home with you and not have you being mine. I left because I promised to protect you and I thought that was what I was doing. I left because I couldn't stand the thought of not being with you, but I also thought it was too soon after your relationship fell apart to even broach the subject."

My chest was heaving by this point, but at least the jumble was vanishing, and finding the words I needed was starting to come easier. "The thing is, Linds, I thought leaving you would protect you from *me*. From the feelings I had for you when I didn't think you could possibly be in a place where you could reciprocate."

Moisture clung to her lashes and her teeth sank into her lower lip. "That wasn't for you to decide."

A smirk crept onto my lips when I remembered Kavan saying those exact same words to me when we'd first gotten back. I shook my head and brought my forehead down to hers. "So I've been told. When I left that morning though, I wasn't thinking about it like that. I never meant to hurt you. In fact, I was trying to save you from being hurt."

"I don't need you to save me, Jaxon." Her voice was quiet and laced with pain, but she hadn't pushed me away yet. "How could you not have realized how much it would hurt me to be walked out on for the second time in little over a week? Especially after the night we had together."

Agony twisted my insides into knots. "I'm so sorry, baby. I don't know how I didn't realize it. I just didn't. I was so caught up in what I thought was right that I never stopped to consider just how fucking wrong I might be."

"You were, Jaxon. Wrong, I mean."

"I know," I whispered, winding one arm around her waist and holding her to me. "I wish there was a way to go back. I wish I could take away all the pain I caused you. I'd rather have been tortured for a week than to have had you feeling that way for even a minute."

"I hope you're ready to sign up for a couple of years of torture then," she mumbled, "because if it's a week for every minute, it's going to be a lot of weeks."

"If it would take your pain away, I'd do it in a heartbeat," I said firmly. "That being said, I'm also glad I left."

She stiffened against me, and I rushed out my explanation for that statement. "If I hadn't left the way I had, I never would have been forced to really face how I feel about you. After spending every minute together and then suddenly no longer having you in my life, it became glaringly obvious how much I care about you."

"You needed to hurt me to realize how much you love me?" she asked, her voice strained. "I hope you know how fucked up that sounds."

"I do, but I didn't mean that I'm glad you got hurt. I will never, ever forgive myself for hurting you and I know you probably won't forgive me either. What I meant was that I never even let myself consider that I'd fallen in love with you because I thought it was way too fast."

Lindsay kept quiet, hearing me out while my heart thundered underneath her ear. "It took losing you for me to realize that just because it happened fast didn't make it any less true. I fell head over fucking heels for you, so fast and so hard that I didn't even realize it was happening until it was too late."

"How do I know you're not lying?"

"Why would I lie to you about this?" I pulled back to look into her eyes, stroking my thumb along her cheekbone. "Why would I leave an Air Force convention where the only thing I did was talk about you to a total stranger, only to come here to tell you everything? You've already told me my job is safe, and I trusted you when you said it. There's no reason for me to be lying, and I'm not."

"I don't mean to sound like a broken record, but I just don't know how to trust you about any of this. I trusted you so completely, and yet you took that trust and tossed it against the bungalow walls and left it shattered all over the floors. I can't think of any ulterior motives for you to be here, but I also can't just forget how I felt when I woke up without you."

Panic flared up inside me. I hadn't thought this would be easy, but I also still hadn't quite realized the extent of the damage I'd caused to our relationship.

"There's nothing I can say that will make you trust me again, but if you'll let me, I'll spend every day for the rest of my life proving it to you."

"The rest of your life?" Her eyes flew wide open. "Are you—"

"No." I laughed softly, closing my eyes as I wound a hand into her hair again. "I'm not proposing. I would if I thought it would help convince you of how serious I am, but I don't think it would, and I'm not fucking up again, Lindsay."

Her chest deflated against mine as she let out a relieved sigh. "Thank God."

"I will tell you this, though. You're the only woman I want. I am going to marry you one day if you'll have me. I promise that by the time I ask, you'll know with every fiber of your being how much I love you and I would rather die before I hurt you again."

"Die? That's a little dramatic." The slight lightness in her tone sparked the kind of hope in my chest that I'd never felt before.

"It might be dramatic, but it's also true. I might not be asking you to marry me, but that doesn't mean that I'm not making promises I intend on keeping. I will love you for the rest of my life, even though I'm not putting a ring on your finger tonight. I'm yours, Linds. What you do with me is up to you, but it doesn't make me any less yours."

When she pulled away, I thought it was over. I thought she was about to tell me that my five minutes were up and to get the fuck out of her office. But then she looked up at me, and my knees damn near buckled in relief.

"It might only have been a week, Jaxon. I know some people will think that we're crazy or infatuated or maybe even that we're just plain stupid, but I love you too."

My heart swelled to three times its normal size, but she wasn't done yet. She planted her palms over my chest, one of them directly over the organ that felt like it was only beating for her now.

"I wasn't ready to admit that was what I was feeling back on the island either, but I planned on talking to you that morning. I wanted to tell you that my feelings were real and to ask if you felt the same way."

I groaned. "Fuck. I'm such an idiot. I could've saved us both so much fucking heartache if I'd stayed for that conversation."

"Maybe, but like you said, the time apart really did put things in perspective. You are an idiot, though. I'm just thankful that you're *my* idiot."

"All yours, Linds. Forever. If people think that makes me crazy, they can all go fuck themselves."

"Eloquently put, as always." She trembled in my arms and I froze, again thinking that she was crying until I looked down and realized she was laughing. "This time, however, I agree with you completely. I don't care what anyone else thinks."

"The time we spent apart might have helped put things in perspective, but I'm pretty done with that now. I never want to be away from you ever again."

"That might prove to be a little difficult, considering we've both got jobs to do and yours requires you being away all the time."

"Yeah." I lowered my head and nuzzled her neck. "I've been thinking about that, and I have a plan. I'm too young to retire as a pilot, but—"

"I'd never ask you to do that. I was just teasing." She pressed a kiss to my chest. "I know this thing in here would wither up if you had to stop flying."

"The only thing that would make it wither up would be losing you." I said it without any hesitation whatsoever. "There's a position available as a senior ground instructor. I've already discussed it with Steve, and he's agreed to letting me split my time between flying and instructing. They've been on my ass about teaching for a while actually."

"That's funny. I thought my department was responsible for

appointing people to available positions." She smiled. "Luckily, you know someone in HR who knows you'll be perfect for the job. I'll be sure to put in a good word for you, even if I won't be able to handle the appointment myself. Conflict of interest and all."

"Why do you have a conflict?" I asked, my grin already spreading.

She shrugged, her eyes shining as she looked up into mine. "I can't exactly appoint my boyfriend who swept me off my feet in every way imaginable, now can I?"

"Boyfriend?" I asked the question with my mouth so close to hers that our lips were brushing when they moved.

"Boyfriend," she said decisively. "Possibly future husband if he plays his cards right."

"I like the sound of that." Realizing for the first time since the conversation started that we were still standing in the hallway outside her office, I curled my hands around hers on my chest and cocked my head. "Since we've established that I don't want to be away from you for longer than strictly necessary for us to do our jobs, are we going to your place or mine?"

"Mine," she whispered. "We can figure the rest out later."

CHAPTER 39

LINDSAY

Jaxon's lips found mine as soon as my front door closed behind us, and feeling them there again was the best thing I'd ever felt. I never wanted to stop kissing him again, even if I knew we'd have to stop at some point.

I couldn't quite believe that he was here with me, that he'd come after me and flat out told me he was fighting for us. While I knew that everything between us wouldn't just snap back to the way it had been, I had a feeling things would get even better from here on out.

My heart wasn't ready to let all its guards down, and I still had to figure out how I would ever trust any man enough to say yes to marrying him, but if anyone was going to get me there, it was Jaxon.

Definitely not now but eventually.

In the meantime, I was going to enjoy having him back in my life and getting to know us the way that we would be together as a real couple. Sure, he'd made a mistake, and it'd hurt like nothing before it, but one mistake shouldn't steal the chance from both of us to see what we could become.

I'd also realized while he'd been talking that I wasn't blameless in what had happened. He'd left without saying goodbye, but I hadn't exactly given him any reason to think that I wanted him to stay.

In hindsight and now that I'd heard his side of the story, I could understand why he'd done it. It actually kind of spoke to how deeply he cared about me that he was willing to put himself through all that for me.

On our way to my place, he'd told me how much it'd hurt him to leave like that. In the end, we could both have saved the other a lot of pain and heartbreak if we'd just communicated our feelings properly. So that was what we had agreed on doing from now on.

No more waiting, no more wondering, and no more making decisions about what was best for the other without talking about it. We were sealing those promises to one another with these kisses, but they were also slowly turning into something more.

I writhed against him, need ricocheting around inside me. He was as hard as steel against my stomach as he continued to kiss me like he'd never kissed me before.

Large, powerful hands kneaded my breasts over my shirt, his thumbs dragging over my stiff nipples. A shiver ran through me, settling into a throbbing ache between my legs.

"You okay?" Jaxon asked breathlessly between kisses.

"Yeah, I'm fine, just..."

He gave me a sexy smile. "Overwhelmed? Me too. This doesn't have to lead anywhere tonight. Just so you know."

I nodded but bunched the material of his shirt between my fingers. "Fair enough. It doesn't have to, but I want it to. If you'd rather talk some more, we can—"

His lips slammed back into mine, his hands dropping to my butt before he lifted me up and held me against him. Shifting his hands to my thighs, he broke away to cock his head at me. "I'd love to talk some more, but I love you, and I fucking want you more than anything. All I meant was that if you don't want this tonight, it'd be okay. I needed to put it out there before we kept kissing like that."

I crossed my ankles behind his firm butt and pointed down the hall. "My bedroom is that way, and thanks, but trust me when I tell you that I want this too."

Barely aware of our surroundings, I was fixated on Jaxon's gaze as he walked us toward the bedroom. There was raw, carnal need in his eyes, but that fierce possessiveness I'd noticed before was back.

What was new was how he looked at me with so much love that it made my breath catch. It also made my heart expand and my body ache for him.

When we finally reached my bedroom, he gently laid me down on my mattress. He smiled and unzipped the back of the pencil skirt I'd worn to work before dropping to his knees to remove my heels and my panties.

He planted a soft kiss on my lower belly that made me wish it'd been just a little lower, making a moan tear out of me. Glancing up, his eyes lingered on mine as he leaned forward to kiss me again. "I won't drag it out, baby. I promise. Just bear with me for a minute, okay?"

I nodded as he pushed himself up to his feet and made quick work of the rest of my clothes. Once I was completely exposed to him, he crawled onto the bed with me and brought his mouth to mine.

There was such a connection between us that it ignited something deep in my soul but also stoked my need into something that was more than just physical. There was the physical need as well, but it was also so much more than that.

It was the need to be joined with him on a level that went deeper. I wanted to find the warm corner of his heart he claimed was mine and to crawl into it for the rest of time.

His fingers curled around the back of my neck, his tongue sliding into my mouth. He stroked it over mine. Gifted fingers caressed my bare breasts until I was gasping and trembling, moaning again.

Jaxon's warm mouth moved down to my chest while his fingers started a slow journey down. I spread my legs wider, urging him to move faster. The air felt cool against my overheated center, but I knew it wouldn't last long.

His gaze rose to mine as his fingers found their mark. I curled my hands into fists, feeling ready to explode while he seemed perfectly calm. On closer inspection, I could see that he wasn't. His pupils were dilated and his movements almost jerky from how hard he was trying to restrain himself.

"Don't, Jaxon. Just be in the moment with me. Don't hold back because you're trying to punish yourself for something."

Exhaling slowly, he nodded and disappeared from the bed. He stood at the foot of it, the quiet rustle of his clothing the only sound in the room as I held my breath.

Beautiful, insanely sexy, and stupidly handsome didn't begin to describe him naked. It didn't matter how many times I'd seen him that way before, it would always make my heart race and my core clench with need. He was perfect with all those hard lines and smooth, inked skin.

When he climbed onto the bed again, he lay down beside me and stroked his fingers over me. "You are so fucking sexy. I can't actually believe I'm getting to touch you again."

"I was just thinking the same thing." He molded his palm over my center, and the sudden pressure where I needed it so damn badly made me see stars.

My back arched when his fingers moved between my folds. Tingles erupted over my skin as he pushed a finger into me. "God, Jaxon. I wish I could tell you what you do to me."

Groaning against my skin, he slowly worked another finger into me. "You don't have to tell me, Linds. I already know because you do the same to me."

"I'm two seconds away from exploding and you've barely touched me." I shuddered when his mouth started traveling lower.

He chuckled, his warm breath fanning across my heated skin when he positioned himself between my legs. "I'm two seconds away from exploding, and I've barely touched you, but you haven't touched me at all."

"Because I can't reach."

"I'm keeping it that way for a reason." Pushing his fingers deeper into me, he brought his tongue to my slit and licked me from top to bottom. "If you touch me right now, it's game over and I can't have that."

Fireworks exploded behind my eyelids when his tongue circled my clit. I stopped arguing. Stopped even breathing.

My body was going to be blown to debris when this orgasm hit. I gripped the sheets harder, trying to anchor myself against the astonishing intensity of the sensations racing through me.

My hands flew to his hair, tugging the soft, golden-brown strands. Jaxon read me perfectly, knowing exactly what I needed to push me over the edge.

He brought his lips to my clit and sucked the little bud between them, flicking it with his tongue at the same time. It sent me skyrocketing, my body trembling as I cried out. All those sensations crashed into me, and I let them take me to that place where nothing existed but bliss.

I went limp after screaming his name.

When I finally came to again, Jaxon was wearing a satisfied smile. But it was tight and strained.

My limbs were still quivering from the force of my orgasm, but I managed to sit up. He watched me with heavily lidded eyes. "What are you doing?"

"Showing you that I want to worship and love you the same as you did me." My voice came out raspy, but I meant every word.

He looked like he wanted to argue until I shook my head, put my hands on his broad chest, and pushed down lightly. He lay down on the mattress, his dark eyes fixed on mine.

I did the same things as he had done at the beginning, moving slowly to kiss his lips while my hands explored his unbelievable body. I traced the hard ridges of his torso and the toned muscles in his arms.

My fingertips trailed to his belly button, circling it once or twice before I found the smattering of hairs that formed the happiest of trails to his thick erection. He groaned into my mouth when I tangled my fingers into them.

I swallowed the sound, and Jaxon's hands gripped my hips, his fingers digging into my skin. My hands gripped his thighs, my thumbs resting a hair's breadth away from the apex of them. I brushed against him every so often as my mouth made its way down.

Only stopping when he was inches away from my lips, I brought a hand up to wrap it around his base. Blood throbbed in the veins under his skin, and he sucked in a sharp breath as I stroked him.

The muscles in his throat worked and he cursed when I closed my mouth over his tip, licking across the slit to taste the liquid that had gathered there. His hips bucked clear off the bed, and his stomach dipped on a deep breath.

His hands burrowed into my loose hair, gripping it tight. "Fuck, Linds."

I felt his need as acutely as my own, my own stomach flipping at the thought that I was responsible for his pleasure. Maybe I needed some time to work my way back to trusting him, but he had placed his body and heart in my hands, and I intended on taking the very best care possible of everything he had entrusted to me.

Sliding my mouth down his length and hollowing my cheeks, I used my hands to massage him where I couldn't reach him with my mouth. I swirled my tongue around his broad head and over the nerves bundled beneath it.

He released a loud moan and his hips bucked. Then he was tugging on my shoulders and pulling me off him. Jaxon's eyes were wild, his breathing ragged. "Condom?"

"I don't have any."

He froze. "Neither do I."

"I'm still on birth control," I said. "Have you been with anyone else?"

"Fuck no." He sounded almost offended before a pained expression contorted his face. "You?"

"Hell no."

His answering grin was as relieved as it was damn hot. He rose over me, resting the bulk of his weight on his elbows.

As I lay underneath him, the feeling of his bare skin against mine was exquisite. He fit himself to me, took my mouth in a kiss that made my toes curl, and pushed in slowly. Rocking against me, his fingers wrapped around my thighs and he set a rhythm that soon started building that familiar pressure again.

He wound the tension tighter, stroked into me in a way that pushed me higher with every thrust. Our slick skin was plastered together, our hips moving fast as we climbed to our respective peaks. When he moaned my name and tensed against me, his whole body shuddered and mine erupted with pleasure at the same time.

Long waves of it rocked through me while Jaxon buried his face in my neck, his hot breath ghosting across my skin. Bringing his head up when our moans had eventually quieted, he pushed my hair off my damp forehead and smiled softly. "I love you, Lindsay."

"You can't leave me again," I whispered against his lips. I would never tire of hearing him tell me that he loved me or telling him how much I loved him, but it'd been a long day and I was too afraid sleep would pull me under.

Having made the mistake of keeping quiet once about what was going on in my head before we fell asleep, I needed to get the words out right now. "I'm serious, Jaxon. I can't go through that again. If I wake up tomorrow and you're not here, I don't know what I'll do."

"You don't have to worry about it, love. Maybe Big Mac was right, and some weird stars did align, but they're aligned now. I'll be here tomorrow morning and every morning after that until you kick me out."

I propped myself up on my elbow and scooted up to kiss him, pouring every gushy emotion I never thought I'd feel into him. His arms circled around my waist, and without breaking the kiss, he rolled us over so he was hovering above me, his eyes burning with intensity as they locked on mine.

"I'm staying right here," he murmured. "I'm not going anywhere. Go to sleep, snookums. I'll be here when you wake up."

My nose wrinkled. "Snookums? Really? We're doing the nick-names thing again?"

"We are. I'm really looking forward to seeing how creative we're going to have gotten by the time we celebrate our ten-year anniversary back in Fiji."

My heart galloped as I kissed the tip of his nose. "Okay, buttercup.

Challenge accepted, but you're not allowed to complain about a single one."

"I won't," he said as I cuddled into his side, his chest rumbling with laughter. "I told you already. I'm yours to do with what you want. Do your worst. As long as I get to be here to hear each and every one of them."

With those words and the sound of his laughter in my ears, I finally closed my eyes and slept peacefully. When I woke up the next morning, he'd kept his promise. He was still there, still holding me, still loving me.

It didn't mean everything was fine between us or that I trusted him with all my heart and soul, but it was one step closer. Everything else would come with time, and at least this time, we had it. There was no clock counting down to the end of our relationship, and what we made of it was up to us.

EPILOGUE

LINDSAY

ONE YEAR LATER

E very little girl grew up dreaming about her wedding day. I
might not have counted myself among those little girls before,
but I'd sure as hell made up for all the dreaming I'd missed, ever since
Jaxon had walked back into my life.

As he'd promised that night when we'd made up exactly one year
ago today, he hadn't asked me to marry him yet. Even though I knew
now that he loved me with every fiber of his being and that he would
never hurt me again.

It didn't matter, though, because I really did trust him now. I knew
that when the time was right, we'd be jetting back to Fiji to say our
vows. We hadn't talked about it, but that was what I wanted, and I
knew it was what he wanted too.

Once, a couple of months ago, I'd found the resort's website open
on our computer at home. Open to the page featuring their wedding
options and packages.

The excitement I'd felt when I found it and it confirmed that we were on the same page—literally and metaphorically—still hadn't completely evaporated. I wasn't sure it ever would.

This last year with him had been the best of my life. It wasn't so much the wedding I was looking forward to so much as finally really being married to him.

I woke up every morning in his arms, and fell asleep the same way at night. If anyone had thought that what we felt about each other would mellow out over time, they'd have been wrong.

Ember had even admitted to me earlier how very wrong she, for one, had been. Kavan and Jaxon's mom, however, weren't surprised at all.

If anything, our feelings for each other had only grown and become deeper. Which was why, about six months in, we'd both given our notice at the places we'd been renting and bought a house together.

The renovations had been murder, but I'd come to the conclusion that if a couple can survive that, they had to be able to survive nearly anything. As I turned off the highway into our suburban neighborhood, I hit the call button on my steering wheel and my boyfriend's gorgeous voice flowed through my speakers a second later.

"Hey, beautiful. You on your way home?"

"Yep. Do we need anything? Also, 'beautiful' isn't your most creative one so far."

He laughed. "True, but it doesn't need to be creative to be the truth. We don't need anything. I stopped on my way home. Just get here fast and safe. I've got something for you."

A legit yelp tore out of me. "Is it Ethan? Is he finally back?"

"Way to ruin the surprise," he grumbled, and I heard my brother's laughter in the background. "He can't wait to see you either, cupcake."

"I'll be there soon." I hung up without telling him that I wasn't his roomie in prison and that, as such, he couldn't call me cupcake. I'd be home soon enough and then I could tell him in person.

Joy spread through my veins at the thought that I'd be seeing my brother again in just a few minutes. He'd left only about a week after that night that he showed up on my doorstep. We'd stayed in touch this time, but video calls and emails just weren't the same as seeing him for real.

Surprisingly, I wasn't the only one staying in touch with Ethan. The guys had figured out pretty quickly after Jaxon and I had gotten together that they'd met before.

The morning after our reunion, it turned out we'd both texted my brother to let him know what'd happened and that we'd made up. They put two and two together, and I'd learned that the stranger Jaxon had been speaking to about me all night at that convention he'd been at was my brother.

Apparently, I had Ethan to thank for convincing Jaxon to fight for me. *Imagine that.*

Big Mac had had a huge laugh about it when we'd told him. According to him, it'd been serendipity and simply more proof that we were fated to be together.

Maybe it's fate. Maybe it's not. Whatever it was, I'd never been happier.

Jaxon had landed the position as instructor—with no help from me. He hadn't been kidding when he'd said they'd been after him to teach for a long time.

Half the damn company converged on him after he'd mentioned to Steve that he might want it. He still flew because I knew he'd never be happy with having his feet permanently on the ground, but he was never gone for longer than two or three days at a time.

Our garage door started rising after I stopped in our driveway, and Jaxon was waiting for me on the other side. He grinned while I parked, then pulled me into his arms as soon as I was out of the car.

"I love you," he said before slanting his lips over mine in a kiss that left me breathless and wanting more. A soft chuckle made his chest vibrate against mine when I pressed myself up against him. "We have company, remember?"

Shit. My brother's here.

Ignoring my body's demands to drag Jaxon into our bedroom—or the kitchen right off the garage for that matter—I straightened up and gave his chest a light push. "I remember. Where is he?"

"Backyard." He snaked his arm around my waist and dropped a kiss on top of my head as we made our way inside. "He's been helping me with something, so he isn't your only surprise today."

"Yeah?" I peered up at him, but his face gave nothing away. "What else?"

"You'll see soon enough." He held me tighter so we could fit through the door without the need for us to let go of one another. "I think you're going to like it, though. I fucking hope you are."

"I will." It didn't really matter what the surprise was. If it came from Jaxon, I always loved it. Unless of course the surprise was me waking up without him, but we didn't really even talk about that anymore.

Our house was my favorite place in the world. It ranked above even Fiji, but only because this was *ours*. We'd picked out every part of it together to make it into exactly what we wanted.

Elements from the bungalow in Fiji were included, but we'd also installed large windows that let in plenty of natural light. The kitchen was a real farm-style space with a table large enough to feed a family of eight, which I knew Jaxon was hoping to fill with our children one day, but six kids was pushing it just a bit too far. Three max. The other three seats at the table could remain open for their spouses one day.

We'd filled our walls with photographs of all the adventures we'd been on together, including kayaking, snowboarding, sport shooting, and so many others. Jaxon caught me looking at them as we walked past, and kissed my temple.

"Life with you is my favorite adventure, my love," he said, and my heart skipped a beat as a big, soppy smile spread on my face.

He laughed and held me tighter until my brother came walking in from outside. Ethan opened his arms and I ran into them. "You're finally back! Please don't tell me you're leaving again soon."

"We can talk about all that later." He hugged me tight. "It's good to see you, sis. This is a nice place you've got here."

"Thanks. I'm assuming Jaxon's already given you a tour?"

His eyes sparkled when he released me and nodded. "My favorite part is the backyard. It's magical."

Jaxon made a soft noise behind me, his palm on my lower back. "You two are just spoiling all the surprises today, aren't you?"

"Why is the backyard a surprise? And what's so magical about it?" I spun to face him, but he just shrugged and shot my brother a look.

"Why don't you go have a look?" Ethan suggested before turning and striding back outside.

"What have you done?" I asked, but Jaxon just pressed gently against my back.

His soft touch spurred me into motion, my curiosity making me increase my pace. Jaxon kept up easily, a strange, nervous energy suddenly radiating from him.

I wanted to question him some more, but then we walked out onto our patio, and it all suddenly made sense. Our backyard wasn't huge, but they'd completely transformed it.

Twinkling lights were strung in the trees, lanterns hung from some of the lower branches, and there were rose petals covering the grass, but that wasn't nearly the biggest surprise.

In the center of the yard was a makeshift outdoor kitchen. It was bathed in the orange glow from the lights and the soft, late afternoon sunlight. Standing behind a gas-burner with a spatula in his hand, the apron that read 'If The Cook Ain't Fat, Don't Eat The Food' tied around his neck, and a gigantic smile on his face, was none other than Big Mac himself.

"What are you doing here?" I asked before launching myself at him.

He caught me in his meaty arms, lifting me up and spinning me around. "Jaxon flew me in to make you dinner. I've got to say, I've received a lot of compliments in my life, but this is the biggest one ever."

After I finished hugging our friend and the man who'd been rooting for us from the start, I pivoted to face Jaxon. "You flew him in just to make us dinner? I love it, but that's ridiculous."

"Not just to make us dinner." He shifted on his feet, and that nervous energy was back. Ethan clapped him on the shoulder and murmured something I couldn't hear to him, and my boyfriend nodded.

His eyes didn't leave mine while he walked up to me, but he didn't wrap his arms around me as I'd been expecting. I frowned at him, but he simply swiped his tongue over his lips.

"I brought everyone here together tonight because I want to give you one more thing." Something seemed to click inside him, and then the nerves were gone.

Warmth and love dominated his gaze, and his voice was confident and smooth when he spoke while lowering himself down on one knee. "You changed my life, Lindsay Flinn. Being with you felt right from the very first moment that I touched you, and I've only gotten more certain about it since."

I couldn't speak, couldn't even think as I stared down at him. Those melted-honey eyes that had drawn me in right from the beginning were glued to mine, and the corners of his mouth inched up.

"I bought this ring the day after you agreed to give me a second chance." He pulled the box out of his pocket but didn't open it yet. "I knew I had a lot of work to do before I got to ask you to be mine forever in the same way I'd already pledged myself to you. There have been so many times over the last year where I've gotten so close to asking, but I needed to know that you were ready too."

"I'm so ready," I whispered, "but your mom and Kavan are going to kill you for not inviting them to be here."

He smirked. "I did invite them. Kavan and Shira are waiting for our godchild to wake up, and they're picking Mom up on their way over here. Plus, I think we have enough of an audience as it is."

"Wait, don't tell me Mr. I-Can-Do-It-All is nervous?"

Chuckling as he slowly lifted the lid to reveal the most gorgeous, intricately designed ring I'd ever seen, he slowly lifted it up to me. "Nervous? I was seventeen miles past nervous three hours ago. I'm a wreck, Linds. I love you more than anything in the world, and I always will. I lost you once, and I don't know if I would survive losing you again if I've read this wrong."

"I never want to rush you or push you," he said. "I know what happened the last time you trusted someone when you said yes, and even though I will forever be grateful to that asshole for walking out, I know putting that same kind of trust in me won't be easy. I never want to make you feel like I wouldn't wait for you for as long as it takes for you to be ready. I'll wait a hundred years, but I'm asking you today because on the off chance that you are ready, I don't want to wait a day longer than I have to before I'm married to you. I will never leave you again, Linds. I have never wanted anyone as much as I want you. I have never loved anyone the way that I love you."

"You've never rushed me," I said as I touched my fingertips to his cheeks. "In fact, you've been more patient with me than I had any right to expect. I love you too, Jaxon."

"Does than mean you'll be my wife?" Hope so powerful I felt it in my own chest shone from his eyes.

"Yes." I'd hardly gotten the word out before he was sliding the ring onto my finger, getting to his feet, and winding his arms around me. "Thank you for fighting for me."

"Thank you for letting me win." He brought his lips to mine and I felt the promise in his kiss searing into my soul. He would never leave me again, and on our wedding day, I knew I wouldn't have to worry about whether he'd show up.

Jaxon had always shown up for me, even right back at the beginning when I hadn't even known I'd needed him. At his side, I knew I was safe, loved, and cherished. He was my happily ever after, and I couldn't wait to know what it felt like to really be his wife.

Ember, Jaxon's mom, Shira, Kavan, and little baby Hope came rushing through the doors before he even let me go, and we were pulled apart for hugs and congratulations while Ethan introduced everyone to Big Mac.

This was just the beginning of our story, but as I looked around the garden filled with our family and friends, I knew with everything in me that it would be a good one. There was no more doubt in my mind that we had always been destined to be together.

It definitely had been fate. *No more maybe about it.*

The End

ABOUT THE AUTHOR

Hey there. I'm Weston.

Have we met? No? Well, it's time to end that tragedy.

I'm a former firefighter/EMS guy who's picked up the proverbial pen and started writing bad boy romance stories. I co-write with my sister, Ali Parker, but live in Texas with my wife, my two little boys, a dog, and a turtle.

Yep. A turtle. You read that right. Don't be jealous.

You're going to find Billionaires, Bad Boys, Military Guys, and loads of sexiness. Something for everyone hopefully. I'd love to connect with you. Check out the links below and come find me.

Fake It For Me

My Holiday Reunion

Take It Down A Notch

Show Me What You Got

Heartbreaker

She's Mine Now

Say You Do

Made in the USA
Monee, IL
27 October 2020

46190335R00154